AP - - '13

W3/14
W1/17
W1/20

continued . . .

Seeing Is Believing

ERIN McCARTHY

BERKLEY SENSATION, NEW YORK

THE BERKLEY PUBLISHING GROUP
Published by the Penguin Group
Penguin Group (USA) Inc.
375 Hudson Street, New York, New York 10014, USA

USA / Canada / UK / Ireland / Australia / New Zealand / India / South Africa / China

Penguin Books Ltd., Registered Offices: 80 Strand, London WC2R 0RL, England
For more information about the Penguin Group visit penguin.com

SEEING IS BELIEVING

A Berkley Sensation Book / published by arrangement with the author

Berkley Sensation Books are published by The Berkley Publishing Group.
BERKLEY SENSATION® is a registered trademark of Penguin Group (USA) Inc.
The "B" design is a trademark of Penguin Group (USA) Inc.

For information, address: The Berkley Publishing Group,
a division of Penguin Group (USA) Inc.,
375 Hudson Street, New York, New York 10014.

ISBN: 978-0-425-26173-6

PUBLISHING HISTORY
Berkley Sensation mass-market paperback edition / March 2013

PRINTED IN THE UNITED STATES OF AMERICA

10 9 8 7 6 5 4 3 2 1

Cover photo composition by S. Miroque. "Couple" by Miramiska/Shutterstock.
"Dog" by Sundeep Goel/Shutterstock.
Cover design by Rita Frangie.
Interior text design by Kristin del Rosario.

ALWAYS LEARNING   PEARSON

*For all the readers
who loved Piper in* Heiress for Hire,
this one is for you.

Chapter One

Chapter One

THERE WAS A GHOST REACHING OUT FOR HER.

Again.

Piper Tucker had heard the footsteps on the hardwood floor of the parlor and smiled. "Lilly or Emily, whichever twin you are, it is bedtime. No more glasses of water, no more back rubs, no more excuses."

She turned, expecting to see one or both of her eight-year-old cousins she was babysitting. Well, they technically weren't her cousins, since they were the children of Piper's father's ex-wife and her second husband, but that was too complicated for a town like Cuttersville, Ohio. They just called each other cousins.

Only it wasn't cousins coming into the room, biological or otherwise.

It was a ghost.

Dang it. Piper had been hoping to spend the whole

weekend in the house without seeing a single dead person, and here she'd been there for only three hours and already a spectral woman was staring at her. The entity wore a poke bonnet, a dusky mauve gown with a braided pelisse, and button boots. Young, her shadowy face was free of lines or blemishes, and the eyes set in that pale, ethereal frame were deep, thick black. Funeral black. Filled with sorrow. This ghost was Rachel, a woman who had died nearly a hundred and fifty years before of an opium overdose after bludgeoning her indiscreet fiancé.

Piper knew the story about Rachel from her aunt Shelby, her father's ex-wife and the owner of the house. Piper knew that was who she was seeing because she'd encountered the murderess a half dozen times or more since childhood.

"Hi, Rachel. Is there something I can do for you tonight?" Piper fought a sigh. Seeing the pain on the vision's face, sensing her sorrow and confusion, always made Piper feel a little sick to her stomach. Guilty that she was the one ghosts came to, and yet she didn't know what to do to help them.

Rachel didn't move, but the sound of a foot stamping on the floor echoed around the room, ringing loudly in the quiet dark. The one lamp Piper had been using to read a gardening magazine flickered off and back on.

"What's the matter? If you'd tell me how to help you, maybe I could." When she was a kid, ghosts had actually talked to her, unless her memory was playing tricks on her. But she could swear she'd had whole conversations with the people who had appeared in front of her randomly and without warning. But now they never said anything, not Rachel, or the other various spirits she saw around town.

In her teens, Piper had taken to begging them to leave her alone, to go away and bug someone else, but now that she was older, she couldn't bring herself to shoo a soul who'd been restless for more than a century. Piper still wanted to be left alone. She still wanted to be normal, to blend in to the town and in to her family, until no one remembered she had ever lived anywhere but Cuttersville.

Seeing ghosts was her secret. But she didn't yell at them anymore.

Arms stretched out, reaching for her. Eyes beseeching with aching intensity.

"Tell me how to help. I don't understand what you want." Piper gripped the back of the sofa she was sitting on, her throat closing up. She remembered what it was like to feel lonely, vulnerable. Before her father had taken her in when she was eight, she had been unwanted and unloved by her stepfather, and sometimes it didn't take much to drag all those feelings right back up to the surface.

"She did it." The words came from Rachel even though her lips didn't move. Even though the sound seemed to flow and ebb and surround Piper like a cloud, misty and shifting.

A clap of thunder made Piper jump on the couch. It had been threatening to rain all day, and she figured this was appropriate timing. "Who did what?" Was Rachel really talking to Piper or had she imagined it? Now she wasn't sure.

This was why she hated being the weirdo who attracted more ghosts than a graveyard on Halloween. Most days she didn't even do all that well with people who were still alive. She certainly had no social skills when it came to the dead. And she couldn't exactly invite Rachel to sit down and have some iced tea and tell her all about it.

"She did it."

Okay. Piper needed a little more to go on than that.

Before Piper could ask for clarification, a knock on the front door had her sitting straight up. "Geez, oh Pete." Would anyone else like to startle the heck out of her? She was not a jumpy sort, but she didn't like being caught unaware.

Clutching her chest, she stood up, patting her pocket to make sure she still had her cell phone. Rachel was already dissipating. The spirit didn't like Shelby's husband, Boston, and made a hobby out of tossing plates at him from time to time, but as far as Piper knew, no one had actually seen the ghost but her. Rachel wouldn't appreciate a visitor.

The clock on the wall read 10:03, and Piper hesitated as she headed for the door. It was awfully late for anyone to be stopping by, and Boston and Shelby had gone to Cincinnati for the whole weekend.

A quick glance through the peephole showed a man's head, too distorted for Piper to identify him. His head and shoulders looked rain soaked, which earned some sympathy. But while Piper was compassionate, she wasn't a complete idiot.

"Can I help you?" she called through the door, hand on her cell phone button in case he axed his way through to her and a call to 911 was needed.

"Shel, it's Brady. Let me in, damn it. I'm drowning out here."

Brady. The name brought a rush of pleasure she wasn't all that sure she was entitled to.

"Brady?" she said in astonishment. Glancing down at her pajama shorts and tank top, she grimaced. Not exactly what she wanted to be wearing when encountering the man of her childhood dreams, but she opened the door anyway. "What are you doing here?"

"Standing on the damn porch . . ." Brady Stritmeyer locked eyes with her, his expression surprised. "Hi, uh, sorry. I thought you were Shelby. Is she or Boston here?"

He didn't recognize her. That was a little deflating even as Piper reasoned Brady hadn't seen her in twelve years, since she was all of eleven years old and he had been eighteen, preoccupied with getting out of Cuttersville.

"They're in Cincinnati for the weekend and I'm babysitting the twins. I don't think they were expecting you." Piper moved to the side. "Come on in out of the rain."

It had been more than a decade since she'd seen him in person, but over the years she'd seen photos of him from visits Shelby and Boston and the kids had made with Brady in Chicago. She'd always had a crush on him. Always thought he was good-looking. But in the flesh he had a presence that a picture couldn't express.

A couple of heads taller than her, he had short, dark brown hair and a rangy, muscular frame. Droplets of water trailed down his temple and dripped off his stern chin. She couldn't see his eyes in the hazy darkness of the porch, but she knew they were green. Many a pubescent fantasy of hers had been built around those green eyes.

"This is really embarrassing," he said with a half smile. "But you obviously know who I am and I don't recognize you." He stepped into the house, glanced around the hallway, turned back to her, and shrugged. A charming grin flashed at her. "I was thinking about faking it, but you look like you're already onto me."

"That's okay. You've been gone a long time." And never once in twelve years had he come back to visit. Piper wondered why he did now, without even calling his family first.

She tucked her long hair behind her ear and leaned on the door she'd closed. "I'm Piper Tucker."

His eyebrows shot up. "Little Piper? Danny Tucker's daughter?"

When she nodded, he ran his eyes over her, looking a little more closely than she was comfortable with. He smelled like rain, his shoes squeaking on the hardwood floor, and God, she did not want him to see in her face that she'd once cared about him. That she'd wanted him to sweep her off her feet and make her his wife, with the sort of vagueness towards details that thirteen-year-olds are so good at.

"Damn," he said. "You've done some growing since the last time I saw you." He held his palm out in front of his waist. "You couldn't have been much more than this tall when I left."

Plucking at her tank top, trying to pull it lower over her stomach, Piper gave a nervous laugh. "Well, I was only eleven and I was always kind of short." Puberty had come late for her, which the pediatrician had speculated could have been the result of poor nutrition in her early developmental years.

"It looks like it all worked out for you in the end. You turned out just fine, Piper."

Well. That was probably meant to be a compliment, but it landed on her ears offensively. Like while he wouldn't go so far as to call her pretty, she should be lucky she hadn't turned out plain old ugly either. Piper had never had any illusions about her attractiveness. She'd always been gangly and awkward, with eyes too big for her head. A head that had been bald from age six to nine, with hair long enough to ruffle not appearing until she was nearly eleven.

No, she'd never been beautiful like her stepmother, Amanda, but hearing Brady's offhand remark drew out a vulnerability she hated. It lived in her all the time, those deep-rooted childhood insecurities, but most of the time, she ignored them. Having them arise now made her frustrated.

"Thanks," she said briefly, afraid to say anything more.

Brady popped his head into the parlor. "Damn, this place hasn't changed one bit. A new couch, maybe, but everything else is the same. So, the kids all asleep? Is Zach in his room watching TV? I'll go hang with him for a while."

"He's actually at a friend's house. At fourteen, the idea

of spending the weekend with his little sisters and a babysitter was just too mortifying, I guess. He'll be around during the day tomorrow but he won't be sleeping here."

Brady was wandering into the parlor, so Piper followed him. He had pulled a doily off an occasional table and was twirling it around on his finger. "Well, at least this way I won't have to sleep on the floor."

Piper crossed her arms over her chest, distracted by the way his jeans clung to his backside. "What do you mean?"

"I can sleep in Zach's bed tonight."

It took her a second, but when his words filtered through her brain, Piper bit her lip nervously. "You're spending the night?"

"Yep. It's too late to go to my grandmother's. I don't want to wake her up. And I don't get along with my father, so I'm not exactly welcome there. My sister Heather moved to Cincinnati when her husband couldn't find a job here." He held his arms out, doily included, and smiled, a charming, confident smile. "Sorry. You're stuck with me."

Oh, Lord. That's what she was afraid of.

A completely innocent slumber party with Brady Stritmeyer.

That was called a cruel irony.

BRADY SET THE DOILY DOWN AS PIPER GAVE HIM A very forced smile. Clearly, she wasn't thrilled about the idea of him spending the night. He wasn't sure why it mattered. He was thirty-one years old—it wasn't like he needed her to cook for him or anything. Maybe she'd planned on painting her nails or waxing her bikini area and couldn't if he was hanging around.

But even if he had another place to stay, he wasn't sure

he wanted to go anywhere. It was fascinating to watch Piper, to study all the changes twelve years had brought to her face and her body.

Jesus, her body. She had just that right combination of curves that told a man this was definitely a woman, without being overblown and distracting. Her little cotton shorts were hugging her round ass, and despite the fact that she kept crossing her arms over her chest, he had seen the outline of her full breasts. Caught a glimpse of her taut nipples.

And when she'd first opened the door, and the light from the hallway had hovered behind her, all that hair had tumbled down over her shoulders and breasts and he'd felt a kick of sexual awareness. An instant attraction.

Now that he knew it was Piper Tucker, the hair amazed him even more. He remembered her as a shy little girl clinging to her father, her bald head covered with a hat all the time. No wonder he hadn't recognized her.

Piper was a sensual, exotic woman now.

"Sit down with me, Piper, and tell me what you've been up to for the last twelve years." Brady dropped onto the couch and patted the seat next to him. He would behave himself now that he knew who she was. He was confused enough about his life without dragging someone else into it, and Piper was too young for him anyway.

Not to mention that her father was bigger than he was.

Yet it annoyed him when she sat in the chair across from him, instead of on the couch. She crossed her legs and hugged them to her chest and shrugged.

"Well, you know, there was middle school and high school. Then college. Now I'm one of the two kindergarten teachers at the grade school."

"Hey, that's cool. You must like kids if you teach school and still babysit on the weekends."

"Well, Boston and Shelby are like family, and I love

Emily and Lilly. I like spending time with them. And it's only the first week in September, so school's only been in for two weeks. I've had all summer to rest." She gave him a shy smile that challenged his decision to be nothing more than an affectionate cousinly sort to her.

Women in Chicago didn't smile like that. At least not those he worked with day in and day out at a marketing firm. Or he had, until he'd been laid off three days earlier. Professional women were confident, aggressive, independent. He liked that.

But he liked that smile on Piper's face, too. More than he should.

"How are your dad and mom?" he asked. He'd seen Amanda a few years back when she'd been visiting her father in Chicago, but they had talked mostly about the city, the good restaurants to hit, and Brady's job. Amanda had only briefly mentioned that Piper was in college, and Brady hadn't given much thought to what was going on back here in Cuttersville.

It felt odd to be back home, in a house that hadn't changed, even as everything around it had. Brady had thought that he would be swamped with emotion when he came back after his self-imposed exile, but really so far he'd felt nothing but a mild sort of pleasure and curiosity.

"Great. My dad's looking at a good crop this year, and my mom sort of has her hands in everything. She raises purebred poodles, sells real estate, and is president of the PTA at my brothers' school."

That was kind of a humorous image. When Brady had first met Amanda fifteen years earlier, she had been a bored rich girl. "No kidding? And what about you, Piper? You living in town now? Got a boyfriend or a husband or anything?"

It would be easier if she did. Stop him from thinking

thoughts about her naked body that he shouldn't be thinking.

But a hint of color rose in her cheeks. "No, no boyfriend or fiancé. And I still live with my parents in the farmhouse. I guess that sounds kind of lame, doesn't it? Especially to someone like you who left home right out of high school."

He'd left home all right, chomping at the bit to get the hell out of Cuttersville. And twelve years later he was starting to wonder what he'd been running from. The success he'd wanted, expected to find in Chicago or New York, hadn't arrived, and he had given up painting altogether three years ago. It hurt to pick up a pencil or brush and know that he couldn't replicate on paper what he saw in his mind.

"If you're happy, then there's nothing lame about it."

She nodded, then said, "Do you want me to put your shirt in the dryer? The shoulders are soaking wet."

He'd forgotten about the damp cotton clinging to his skin. The house didn't have air-conditioning, and it was still summer temperatures. He wasn't cold. But neither was he going to refuse a perfectly legit chance to take his shirt off in front of her and see her reaction.

"Thanks." Brady peeled it off, and wondered what the hell he was doing. Hadn't he just told himself this girl—seven big, long years younger than him—was off-limits? And here he was going for the flirt.

But he supposed every man had a bad habit. Some drank, others smoked, quite a few gambled to excess, and hell, some did all three. His weakness was women. He liked to flirt, liked to make women smile and laugh. He loved to wine and dine and sixty-nine a woman. Nothing wrong with that if both parties knew the score. Brady wasn't the settling-down kind. He had been born restless, and this trip back to Nowheresville for no good reason was further proof of that. He should be back in Chicago, pounding the pavement for a job, yet he'd decided to come home for some strange reason.

Because he'd found himself angry and bitter and maybe even a little scared for the first time in his whole life. That was why he'd come home. Like being back in Cuttersville would solve any of the mess his life had become.

But he might as well enjoy himself while he was here.

So he bunched up his shirt and stood, stretching a little so she had a good shot of the pecs and his ripped stomach. All those hours at the gym should be worth something. "The dryer still in the basement? I'll just toss it in."

Piper's eyes had gone wide. He was almost sorry he'd stripped the T-shirt off. She looked horrified, not flirtatious. But then her eyes dropped down, just a little, and she ran her tongue across thick, plump lips. "Oh, I'll get it," she said, her voice a sweet, husky whisper.

Damn, he knew that look, felt that vibe, could practically smell the attraction that had sprung up between them. Good thing the twins were upstairs sleeping or he'd be severely tempted to taste Piper Tucker from tip to toe.

This was not a woman he could fool around with.

It was a mantra he was going to have to repeat all week long. Along with the friendly little reminder to himself that Shelby would tear his head off, and Danny Tucker would rip something even more important off him, if they found out he was fooling around with Piper. And Amanda? Hell, she might be the worst of all. She wouldn't tear something off Brady. She'd string him up by his nuts, spray him with honey, and let the bees at him.

Piper was extra special to them, because Danny hadn't known she existed until she was eight years old and her worthless stepfather had dumped her in Danny's driveway.

Not a woman he should be messing around with. Repeat ten times twice daily and maybe it would sink in.

Yet he still found himself moving in just a little too close to her when he handed over the shirt. "That's sweet of you. I left my travel bag in the trunk."

"No problem. I . . ." Piper looked over his shoulder.

"What?" Brady half turned, expecting to see one of the kids standing in the doorway. Good thing he hadn't given in to his very inappropriate urge to kiss her.

"Nothing." Piper darted her eyes back to him. Then behind him again. Her cheeks flushed. Her head tilted, sending her wavy light brown hair cascading over her forehead and right eye.

"What are you looking at?" She obviously saw something back there. "A mouse?"

"No. Nothing." Step one, step two, she shifted around to his side and stood stiffly, tugging her tank top down again.

Then Brady knew what it was. What he'd forgotten about Piper Tucker from all those years ago, the summer he had been fifteen and she'd arrived in town.

"You still see ghosts, don't you?"

Chapter Two

❧

PIPER STARED AT BRADY IN ASTONISHMENT. "I . . .
I . . . don't have any idea what you're talking about."

Only she wasn't all that great of a liar. She couldn't even
look him in the eye as she spoke.

But she wasn't about to admit that a ghost of a man with
blond hair was standing right behind Brady, smiling and
nodding his head up and down.

"Come on, Piper. I remember. You used to ask me to
draw pictures for you. Pictures of the ghosts you saw."

Dang. She couldn't believe it. Why would he remember
something like that? And why were they having this conversation while he wasn't wearing a shirt? She had almost
whimpered when he'd exposed his chest to her. Brady had
filled out a bit in the last twelve years. In all the right places.

"I was just a kid. I had an active imagination." Her parents had forgotten about her imaginary friends and ghost

sightings. Or at least they never mentioned them to her anymore. It wasn't something Piper ever wanted to discuss with anyone, least of all Brady Stritmeyer, a lifelong crush she clearly hadn't quite gotten over.

"Bullshit," he said.

She was surprised that he hadn't just dropped it. And that he was swearing at her. Raising an eyebrow at him, Piper clutched his damp shirt, glad she had it to mask her clammy and trembling hands. If there was one thing she was good at, it was changing the focus of a conversation from her to someone else. So she said, "I do remember the one time I had you sketch my mom in Victorian clothes. She was so upset that her hair was pinned back like that, even in a drawing, but she made an effort to fake that she liked it. How is Chicago, by the way? My mom said you work at a marketing company. That sounds interesting."

It hadn't seemed like a good fit to Piper, but then she had reminded herself she knew nothing about him except the impressions of an eight-year-old girl of a teenage boy. People matured, changed. Not that she had changed much, but maybe he had.

"It's not really interesting at all." He gave her a slow grin, shaking his head. "Don't try to change the subject on me, Piper. That sketch you had me draw was the ghost in the mirror. I remember it distinctly. You were all sorts of worked up about it, insisting she had something to say."

Piper felt her cheeks heat. She remembered it distinctly, too, and it embarrassed the hell out of her. She was standing in front of a shirtless man—something that didn't happen all that often to her—and she was being reminded of the odd little kid she'd been.

"You don't really believe in ghosts, do you?" she asked him. Most people didn't. Or if they did, they still thought the person who saw them, who could talk to them, was strange.

"I'm not sure if I do or not," Brady said with a shrug. "There were certainly a lot of unexplainable noises and doors closing around this house back in the day. If it wasn't ghosts, I don't know what it was." He studied her so intently that she fought the urge to squirm. "Do you believe in ghosts?"

It was a test. She could feel it. So she stared him straight in the eye, heart pounding too swiftly to be normal, and lied. "No."

Then she blew it by darting her eyes to look past his shoulder. The ghost had started waving, which was distracting and weird. The movement caught her attention and she reacted by looking, which of course Brady noticed. He half turned.

"What's behind me, Piper? Red-Eyed Rachel?"

No, she was in the doorway to the kitchen. Piper could see her out of her peripheral vision. Knowing she couldn't form another lie on her lips, she just shook her head and figured he could interpret that however he chose.

"Nothing? No ghosts?"

She fisted his shirt tighter in her hands. Why didn't he just drop it? "I should get your shirt in the dryer."

Whatever reaction she expected from him, it wasn't for him to turn and punch the Blond Man in the direction of the gut.

"No!" she shrieked instinctively. It didn't matter that the ghost was dead and couldn't feel anything. It was so shocking, so disrespectful, she couldn't prevent her reaction. Then she clapped her hand over her mouth when he turned back to her, smug.

"I knew it." He tilted his head and said over his shoulder,

"I'm sorry, whoever you are. But I was trying to prove a point."

Piper left her hand fall. "He's not there anymore. You scared him, I think." There was no point in denying her reaction. But she didn't feel like sticking around to have Brady gloat or grill her on her freakish ability. So she headed for the basement door off the kitchen, skirting past Rachel, the cold of the beseeching apparition tripping goose bumps over her arms.

He followed her. She could feel his presence falling into step behind her, but she refused to look. Flicking the switch at the top of the basement steps, she tried not to think about how much she hated Shelby and Boston's basement. The house was almost a hundred and fifty years old and the basement was a true hole in the ground. Support walls had been added over the years and the laundry area was lit with flourescent bulbs, but the dark still clung to the corners and there was a musty, decaying smell. When she had been about fourteen she'd seen a dark shape moving around down there, a malevolent spirit that didn't seem quite human, and she'd avoided it ever since.

"I didn't mean to scare anyone. And I didn't mean to upset you," Brady said behind her.

Hanging on to the railing, she took the rickety steps down into the gloom. "I'm not upset." Lie. Total lie. Piper despised lying to anyone else, or most importantly, to herself, but she didn't want to admit to Brady that she didn't like to be Ghost Girl to anyone, least of all to him.

She hesitated at the bottom of the stairs and he bumped into her, his thighs brushing her backside in her barely there cotton shorts, his bare chest warm against her back for a brief second.

"Sorry." His hands touched her arms as if to steady himself.

She was grateful he couldn't see the burn in her cheeks in the dark. The goose bumps were back, full force, and she was painfully aware that she wasn't wearing a bra and he wasn't wearing a shirt. "It's fine." But it really wasn't. She wasn't good at casual flirtation. She took everything too seriously, too literal.

So when he turned her around, slowly, she let him, but she dropped her eyes, not wanting him to see her confusion. For a guy like Brady, touching a woman's arms in the dark was no big deal, she was sure. The same couldn't be said for her. She wasn't particularly experienced with men. Actually, come to think of it, she had no experience with men. Over the years, she'd had small pockets of interaction with boys, but not men. Brady was over thirty years old and she felt like a child next to him.

"I didn't hurt the ghost, did I? It was kind of impulsive, actually, just trying to get a reaction from you. I'm not going to get sucked into hell or anything, am I?"

Piper raised her eyes to study his face in the murky light, astonished. "How would I know?" she asked him, honestly.

He gave a soft laugh. "I don't know. I guess I thought if you can see them, you know what they want."

"No. I have no idea what they want. But that spirit just disappeared, like the smoke in the breeze when Boston lights a cigar on the front porch. So I think you're safe." Piper wasn't feeling particularly safe in the basement, though. There was a tingle on the back of her neck and she was uncomfortable not being able to see the room behind her.

"I think it's cool that you see ghosts. It makes you special. I wish I had a talent of some kind."

If that was special, God could keep it. She didn't want any part of being different. She frowned at Brady. "You do have talent. You're an amazing artist." That was something he created, not something that just showed up like dead flotsam bobbing around him.

He shrugged, his muscular shoulder raising upwards, a disparaging smirk on his handsome face. "I was mediocre at best and now I'm not anything. I don't paint anymore."

"You don't?" Piper was almost as shocked as when he'd sucker-punched the ghost. "But you're so talented." She remembered the way he had been able to pick up a sketch-book and produce a lifelike image in just a matter of minutes. He had painted butterflies on her bedroom wall and she had danced around her room, pretending she was as graceful and beautiful as those monarchs he had created. She couldn't believe that he could have insecurities about his abilities. Insecurities at all. She tended to think those were her province and hers alone.

"No, I'm really not. I'm average." His voice was soft, distracted, like he wasn't really thinking about his artistic career at all.

The way he was looking at her . . .

Piper swallowed, heat coiling between her thighs into a hard knot of desire.

"I can't get over your hair," he murmured, his finger reaching out to brush it off her cheek. "It's beautiful. And it feels as good as it looks."

"Thank you." Her hair was too long, she knew that. It wasn't stylish to have it so thick and wavy, cascading down the middle of her back. But she had a hard time cutting it. Part of her irrationally feared if she cut it, it wouldn't grow back. And sometimes, when she debated a cut that would expose more of her face, she could hear her stepfather's voice reaching out from the past like a horsewhip to tell her that she was disgusting, that no one should ever have to look at her ugly mug.

That Brady, of all people, would look at her the way he was, meant a lot to her, even if he was just being nice.

The corner of his mouth turned up. "You don't believe me, do you?"

It was too close to the truth and she didn't like it. "You ask a lot of questions," she told him. "The twins ask less questions than you do."

He laughed. "Sorry. Guess I should back off." Shifting to the right, Brady took the shirt out of her hands and moved towards the washer and dryer.

Disappointed by his defection, she cursed that she still hadn't completely conquered her childhood habit of blurting out whatever she was thinking. If she was savvier about these kinds of things, she would have smiled and laughed. She would have leaned closer to him or done some such nonsense that she had never learned. Amanda was a class-A flirt, but that particular talent didn't pass from stepmother to stepchild, not even after years of watching her mom coax and cajole whatever she wanted out of her father by flashing him a little leg or trailing her nails down his chest. Piper couldn't think on her feet like that.

She just said whatever came to mind or she said nothing at all.

Which apparently resulted in men walking away from her. While she might not know what to do with Brady Stritmeyer all in her personal space, she didn't like him vacating it either.

Piper glanced down at her taut nipples and sighed, silently apologizing to them.

For a brief few minutes, the girls had optimistically thought they were going to get to come out and play, and she was sorry to say that wasn't going to be the case.

Not with Brady, anyway. Actually, it wasn't ever really

the case. Crossing her arms over her chest, she followed him to the dryer, watching the pull of his jeans over his butt as he bent over.

A girl could look.

Brady turned and caught her.

And a girl could get busted looking.

HITTING VARIOUS BUTTONS ON THE DRYER, NOT REALLY sure how the ancient thing worked, Brady tried to get a grip on himself. He was in trouble. Real, honest-to-God, he-was-going-to-lose-his-testicles kind of trouble. Because he had seriously been contemplating kissing Piper Tucker.

What the hell was wrong with him?

Not only was he considering going there with a woman who was totally off-limits if he wanted to live, he had confessed he wasn't painting without hesitation. He didn't talk to anyone about his failed attempt at being an artist. Not a single person. He went to his soul-sucking job and he went home and he went out with various friends and women and he pretended that nothing was wrong when everything was.

He was a first-rate fake, having perfected the art of happy-go-lucky man around town. It was the only art he had been successful at. Yet no one knew that, and he had told Piper all of twenty minutes after being in her company.

But it was those eyes. They were enormous, giant pools of understanding, and they looked at him like he was something important. It was disarming. Appealing. It had been a long time since he had looked at a woman and thought she was as beautiful as he thought Piper Tucker was. Her cheeks were flushed with health and color, her lips were full, her eyes the rich color of hot chocolate. And her hair . . .

It made him think of period films where the proper lady was shown in her boudoir with a lace nightgown on, her thick, luscious hair spilling around her as she brushed it with an elegant comb, contemplating getting fucked by her secret lover.

Brady kind of wanted to be the secret lover. Like, a lot.

Which made him an idiot.

He turned to her in frustration, and not just because of the stupid dryer. "This thing is a thousand years old. I can't figure it out."

Piper reached around him and pushed a button. The dryer started up immediately.

"That was too easy," he told her.

"It dries clothes just as well as it would if it were complicated."

Brady laughed. That was a Cuttersville kind of comment if ever he had heard one. Piper sounded like his grandmother.

Not that she reminded him of his grandmother at all. Nope. His grandmother was old, for one thing, but Jessie Stritmeyer was outspoken, bossy, calculating. There was none of that in Piper. Nor did he ever see her wearing those bedazzled baseball caps his grandmother had always favored. Which made him nostalgic, and glad he'd decided to come back home. It had been five years since he'd seen Gran.

"Good point." He leaned on the dryer and crossed his ankles, feeling a little vain. He wanted Piper to steal another glance at his bare chest. But she wasn't even looking at him.

"Did you see that?" she asked, taking a step closer to him as she studied the far corner of the basement.

He didn't see anything but plastic storage containers and cobwebs. "What am I supposed to see?"

"Something moved."

"A small something, like a mouse, or a big something, like a cat?" Either way, he wasn't sure it mattered. It was a dirty old basement. All kinds of shit was probably living in it.

Piper shook her head. "Like a person size."

Brady strained to see into the dark. "I don't see anything." If a homeless bum was squatting in Shel and Boston's basement, even the shadowy corners wouldn't cover that up, so he figured they were safe.

"It went under the stairs."

She sounded afraid. Her voice had dropped down to a whisper and she had maneuvered herself so that she was on the opposite side of him from where she had seen whatever she had seen. This would be an excellent opportunity for him to show that he was no wimp. He could go under filthy stairs and face down a fictitious ax murderer. Maybe even a real ax murderer. Then maybe she would fall into his arms in relief and press her braless breasts against his bare chest.

What he should not do was try to punch another ghost. That little impulse had clearly upset her. He wasn't sure he believed in ghosts exactly, but then again, he had certainly seen enough evidence of them, especially in this house when he was a teenager. There was no other explanation for some of the things that had happened, and Piper clearly saw something. Which meant there were either ghosts or she was insane, and he really didn't think that the latter was the case. So if a living person running around the basement was unlikely, the logical conclusion would be that Piper had seen a spirit. He'd certainly believed in ghosts when he was fifteen, so it surprised him a little that he even had any skepticism. Maybe the city had taught him that.

He wasn't sure he liked it.

"What did it look like?" He found himself whispering back, though he wasn't really sure why they needed to whisper. All they needed was a creepy music soundtrack playing, and they'd be in a horror film.

"A black blob."

That was specific. "Have you seen it before?" Brady moved forward, his gym shoes crunching on the old shifting and dusty tiles.

She hesitated.

He looked back at her. "You can tell me." He meant that. He wasn't going to judge her. He did think it was cool that she saw something other people couldn't. What happened to someone to allow that? Were they born that way? Was their mind somehow more elevated or open than other people's? Whatever it was, it was cool to be able to do something most people couldn't. He wished he could say that about himself.

"When I was a teenager, I saw something down here like that, just a black blob. It really scared the bejeezus out of me. I don't come down here unless I have to."

Which made her taking his shirt to the dryer a very sweet gesture. Brady was genuinely touched. At the same time, he was pissed that something dared to scare Piper. What kind of an asshole ghost was this guy? "Don't worry. I've got it."

Big man in the basement, that was him. He mentally eye-rolled himself. About the most danger he'd ever been in was when he'd fallen out of his girlfriend's bedroom at fifteen to avoid getting caught by her father. He dodged traffic, not bullets.

Piper made a sound in the back of her throat as he took a step forward. She looked torn between not wanting to go with him and not wanting to be left behind. Brady figured he might as well take advantage of the opportunity. "Come on," he said, and took her hand in his. Not even her father could object to a little hand-holding in the face of malevolent spirits.

Her hand was tiny in his, and she squeezed back with a

pressure he wasn't expecting. It had been a long-ass time since he had held hands with a woman, because most women he knew were too independent for it, and he had to admit, he kind of liked it. He dug feeling like the big strong man next to her instead of the loser who couldn't buy a career woman dinner and a night on the town. As he walked, Piper inched in even closer to him, until their hips were bumping.

"Is this the right way?" he asked her.

"Yes. There." She pointed to the corner under the stairs.

All Brady could see was a stack of boxes and old shelving with floral contact paper on it in avocado green and brown. An ancient blender rested on one, but the others were empty. "Okay, let's just take a closer look."

He didn't think he was going to see anything at all. It was a matter of whether Piper was going to see anything or not. All he could do was just look around and wait for an all clear from her.

"So, do you see anything?" he asked, turning to see her face.

What he didn't expect was her eyes to go wide and a bloodcurdling scream to leave her mouth.

Chapter Three

❦

"WHAT? WHAT'S WRONG? WHAT DO YOU SEE?"

It took Piper a second to slow down her heart rate as she pointed behind Brady to the blender on the shelf. "Oh, my God, that is the biggest spider I've ever seen in my life!"

She hated spiders. They eased into places you weren't expecting them, like silent, furry intruders, and this one was huge. A silver dollar was smaller than that arachnid. She could slap a saddle on it and ride it to the back field for God's sake. It was so enormous that she forgot about the black shadow and the fact that she was holding hands with her childhood fantasy.

Brady's mouth dropped and he loosened his grip on her hand. "Are you kidding me? You're screaming over a spider? Jesus, I thought a killer clown was under the stairs or something."

That startled Piper out of her fear. "A killer clown? Why would there be a clown down here?"

He shrugged. "I don't know. But what's scarier than a clown? Not much. Be honest." He shook their mutually clasped hands to emphasis his point. "A painted-on smile? Come on, that's messed up."

Piper fought a smile at his decided opinion. Clowns didn't particularly scare her, but if one was under the stairwell with a butcher knife, she certainly wouldn't be amused. "I've never been to the circus."

"Well, don't go. And when you have kids, don't take them either," Brady said vehemently. He looked behind him, scanning under the stairs. "But other than a spider, is it all clear? I don't see anything, but the question is, do you see anything?"

She shook her head. Whatever it was, it was no longer hanging around. "But do you think you could kill the spider?" She hated to ask, but she hated the thought of that thing crawling towards her even more.

"I don't even see it."

"It's on that shelf next to the blender. It's moving." An involuntary shudder coursed through her. She knew it was an irrational fear but she couldn't stop it. That was why it was called irrational.

"You grew up on a farm. You must have seen lots of critters running around." Brady obligingly moved towards the spider.

Piper forgot her fear when he bent over, his jeans pulling taut over his backside. She really appreciated the way that denim hugged every inch of his firm butt. "Um . . ." What was the question? She forced her attention back to the matter at hand. "We had five dogs running around. Plus a barn cat. They take care of everything moving."

"Five dogs? Geez. Please tell me they are not all teacup poodles."

"No. Baby, my mom's first dog, is a senior, but still kicking. There's another poodle, Samson, who is twelve. Then two golden retrievers and a beagle mix." Her mother liked dogs. Her father liked to make her mother happy. "Do you see it?" Piper wasn't coming any closer until that bug was under Brady's boot.

"Yeah, I see it." Reaching way under the stairs, Brady picked up a stack of papers and used it to shove the spider to the edge of the shelf. It dropped to the floor.

Piper looked away out of guilt. The spider really shouldn't have to die because she was a wimp. "Maybe you can take it outside," she said.

"Oops."

Her heart sank. He'd already killed it. "Is it dead?"

"No, it ran under the bottom shelf. I can't reach it."

Piper felt instantly better. "Oh, okay, that's good. I shouldn't have asked you to kill it anyway. It didn't do anything."

Brady didn't answer. He was studying the papers he had used to shove the spider off the shelf. "Hey, check this out."

"What?" She moved towards him, well aware that she had nothing on her feet but flip-flops. If that spider came back and ran over her with its fuzzy appendages, she was going to faint.

"It's an old photocopy of an even older newspaper article. 1887. The headline is 'Scorned woman kills fiancé.'" He held it up. "It's too dark down here to read the actual article, but doesn't that sound like Rachel's story?"

"It does." Piper shivered, and she wasn't sure why. "I guess we can go upstairs and check it out."

The idea of hearing Rachel's story in truth, not from passed-down, potentially exaggerated ghost stories, both intrigued and frightened her. If she read about Rachel, and she sounded evil, Piper might find herself scared of her ghost. If she sounded innocent, then, well, Piper would feel guilty that she couldn't help her. But it didn't sound like she had a choice in the matter. Brady was studying the paper as he went towards the stairs.

"This is so cool. I mean, she was who you saw earlier, right? This is an awesome coincidence."

Piper followed Brady, debating the existence of coincidence. There seemed to have been an awful lot of that in her life, and she wasn't sure what it meant, exactly. Nor did she really want to consider it at the moment. She just wanted to enjoy the fact that quite unexpectedly Brady had shown up at Shelby's when Piper was the one there. Coincidence? Or fate? Either way, it was a good view and she intended to enjoy it while it lasted.

In the kitchen, Brady hopped up onto the kitchen counter, his legs swinging below, banging the cabinets. Using one foot on the other, he pushed off his boots, letting them drop to the vinyl floor with a soft thump. His legs were spread apart, and she found herself wanting to step in between them and kiss him. The thought made her thighs burn. To avoid temptation and humiliation in the form of throwing herself at him, Piper took a seat at the table.

Brady was holding the paper right in front of his face. "This is faded and filthy. This photocopy must have been made thirty or forty years ago. But I think I can make out most of the article."

How lucky for them. Piper just sat and waited.

"Aren't you curious?" he asked her, dropping the paper so he could see her.

She shrugged, propping her chin on her palm. "That's a complicated question. I am curious, but at the same time, I'm not sure how much I want to know."

"Just dive in—that's what I always say."

Easy for him. Brady had always had the confidence to do that. Piper? Not so much.

"Scorned woman kills fiancé. Okay, let's see what went down. 'Mr. Jonathon Stradley got the shock of his life two evenings prior when he set about the ordinary task of fetching his mother a sack of flour from Peterson's Grocery and instead encountered a bloody young miss wandering out of her house at 317 Elm Street.'" Brady looked up and made a face. "Okay, why do we need to know the name of the grocery store? Or her address?"

Piper shrugged. "Maybe the reporter owns the grocery store, too. I personally like the phrasing 'bloody young miss.' That's not something you hear every day."

"Agreed." Brady cleared his throat and continued. "'When questioned by Mr. Stradley, the young lady, whose dress was splattered with fresh blood, admitted that, in fact, her fiancé was quite dead inside the parlor, bludgeoned with a candlestick. Upon entering the house of doom, Mr. Stradley found a comely maid with a pleasing figure screaming in the parlor and the gruesome scene of a young gentleman on the floor bleeding about the head and face. He was quite dead, Mr. Stradley determined.'"

Quite dead. As opposed to sort of dead?

"Huh," Piper said, when Brady paused, giving her a look that showed he thought the writing was as ridiculous as she did. "If this wasn't a real story, I'd have to laugh. I'm not sure what the attractiveness of the maid has to do with anything. And how does the reporter know? He wasn't even there."

"Good point. But it's a small town. Everyone probably knew everyone, so I guess he was trying to score a date with her pleasing figure. Okay, let's see what went down next." Brady picked up reading where he'd left off. "'Mr. Stradley sent a passerby to fetch Mr. Harrison Bingley, the proprietor of the Bingley Funeral Home, who arrived to a scene of chaos. The sweet maid, one Miss Betsy Chambers, who had suffered such a grievous shock upon discovering her mistress soaked in blood over the body of her fiancé, had fainted into Mr. Stradley's arms. The bloody and coldhearted woman, well-known in our community as Miss Rachel Strauss, daughter of Henry and Alice Strauss, appeared to have murdered her fiancé by repeatedly hitting him on the head with a candlestick.'"

Brady rolled his eyes at her.

Piper made a face back at him. "How do they know that?" she asked, feeling incredulous. "They didn't even call the police. Or the sheriff or whoever was in charge in 1887."

"All I know is I'm glad I wasn't accused of a crime back then. This is nuts. This is barely two days after the murder and they're essentially telling you Rachel did it in the paper. I guess they hadn't invented the phrase 'person of interest' yet."

"Obviously." Piper felt the hairs on the back of her neck stand up and she glanced around the kitchen, suddenly feeling like they weren't alone. But she didn't see anything. She wondered whether it was possible for Rachel to hear what they were saying and how she might feel about their conversation.

Brady didn't seem to notice her sudden discomfort. "'While as shocking as this may seem, one will only be more shocked when the full tale of that horrific night is revealed. Upon questioning Miss Chambers and Miss Strauss, it would seem that Miss Strauss's fiancé had forced his unwanted attentions on the beleaguered Miss Chambers and that Miss Strauss, upon discovering her fiancé's perfidy, lifted the brass candlestick off her mother's mahogany fireplace mantle, and struck the head of her fiancé one dozen times until he fell to his death, his lifeblood spilling on the hardwood floors and ruining the sprigged muslin gown of Miss Strauss as it sprayed her with each blow.' "

Piper wasn't sure where to start on the bias in journalism contained in that article. It was written like a gossip column, not a reporting of the facts. "Did the maid count the number of times Rachel hit him? Who stands there and counts while they're watching an assault? That's ridiculous."

"It's also ridiculous that we're being told the mantle is mahogany and what kind of freaking dress she was wearing."

"And I always thought the maid was a party to the fiancé's attentions. That's the way I always heard the story from Shelby."

"Me, too. But remember the maid went on to marry a lawyer or something. It seems pretty obvious from this article that she had some skill in manipulating men. Or that she was attractive enough she didn't even need to do anything more than smile and they thought the best of her. Hell, maybe she married this reporter."

"Some women can definitely do that, bend men to their will." Not her. Piper had never mastered the art of flirting. Of course, that implied she had tried. But the only man who had ever melted when she smiled was her father, and she had tried not to take advantage of that fact.

"Don't you go trying it," Brady teased. "Though I think you could definitely pull off the innocent look if you wanted."

Piper wasn't feeling very innocent looking at his bare chest and the inseam of his jeans. Nor did the label feel like a compliment. She didn't have a lot of experience with men, but that didn't mean she wasn't willing to get down and dirty with the right man. Because she thought she might actually like that. With the right man. Who was not Brady.

"Before or after I hit someone with a candlestick?" she asked.

Brady laughed. "I can't see you doing that no matter what some guy did to you. Wait, though—I thought Rachel did the hitting. But you know, now that you mention it, did Rachel ever actually confess? Or did they just conclude that she did it?"

"What does the rest of the article say?"

" 'Though some might say that the fiancé got what he deserved for his offensive treatment of women, I think most would agree that there are nothing but victims here. Poor Miss Chambers has had the scare of her life, Miss Strauss will be spirited off to prison, I am certain, and Mr. Brady Stritmeyer . . .' "

Brady's voice trailed off and Piper started on her chair. "What? Brady Stritmeyer? Are you serious?" The dead fiancé had the same name as Brady?

"Yeah." Brady looked over at her, his expression stunned. "That's weird. Creepy. I share a name with a murdered guy. 'Mr. Brady Stritmeyer paid the ultimate price for his transgressions, with his life! He will now spend eternity lying in the St. Michael's Presbyterian Church cemetery pondering where he went wrong.' "

The clawing unease was creeping over Piper's skin again. Another coincidence. A huge one. "Did your parents ever say anything about being named after an ancestor?"

"No. And who would name their kid after a dead guy who was whacked with a candlestick for putting the moves on the maid?"

Piper couldn't imagine. "Maybe they didn't know? Maybe they just knew it was a family name but didn't realize he had been killed?" Though that didn't seem likely either. Gossip ran rampant in small towns.

"I don't even know what to say." He frowned at the paper in his hand. "It's just . . . weird. And here I thought my name was mine and mine alone."

"Is that the only article?" It looked like he had more than one piece of paper in his hand.

Brady shuffled the papers. "This other one is just a very short obituary for Miss Rachel Strauss. It just says she died at the Cuttersville Lunatic Asylum and is survived by her parents."

"She supposedly died of an overdose."

"That wouldn't be surprising. They dosed those people into comas back in those days. There was no such thing as mental health counseling." Brady frowned at the papers. "I can't believe it. I have the same name as a dead guy."

"A lot of people have the same name as a dead guy." If you thought about it, there probably weren't a lot of truly 100 percent unique names left anymore.

"No one has your name, I bet. There can't be a ton of Piper Tuckers running around."

"Not that I'm aware of." And technically her name was Piper Danielle Schwartz Tucker, because the Tucker part hadn't belonged to her until she was almost nine, when her father had gotten legal custody. The Schwartz was her mother's name, and sometimes Piper was sorry that it wasn't more in the forefront because it made her feel guilty, like she no longer was acknowledging the woman who gave birth to her.

"I didn't think there were any Brady Stritmeyers either. But apparently one was a man whore who got his head bashed in. It makes me feel very ordinary in comparison. He's notorious. I'm just another cog in the wheel. It kind of sucks."

That was a feeling Piper would never understand. She wanted to be ordinary, normal. She had always craved it. "Yeah, but your head isn't squashed like a post-Halloween pumpkin."

"Good point."

"When I was a kid, I would have done anything to have a name like Emily or Nicole. I didn't want to be a Piper."

He cocked his head at her, feet swinging again. "How did you get that name? Do you know? But it suits you, in my opinion. I can't picture you with something as common as a name like Sara."

"I have no idea. My mom—my biological mom—was really young when she had me. Maybe she saw it on TV or read it in a book or something."

"Do you remember her?"

"Yeah." Usually Piper kept those memories tucked away, cherished and warm, like a loaf of bread in a brick oven. She didn't talk about them unless someone asked. "She laughed and smiled a lot, when she wasn't fighting with my stepdad. She liked to sing to me and to paint my nails. I think of her as a woman-child, you know? She really loved me, but she wasn't completely grown-up herself."

"And now you're the woman-child." He gave her a low, sensual smile.

The words were a bucket of ice water thrown over her desire. That was how he saw her. Still not his peer. Here he was sitting across the room from her and he was asking questions about her childhood, not her adulthood, not who she was now. It was disappointing and frustrating to think that no matter how thick her hair grew, people still saw the odd little duck of a kid she had been.

"I like to think more woman than child," she told him. "I am a teacher with a car payment."

"You do seem quite well-adjusted."

He even managed to make that sound like an insult. Piper gave a snort, sitting up straighter in her chair and crossing her legs on the chair so she sat on her feet. "You mean, despite everything? Yes, I would say I'm fairly well-adjusted. I don't have an imaginary friend anymore." Except for the ghosts.

"Maybe 'well-adjusted' isn't the word I was looking for. Content—that's what you seem. Happy."

"I am," she told him simply. It was the truth. She may have longings, desires, for things she couldn't have like anyone else did, but on the whole, she was a very content person. She had been given a second life at eight, and she was immensely grateful. "I have a great job, a home, a family who loves me." Hair. "What more could I need?"

"A man," he told her with a grin. "Isn't that what every girl wants?"

"No, every girl wants to eat whatever she wants without gaining weight."

Brady laughed. "Fair enough."

Piper gripped her ankles and leaned forward a little. "But I'm a woman-child, according to you . . . so what would I do with a man?"

She knew it would get a reaction. She had been counting on it. It did. His eyes darkened. His feet stilled. Maybe she had learned something about flirting, after all.

"Oh, I can think of a thing or two."

"So can I." Piper moistened her lips.

That Piper could sit there in the bright kitchen, her legs crossed so that he could see almost entirely up her shorts, and say that so innocently made Brady hard. He couldn't control it. He looked at her, she spoke, he had a boner. It had happened more than once already and he'd only been in the house an hour. But there was something so damn hot about a woman who had no idea how gorgeous she was. Who was clearly kind and generous and caring and yet so sensual.

His woman-child comment had offended her. Maybe he had said it on purpose to get this reaction, he wasn't sure. To nudge her into admitting that she was attracted to him, because she was. He could read it in the tilt of her head, the toss of her hair, the way her tongue slipped out to slide along her plump pink lip. If he dipped a finger into her panties, either he would find her damp or he would be able to stroke her into it within seconds.

But she didn't want to go there with him. Not really. Or at least she shouldn't. He had been making out with girls in this very kitchen when Piper was still playing with Barbies. She belonged in the bed of some local yokel who would fill her table with food and her belly with babies.

Not a restless townie who'd failed at his attempts to storm the big city. He'd just muddy her sheets.

So he tried to put a halt to the sexual tension that had strung across the kitchen like the laundry line in Gran's backyard. "You should be getting married to a nice guy, building a house on your dad's farm, and having a baby. That's what you should be doing with a man."

Piper made a face. "Thanks for planning my future for me. Would you like to be my matchmaker, too? After all, you did babysit me once upon a time."

"I did?" He didn't even remember that.

The slight lick of anger across her words softened. "Yes. When my parents went to an appointment with their lawyer over my custody. It was for an hour or two."

Maybe he remembered that, vaguely. But he'd been a self-absorbed teenager and his thoughts had run mostly around sex and how he could get it.

Clearly so much had changed in the past fifteen years. "They must have been desperate for a sitter. And I don't imagine you need my help matchmaking."

"No, I don't suppose I do."

Brady couldn't read her tone. She didn't sound amused, or flirty in return. She sounded annoyed, dropping her feet to the floor without waiting for his response. He had the distinct feeling he'd lost points with Piper, and he didn't like that. At all. He wanted to be . . . what? What the hell did he want to be to her?

He had no clue.

Maybe just someone she thought highly of, which proved that he was an idiot whose ego had taken more than a few hits over the last couple of years.

"I'm going to let Snoopy out then I'm going to bed," Piper told him as she crossed the kitchen and bent over to absently scratch behind the ears of a black Lab who looked old and irritated at having been roused from his blanket by the back door.

"I take it this is Snoopy?" he asked. Shelby might have mentioned a dog a time or two, but not having been back to Cuttersville in twelve years, Brady realized how much of the daily in and out of his family's life he was not a part of anymore. It was a disquieting thought.

"Yes. He doesn't like to go outside when it's raining." She tugged on the dog's collar, all the while giving him coaxing words of encouragement. "Come on, sweetie. You can do it. Just real quick—then I'll let you sleep with me."

Unfortunately, that promise was not for Brady. He'd roll over and shake if it would get him a night snug up against Piper. For a brief second, he considered getting a hotel room. It would certainly be less likely to get him in trouble, but it would require a drive out back by the highway and eighty bucks he didn't particularly have. He could control himself, and Piper looked none too pleased with him anyway, so the moment of danger had most likely passed.

"Wasn't Snoopy the cartoon a beagle?" he asked. It seemed an odd name choice for a Lab, in his opinion.

Piper didn't answer. She just dragged the dog outside, the door slamming behind her automatically. Brady stood there, feeling stupid and useless. He should have offered to take the dog out. What the hell was the matter with him? That was what men in Cuttersville did—they offered to be the one inconvenienced. They didn't let women drag dogs out into rainstorms. It was a politeness that he had found annoying and sexist when he was a kid. Now he thought there was something to be said for taking care of a woman. He felt like he'd been trying to do that in Chicago for years, and no woman he'd met had wanted that infringement on her independence. Or they felt he fell short when it came to financially caring for them. But money didn't factor into the equation in his hometown, and given that he was unemployed, there was something refreshing about that.

It made him a douche bag though, for standing in the kitchen, so he pulled open the door and scanned the backyard for Piper and the dog. He had expected her to be right on the back stoop, but she was in the middle of the yard, her cotton pajamas glowing in the dark. He could hear her muttering.

"What's going on?" he asked, wincing when the cool rain hit his bare chest. "Where's the dog?"

"He found a mole or something and he's digging." Piper turned to him as he approached, shoving a hank of wet hair off her forehead. "First he won't go out, now he won't come in. My mom says dogs are as contrary as men, and I'm inclined to think she's right."

"Considering your mother is married to the least contrary man I've ever met, I don't think she has any business complaining." Brady saw Snoopy's rump raised by the fence, his head burrowed as he pursued something clearly important.

"You're right. My dad is the best."

The soft sincerity in her voice gave Brady yet one more reason to steer clear of her. He could never compare to her father. Ever. Suddenly annoyed, he moved past her, the rain pelting him in the face.

38

"Snoopy!" He clapped his hands twice and used a commanding voice. "Get over here!"

The dog lifted his muzzle and glanced at Brady. He gave a look of longing to the hole he'd been digging.

"In the house! Now!" Brady pointed to the back door, which he'd left ajar. The dog took off running, bounding up the steps and back into the kitchen.

"How did you do that?" Piper asked. "He never listens to me."

"I have a way with dogs." More so than women, at the moment, it seemed. "Come on inside before you get soaked through."

"I think it's too late," Piper said. When she stepped into the kitchen and stopped under the circle of light the old schoolhouse lamp created over her, Brady almost had a heart attack.

"Jesus Christ," he said, before he could clamp his jaw shut. The front of her tank top had taken the brunt of the rain and was clinging to her like a pale pink second skin. Her nipples were clearly visible, the rounded curve of her breasts obvious and delectable. The shorts were damp, too, hugging her hips and giving him a view of her panty line as it came to a V between her legs. Raindrops trailed down her legs to her bare ankles, and down her neck across her curved shoulders. He wanted to lick every last drop off of her with his tongue. He wanted to peel those wet clothes from her and see the goose bumps raise on her pink flesh. He wanted to bite that lower lip, so plump and juicy, her skin dewy and fresh from the night shower. He wanted to run his fingers through that luxurious hair and tip her head back so he could taste every single inch of her until she cried out his name in ecstasy.

"What?" She glanced down bewildered, then blushed. "Oh!" Her arms crossed over her chest, which only served to push them up higher, two perky mounds of temptation.

"I'm going upstairs," he told her roughly, trying to wrench his eyes off her breasts, but not quite capable of it. "I suggest you change." Before he did things to her that she would regret. He was sure he wouldn't regret them, but she might.

He just about ran for the stairs. He was strong, but there was only so much a man could be expected to resist.

She followed him, damn her. "Brady!"

With a sigh, he stopped at the bottom of the stairs and pivoted. "Yeah?"

"Please don't tell anyone that . . ." She hesitated, running her fingers through her hair in a gesture that tugged her tank top up to expose her skin.

He didn't think she had any idea how close she was to being taken against the nearest wall. "That what?" That he was about to explode from lust?

"About the, you know, ghost thing. I don't want people to know."

He studied her. She looked very uncomfortable. "This town bills itself as Ohio's Most Haunted Town. I don't think anyone is going to think it's odd. In fact, you'd probably be a celebrity."

"I don't want to be a celebrity. I don't want to be anything." Then she flinched.

He followed her gaze, which had shifted over his shoulder. There was nothing behind him, yet she clearly saw something. "What is it?"

"A killer clown," she said, deadpan.

So Piper Tucker had a sense of humor, after all. Brady cracked a laugh. "That's a good one. Okay, I won't tell anyone."

"Thanks."

His damp skin was starting to itch. The rest of him had been itching for an hour. "Damn, it's a good thing I'm not staying here long."

"Why is that?"

He shook his head. "Because I have a feeling your daddy just might shoot me for the thoughts I'm having."

Her mouth formed an "O" and her eyebrows shot up. Her eyes darkened and her breathing deepened. "My daddy doesn't need to know."

Brady almost groaned. She was a foot away from him, damp and delicious, her nipples still straining against the wet top, her cheeks stained with a pretty blush of desire. This was what he got for playing with fire. The burn of temptation to take what was being offered him, however subtly.

He felt like a total dirtbag. Like the serpent offering Eve the apple. In fact, Piper kind of even looked like Eve with that creamy skin and long, wavy hair.

"I haven't always done the right thing in my life, but I'm going to do the right thing now and go to sleep in Zach's bed alone." He took a step backwards in retreat, which wasn't easy. His fingers were itching to tweak her nipple. Then he ruined the force of his statement by adding, "But if you come in and join me, I don't think I could say no."

"You're not . . . You're not really . . . um, attracted, to me, are you?" She looked a little bewildered by the thought.

He had no idea what was so confusing about his erection. He was hard and she had to see that. The tension between them all night had been palpable. Surely she wasn't doubting it. But given the look on her face, she most certainly was. "Oh, I'm attracted to you, alright. I want to eat you—that's how good you look to me. You're like chili con queso that I want to shove into my face." Maybe that would make it clear.

Those innocent eyes widened with shock and understanding and then a spark of lust, like he'd seen earlier when she had stared at him, wetting those plump lips.

Brady swallowed hard. Rein it in, asshole. "But that doesn't mean I should do anything about it."

"I've never had a man want to eat me before. I think . . ." Her voice dropped to a husky, sensual whisper. "I think I would like that."

Oh, God. He was going to die. He was going to explode from lust and then he was going to hell for having this conversation. Or worse, he would die and be forced to troll this house as a ghost, watching other people have sex while he stood mutely by, a dead eunuch. It wasn't a pleasant future.

He had always been impulsive. The kind who reacted first, thought later. With concerted effort, he reminded himself of all the reasons he couldn't just dive onto Piper Tucker's breasts like a famine-struck infant. Must. Retreat. Now.

"Sometimes things we like aren't always good for us. I don't think I would be good for you, Piper." Then he bounded up the stairs, two at a time, not giving her a chance to reply, self-preservation winning out over manners.

"Brady?" she said softly, her voice drifting up the stairs in the dark to caress him.

He paused. "Yeah?"

"Zach's room is the second on the left. The blue bedroom. Try not to wake up the girls, please. They're light sleepers."

Oh, yeah, the children who were currently in the house, his cousin's twins. Now he really felt like an ass for what he had just said. He didn't even look back at her. "See you in the morning, Piper."

"Night, Brady," she whispered, and the words stirred a longing in him he didn't even know had existed.

A desire for a life where he climbed the stairs in a dark house with a woman and children surrounding him in it. His woman and his children.

Brady just about dove into Zach's bedroom. My God. Sudden unemployment had affected him worse than he had realized.

His gran had always told him he wasn't the marrying kind, and she was right.

He was almost sure of it.

PIPER EYED THE CLOSED DOOR TO ZACH'S BEDROOM and pictured Brady lying behind it on the twin bed with plaid sheets. It seemed maybe he was attracted to her, after all. Either that or he was willing to sleep with any woman who came within two feet of him and was single. He certainly looked at her like he was attracted to her, specifically, and he had compared her to a chip dip. But then, could she really be sure what that meant exactly? Was he attracted to her or just women in general? Her knowledge of interpreting men's expressions could fit in a thimble. For a mouse seamstress.

In high school she had dated Chris Anders briefly. Then in college she had spent her sophomore year in a roller coaster of a relationship with a smart and attractive business major named Seth who was the president of the Young Republicans club. He should have been the head of the Assholes of America club as well. He had taken every single one of her insecurities and had used them against her until she had finally wised up and walked.

These days she spent her time interpreting the expressions of five-year-olds, which generally included pouting, hunger, the urgent need for the restroom, or post-lunch wild-eyed vacancy. None of which were helpful in determining a grown man's sexual intention. She didn't think.

But he'd said he wanted to eat her. Surely she could trust that. Men didn't just compare women to a meal if they were mildly interested or just feeling the effects of blue balls. He would have sex with her if she pushed the issue—she was almost entirely sort of sure of it.

There was no sound from behind the closed door. No snoring. No tossing and turning. No desperate plea for her to join him.

Exasperated at herself, Piper turned and went into Shelby and Boston's room, shivering in her wet pajamas as she gently closed the door and leaned against it.

"Get a backbone," she whispered to herself. If she wanted to go in there, she should have just turned the knob and gone in. But that wasn't her. She didn't have the courage to take what she wanted so boldly. She also knew beyond a shadow of a doubt that she would not be woman enough in bed for Brady, no matter how offended she chose to get at his labeling her a woman-child. In that regard, compared to him, she was.

Not to mention the truth she saw constantly in her classroom: that it was never wise to play with toys you couldn't keep. It was just too hard to let them go.

She peeled off her tank top, goose bumps rising on her damp skin, her nipples painfully hard. Draping it on the windowsill, she stripped off her shorts and panties as well. Standing there naked in the dark, staring out at the rain trailing down the window in driving rivulets, she was very much aware of her body. The goose bumps on her skin, the ache between her thighs, the brush of air across her backside. She didn't spend a lot of time naked, given that she still lived with her parents and her little brothers. It felt decadent to stand there, her frizzy damp hair teasing across her back and her bare breasts, flesh warming to the temperature of the stuffy room now that her wet pajamas were off.

Sensual. Like the woman that she knew she was. Piper stood up straighter, raking her hands through her thick hair. She always loved to feel her hair, to bury her fingers in its richness, to feel it brush against her back and her breasts, to hold it between two fingers and idly twist it, to drag its weight up on top in a messy knot. All those things she had longed to do as a little girl.

Glancing at the door, she changed her mind. She could do this. She could stroll in there and take what she wanted from Brady. She could prove that she was an adult. She could indulge in one night with her childhood crush knowing that it wouldn't result in anything. There weren't enough times in her life when she gave herself credit. She had survived abandonment, being bald, feeling like the odd kid out next to her beautiful blond baby brothers. She had lived her life quietly and diplomatically, and she was good with that.

But tonight, just for once, before he walked out and the opportunity was never there again, Piper wanted to be selfish. She wanted to feel sexy, and she wanted to be satisfied.

Grabbing the robe she had brought for traversing back and forth to the shower, she pushed her arms through the sleeves. It would have been really bold to stroll in there naked, but she couldn't risk it with the girls in the house. Nor did she think she was really capable of being that sassy. Not yet, anyway.

Belting it, she opened the door and moved into the hallway, letting her eyes adjust to the darkness of the windowless corridor. Then she moved towards the blue bedroom.

Only to halt when she realized that Rachel was standing in front of the door, shoulders drooping with sorrow. Piper drew up short. "Oh, geez. Rachel, give a girl a little warning."

The spirit didn't respond. She just stared at Piper.

With . . . disapproval? Piper's cheeks went hot. Why did she feel like she was being called out by a ghost?

"If I want to sleep with him, it's none of your business," she whispered, feeling foolish even as the words came out of her mouth. She was explaining herself to a dead woman. That was just dumb. And maybe an indication that she wasn't as sure of herself as she liked to think.

Rachel shook her head, a silent tear rolling down her opaque face.

Which left Piper in a conundrum. Did she reach through Rachel to turn the knob? Did she try to scare her off? Or did she abandon the slutty ship she was on and go back to dry-dock in her room?

There was no way she could stick her hand through a ghost. It would be like touching her eyeball. She just couldn't do it. The very thought made her queasy. Nor could she shoo her, which just seemed cruel. Hell, maybe Rachel was purposely blocking her entry into Brady's room. Maybe the ghost had more sense than she did. Piper sighed. Seduction didn't really suit her anyways.

She was about to retreat in defeat when Brady opened the door, causing her to jump and Rachel to disappear in a blink. "Oh!"

"Are you okay? I thought I heard you talking out here."

Piper nodded, her tongue suddenly stuck to the roof of her mouth. Brady was in his underwear. Tight boxer briefs that showed firm thighs and an oversized package. The kind that would require extra postage down at the Cuttersville post office.

Good Lord in heaven.

She was both intrigued and horrified.

"So what were you doing?" Brady pressed.

Prying her tongue down, she forced her gaze up to meet his. "Going to the bathroom," she managed to lie. "Sorry for disturbing you, Brady."

But she realized Brady was no longer listening to her. He was staring at her chest.

A glance down showed that the robe had shifted. Her left

breast was about 50 percent exposed. Including the edge of her nipple.

Before she could react, paralyzed by the horror of her failed attempt at sexy, Brady reached out and yanked the robe closed. Gripping both lapels, his face close to hers, he said grimly, "You're going to kill me. Pick a door now and use it before I remove your free will from the equation, and then feel guilty as hell about it."

Before she could think, respond, scoff at herself doing anything against her will, or overanalyze what his feeling guilty really meant, a low, keening wail started up down the hall. At first she thought it was one of the twins, but Brady didn't seem to notice, and the sound wasn't right.

It was unearthly. Starting, she turned to the right. It was Rachel, making the most god-awful sound of frustration and despair Piper had ever heard in her life.

"You don't hear that, do you?" she asked Brady.

"Hear what?"

"Never mind." Piper moved towards Rachel, intent on shushing her, soothing her, anything to get that sound to stop. But the minute she took a step in her direction, the wailing cut off. It annoyed Piper. Why couldn't she ever just be normal? Why couldn't she attempt to flirt with a man without a dead woman getting involved in the business?

Her heart was pounding in irritation and anxiety, and she could feel her face flushing with embarrassed heat. That was it. She was in this far, she was going all the way. Brushing past Brady, she went back into Shelby and Boston's bedroom, right inside the doorway, and pivoted to face Brady again.

And she dropped her robe.

If this failed, she would most likely dig herself a hole quicker than Snoopy and dive into it to die of mortification.

If it succeeded, well, she might just be too nervous to enjoy herself.

But she was naked and something had to happen one way or the other, so she tried not to squirm as she waited for his reaction.

She didn't have to wait long.

With a muttered curse Brady took her by the hand and just about yanked her arm out of the socket as he dragged her farther into the bedroom.

After he locked the door behind him.

Piper's heart kicked into overdrive, but before she could say a word he was all over her like stink on hogs.

Yeah, he was attracted to her. Thank you, baby Jesus.

Chapter Four

BRADY MIGHT HAVE STOPPED TO CONTEMPLATE THIS rather unusual turn of events in his evening if he could remember how to think. At the moment, he seemed to have forgotten how. The second Piper dropped her robe he'd momentarily gone blind, followed by mute, capped off with paralysis.

Then every nerve in his body had fired up at once like a pottery kiln.

It started in his cock, like a blast of pure energy that rushed out to every limb, so that he ached and burned and his skin felt like it was melting. His mouth went hot. His hand twitched. Piper in damp shorts and a clinging tank top had been noteworthy. Arousing. Intriguing. Piper naked was awe-inspiring. She stood there just inside the doorway, chest rising up and down rapidly, a pink bloom in her cheeks, eyes wide with what he suspected was a little bit of shock at what she had just done, and Brady could honestly say that in all his doggish days of doing women he'd never seen one quite as beautiful.

Her body was perfect. It was lush, with full breasts, dusky nipples, and womanly hips. Her waist nipped in, and her arms were natural, not beaten into muscular submission by thousands of hours at the gym. She looked soft and ripe and delicious, like a strawberry straight off the vine. If there had ever been a possibility that he would refrain from touching her, the sight of her naked was a game changer. Not the least of which was the way she looked at him, so guileless, so honest. So sweet.

When her tongue peeked out to nervously lick her lip, he finally found the ability to do something other than stand there and gape.

Before he could come to his senses, before she could change her mind, he had her by the hand and was dragging her farther back into Shelby and Boston's bedroom, aware of two needs—to remove her naked body from the open doorway where they could be busted by small children at any given moment, and to place that same naked body on the largest vertical surface available so he could bang her brains out as soon as possible.

He paused in dragging her to close the door as quietly as he could under the urgent circumstances and lock it. Then he brought her head to his and did what he had been fixating on for the last two hours.

Brady kissed little Piper Tucker. Only she wasn't little anymore. She was a full-grown woman with breasts worth fighting a war for, and as they pressed up against his bare chest, her lips softly parting for his, Brady groaned. He had never stood a chance. Wily women, he could spar with and dodge. Charming flirts, he could bait and tease.

A woman who bared herself before him and then kissed with the artless tenderness of Piper was not something he could resist. Her hands tentatively trailed up his arms to rest on his biceps while her hair hung between them in a heavy curtain. She smelled like damp rain and peaches. What women smelled like peaches? A farm girl, that was who. One who had spent so much of her life outside that it was woven into the fabric of her skin. That the Tuckers probably didn't grow peaches and they were out of season was totally irrelevant to Brady at the moment. He was just enjoying the light scent, an odd sense of homecoming working its way inside him. This was a hell of a welcome back.

Unable to resist, he cupped her full breast while he kissed her again and again, enjoying the reaction she gave him. When his finger brushed over her nipple she gave a little gasp, right into his mouth, their breath intermingling in a simple and base eroticism that shocked him in its intensity. They were making out, plain and simple, with the frantic need of teenagers, and he couldn't even remember the last time he had done that. He kissed to initiate seduction. A few well-placed darts with the tongue before he moved on to greener pastures down south on a woman, giving her a requisite orgasm with his mouth before he could slide in and stroke himself to satisfaction.

It had been years since he'd done this, a kiss just for a kiss. Just because it felt wonderful to feel his mouth on a woman's, to have her fingers pluck restlessly at his chest, her hip press against his cock with more desperation than calculation. She waited for him to direct, kept her hands away from his erection or his ass, and the desire he felt to have her grope him surprised him. At the same time, he liked her passivity, the way she let him take the lead. It made him feel manly, alpha, aggressive.

The floorboards creaked beneath his feet as he shifted, reaching his arm down under the perkiness of her backside and lifting her up into his arms.

"Oh!" she said, startled as he swept her off her feet.

Hell, she couldn't be any more shocked than him. He didn't think he'd ever pulled this particular move. But carrying Piper to bed seemed to make sense and he was caught up in the moment, damn it. Might as well go all the way with it. The moonlight was streaming in the window, the rain softly pelting the glass as he strode across the room with her warm, naked body in his arms. If there was a split second of hesitation when he placed her on his cousin's bed, it didn't last long enough to be of any consequence. Shelby wasn't going to find out, and as far as Brady was concerned at the moment, the only female who even existed was Piper.

She was looking up at him with naked desire, her fingers pulling her lustrous hair out from behind her back so it wouldn't tug. It spread out on either side of her, a wavy thick border to her luscious breasts and flesh. He couldn't say that her hair was any particular color. It was more a fascinating collage of browns and goldenrods, ranging from espresso to toffee to wheat, all overlaying one another. At the top of her head, it was straight, then as it descended to her temples, it began to wave, and by the time it reached her chin, it corkscrewed on down past her breasts.

"You're so beautiful," he said, knowing it was stupid and trite, but sincerely meaning it. She was all things pink and soft and feminine.

He wasn't sure what he expected her to say. Maybe nothing. Maybe protest. Blush. But she didn't. She said, with a sincere politeness he hadn't heard in a long time, "Thank you. I appreciate it."

Whether that was for the compliment or the fact that he had taken her to bed, he wasn't entirely sure. He just knew that while Piper may have been letting him take the lead, she was directing him more than she knew. He bent over and kissed her softly, running his hand over her shoulder, down her arm, watching the goose bumps rise on her skin. This would be when he normally took a woman's thighs in his hands, spread her, and worked her clitoris with his tongue until she came. Some came with hard bursts, arching and clawing, others with tight control. But all loosened and dampened so he could push inside and take his pleasure, sometimes after a nice, long cock sucking, depending on the woman.

But none of that felt right here. It all seemed too orchestrated, too remote. Funny how the most intimate of acts, oral sex, could feel more distant than kissing and touching a woman. He just wanted to feel Piper. To touch her. So he kissed her again and again, his tongue making sweet inroads into her moist mouth, while he lay over her, not crushing her, but brushing his body over hers, his right hand gliding softly over her arm, her breast, her belly, her hip.

Their mouths were swollen, her eyes glazed as she gazed up at him, her hands lightly on the waistband of his boxer briefs. The air was humid from the rain, the last remnants of summer clinging to the house, all quiet but for the soft drumming of the storm remnants and their ragged breathing. He almost thought this brush and tangle of lips, this slumberous mating of their mouths, could be enough to satisfy him.

Almost.

But when she gave a tug at his briefs, he knew it was a lost cause. He was going in, and Lord knew when he'd be coming back out.

Piper tried to catch her breath, her inner thighs on fire as Brady kissed her senseless. She would have thought that he would go right for the good stuff, either oral sex, or straight-up tab-A-in-slot-B penetration. She was prepared for that, had known precisely what she was getting into. You don't drop your robe with a man you hardly know and expect a whole lot of romance. It just didn't work that way, and she'd known that and had done it anyway.

Yet Brady was proving to be quite the man of mystery. He had picked her up in a move that had nearly had her orgasming in his arms, then had spent she wasn't even sure how long kissing her senseless, his hands roaming, but in a way that was more loverlike than one-night stand. He was throwing her off. Making her feel vulnerable. But at the same time, she knew that this was perfect. That if it had gone down the other way, she wouldn't have enjoyed it as much. It would have been a gesture, a brazen, I'm-a-woman statement, but it wouldn't have been her. This was more her. It was like he had been able to understand that, to offer her exactly what she needed, to have her relaxed and pliant and so very, very turned on.

She was so achy, so desperate for more, for a sense of completion, that she started to move beneath him, trying to force him to take stronger action. He didn't. He didn't even slide a finger between her legs. He randomly, and without any real sense of purpose, would flicker across her nipple, but that was it, and she was going to die. She decided that it was absolutely true, that bullshit lie boys told girls at fifteen, that if they didn't have sex they would die. Piper was going to expire into an early grave if Brady didn't stop being so gentlemanly and take his boxers off and take her. Oral sex right now would kill her as well. It would frankly be more than she could handle. She just wanted him inside her thrusting away the ache, stripping it out of her with his impressive erection.

So she reached for his boxers, trying to tug the tight cotton down. Brady sucked in a sharp breath, and Piper realized that he wasn't as unaffected as she'd thought. He looked like he was in pain, and he swallowed hard, his hand coming over hers to pause her movements. "You sure? Because once it's out, there's no going back."

Like she could stop now. It was the most ridiculous thing she'd ever heard. She nodded. "I'm sure."

"I thought you'd say that," he murmured, brushing a kiss across her temple. "Thank God."

In the back of her mind she thought about the lack of a condom, her father's awkward warnings rising up to taunt her. Starting at the age of twelve, he'd barraged her with statistics and information, and an honesty about her own conception that she could have frankly done without. Piper figured he'd been worried that she'd shared some sort of sexual gene with her mother, and he'd watched her like a hawk throughout middle school and high school, but Piper had never been aggressive that way. She kept her needs quietly addressed and to herself, like most things in her life.

But not tonight. And she wasn't sixteen and she was on the pill, so she wasn't going to worry about the lack of a condom. As if she could find the willpower to stop him at this point.

While she wrestled mentally, Brady divested himself of his boxers and poised between her thighs, bumping lightly against her, his finger toying with her clitoris, but the pause was brief. Before she could even think to urge him on, he was pressing inside her with an erection of epic proportions. She had been right to ogle when he'd stepped into the hallway. All the breath left her lungs and she froze, her body stretching to accommodate him, giving her a feeling of fullness she'd never experienced.

It had a groan of ecstasy ripping out of her mouth before she could stop it. It should feel uncomfortable, and there was a lot of pressure, yet at the same time, she felt so stuffed, so complete, so tingly and amazing that she couldn't think, couldn't breath.

"Oh, my God," Brady said, his voice strained. "Fuck, Piper, you feel so good."

That she was hearing those words, that she was feeling this, had a flood of moisture rushing to surround him. This was her fantasy coming to life, and it was better than she could have ever imagined. His forehead was dewy from the strain of holding back, and her inner muscles throbbed with anticipation. But she did have the forethought to bring her finger to her lip and give a soft "shh" so he would remember to keep it as quiet as possible.

His head shook back and forth slightly and he whispered, "You're killing me."

Piper lifted her hips. Look who was talking.

He got the message, a naughty grin bursting across his lips. "You're going to be sorry you did that," he said in a low voice.

She didn't think so.

When he started to move, she knew so. No regrets whatsoever. Just pure, raw, blinding ecstasy. She bit her lip so she wouldn't cry out, and knotted her fingers into his back. He buried his own hands in her hair as he established a slow and intense rhythm, his hot breath blasting over her cheek with each long, deep slide into her. This was sex. This was what she'd been waiting to experience. This was two bodies deeply connected, grinding and pressing together to one final mutual goal. There was nothing fancy about it, just him buried inside her, and yet she had never been so aroused, so sensitive, in her entire life. She could feel it building in her, could feel the quivering that started deep in her womb, her head shifting as she reached for it, desperate.

Brady seemed to sense it because he plunged his tongue

inside her mouth, mimicking the thrust of his cock into her, his hips swiveling so that he got the deepest penetration possible. That was all it took. She came, crying out into his mouth, letting him swallow her passion as her body shattered around him. She clung to him, stunned, dragged down under the waves of pleasure, unable to believe she had come to orgasm so quickly, with so little foreplay.

Yet she had, and he seemed to find it exciting. He made little sounds of encouragement before his eyes narrowed and he gave one final thrust as he exploded in his own passion. Piper felt the convulsion of his erection, felt the hot spurt of his desire burst up inside her, and she shuddered as little tremors tripped through her vagina, like fingers tickling up her spine.

And she knew this was both the smartest and the stupidest thing she'd ever done in her entire life.

Brady stared down at Piper, too stunned to speak. He didn't need any warning about being quiet now. He couldn't produce a word if the bed had burst into flames. Actually, it sort of had. Good God. What the fuck had just happened to him?

He hadn't had sex with a woman without a condom since . . . ever. But he had with Piper, without hesitation, and it had felt like everything he loved all rolled up in one. Like fireworks and whiskey and a big old, fat paycheck. But even better.

She was so tight, still clinging to him now as their breathing slowed down, his shoulders relaxing. She had come with an ease that had blown his mind, had sent him crashing into his own orgasm, and he'd had the stupid thought that she had been waiting for him to do that. That he was somehow unique, the man whose touch she craved.

Now that his blood was flooding back to his brain, he felt moronic for even thinking something so weird. She was an adult—clearly—and despite the innocence of her seduction techniques, there was no way he was the first man to give her an internal orgasm. End of story.

But it still felt good knowing he had. Fast, too. That couldn't have been more than five minutes.

Ego suitably puffed back up, Brady flipped his hair back out of his eyes and eased out of her. Now what?

It wasn't every day he had mind-blowing sex in secret with a girl he had babysat. The best way to proceed wasn't entirely clear, and he was feeling strange, off-kilter. Like she had sucked all the sense out of him, and he didn't really trust anything that might come out of his mouth. He had the feeling he might just say something totally stupid and completely lacking in game.

Piper didn't seem to have anything to say either, though, just lying there looking as stunned as he felt, her chest flushed with exertion. Brady briefly worried about the wet spot that was probably being generated on Shelby's bedspread as they lingered there, but decided there wasn't any point in worrying about it. It was too late to feel guilty, and he'd already passed the pervy point of no return about thirty minutes ago.

On his side, he relaxed, his hand resting idly on her belly. Brady tasted a mouthful of her hair, because it was piled up all in front of his face, and because he could. It made a slight crunching sound as he gummed it between his lips, and he decided it didn't taste like anything, but he still liked the feel of it.

"What are you doing?" she asked, sounding as unnerved as he felt.

"Nothing." He sighed. "I should go back to Zach's room. It would be bad to get caught here."

"Yeah, it would."

Was he actually disappointed that she didn't protest? He

was. Insane. He had completely lost his mind. There was no reason he needed to snuggle with Piper all night, and it was damn risky. Innocent children should not see the erection that he'd be sporting again before long, given the proximity of Piper's lush, naked body. It was not cool. He needed to leave. It was neither the time nor the place to pull her close against him and fall asleep with her in his arms.

When, if ever, that would be, he had no clue.

Brady sat up. Then he groped around the bed for his underwear and pulled them on. Piper just watched him in the moonlight, not making any effort to cover up her gorgeous body, which both pleased and pained him. He wanted another go at her. Yet at the same time he was feeling wracked with guilt for not resisting the temptation she had presented.

Because what was he thinking? Seriously? How could anything come out of this other than his nuts in the viselike grip of Danny Tucker? The thought made his dick shrivel. With a sigh, he kissed her on the forehead and said, "See you in the morning."

"Good night."

That was it. Nothing else. Yet he could feel her eyes trained on his back as he crossed the room, could feel the weight of her desire, the smell of their activities sweet and tangy in the air around him, the sexual tension drawing tight again. She wanted more. And so did he.

Brady stood in the hallway for a minute, confused and aroused, not necessarily in that order. He wasn't exactly sure what had just happened, or what was still happening. He couldn't get the image of Piper's mouth opened in a silent cry as she came, her nails digging into his back, out of his mind. It was seared in there, like a brand on his brain.

It had been more than he could have expected, intense and satisfying. Yet he'd done so little, and there was still so much of her he would like to touch and taste and explore. He hadn't even gotten to do much more than palm her breasts, and that was a crime. Because she had a full, creamy, delicious, absolutely off-limits breast, with a cherry-on-top nipple that made his mouth drool just thinking about it. Which had his mind already rationalizing that if he'd already been inside her, why couldn't he suck her nipple? Right? There was logic in that.

Overall, there was no logic in anything he'd done in the last week. He should be back in Chicago looking for a job, not wasting a couple hundred bucks on gas to drive to Cuttersville. Not pawing through old papers that showed that Rachel the candlestick-lobbing chick had a fiancé with the same damn name as him. Not plowing Piper Tucker as thoroughly as the back field in early spring.

The thought of which had him rock solid all over again.

Brady went back to Zach's twin bed and punched the pillow a few times. Tossed and turned. Contemplated how creepy it would be to jack off in a bed that wasn't his own. Then decided that it was a teen boy's bed, so it would hardly be the first time a palm had been rosied there while picturing a perfect breast.

He was feeling a little desperate, so he needed to do something.

Stroking himself lightly, he imagined what it would be like to have Piper on his cock, riding him hard and fast, those beautiful breasts bouncing freely.

Damn it. He squeezed hard.

It had been a long time since he'd had this kind of immediate reaction to a woman, and it was disturbing.

All he knew, as he imagined Piper on top of him, his hand sliding over his hard cock even faster, was that he wasn't going back to Chicago on Sunday, as was his original plan.

He was going to stick around his old stomping grounds for a little while and further renew an old acquaintance or two.

Hopefully while naked.

PIPER WATCHED BRADY WALK ACROSS THE ROOM IN his underwear, his shoulders twisting as he slipped through the door and pulled it softly shut behind him. She could hear him go into Zach's room and flop onto the bed, the frame creaking, the sound so loud that she marveled that they hadn't woken up the girls.

A flush of shame rose up her body. Whatever she had wanted to do with Brady, whatever she had done, it shouldn't have been with the twins in the house. She was horrified at her lack of discretion, her inability to separate her lust from what was right. She loved those girls and she would never want them to see anything inappropriate, hear anything she couldn't explain.

The thought had her out of bed and pulling on her now-dry clothes with trembling fingers, the dampness between her thighs an obvious reminder of what she had done. As was the soreness she felt. What had felt so glorious when it had been happening now felt a little tawdry. She climbed back in bed and tried to remember the certainty she'd felt when Brady had taken her hand, the wonder she'd known when her orgasm had just reached out and yanked her into a freedom of pleasure she'd never experienced before.

That was what she had to think about—remember—tomorrow when it was awkward and she felt guilty.

That for the first time in a long time, maybe ever, she had done something selfish, and it hadn't hurt anybody. It had felt amazing to take what she wanted. Or to be taken, more accurately.

The house was silent, only the occasional pop as the old Victorian settled. The rain had stopped. Yet Piper felt something.

She realized Rachel was standing in front of the bed.

Of course she was. Piper pressed the palm of her hand to the soft tank covering her chest, startled even though she really shouldn't be. "Please stop doing that."

She lay on her back, eyes wide-open, Rachel at the front of her bed, very much aware of Brady in the next room. Was he sleeping? He had the biggest penis she'd ever seen. Not that she'd seen a lot, but still. It was a lot to contend with. Could she fit that in her mouth? She wasn't sure.

Rachel glared at her, and waves of recrimination rolled off her. Or maybe Piper just thought they did. But for some reason she felt like she was being judged. "I'm a grown woman," she told Rachel. "It didn't mean anything."

But that was a lie. Even as she spoke the words she knew it was a lie. And while Brady might have willingly screwed her, more to the point she had screwed herself. It was a real challenge to eat one potato chip and leave the rest of the bag untouched. Brady was going to be in town for a few more days and he was one salty, crunchy hunk of delicious that she wanted to taste all over again.

The way he kissed her . . . Have mercy.

Sighing, Piper gripped the bedsheet and watched her new ghost BFF hovering as clearly as her thoughts of Brady.

It seemed there wasn't going to be any sleep for her that night.

Chapter Five

❧

"HEY, SHEL, WHAT'S UP?" BRADY WAS SURPRISED HIS cousin had answered her cell phone. She wasn't known for even remembering where it was, let alone answering it. But then again, she was probably worried about being away from her kids.

"Brady? I'm fine. How are you?"

Hopping onto the kitchen counter, his favorite place to sit since he'd been tall enough to jump up there, he stared at the note Piper had left him. He'd stayed in bed until he was certain she and the girls were out of the house. Slightly cowardly—okay, a lot cowardly—but he couldn't face eight-year-old twins whose babysitter he had banged until he'd had some coffee. Truthfully, when he saw Piper for the first time since he'd left her naked in the dark, he wanted to be alone with her, though he didn't see that happening anytime soon. Piper's note said they had gone out to the farm so the girls could play with her brothers, and he was welcome to join them. And that there were fresh towels under the sink. And coffee ready to be perked. Fresh eggs in the fridge.

The note was almost a novel, she was being so considerate. She'd left her cell phone number and told him not to worry about Snoopy, that she'd already let the dog out. There was a spare house key sitting next to the note.

Another marked difference between the women of his childhood and the women in the city. Back in Chicago, a woman would have left him before he'd woken up and sent him a brief text that was more or less a breezy thanks and blow-off. Or maybe it was just the women he'd been dating, women who thought more about themselves than anyone else, or were more concerned about appearing in control and unaffected. It cluttered his already jumbled thoughts, clouded his feelings. What did he do with Piper Tucker? Well, aside from what he'd already done, which he'd like to repeat as soon as possible.

But he shouldn't. He should talk to her, thank her for a great time, explain how they both knew it couldn't happen ever again.

That was exactly what he should do.

"So Shel, how is it that you never leave town, yet you manage to do it the one weekend I'm here in Cuttersville?"

"What! You're in Cuttersville? Are you shitting me? Why?" He heard her shifting the phone. "Boston, Brady's in Cuttersville."

Boston's response was too muffled to understand.

Brady put his foot on the kitchen chair across from the counter, stretching his leg and inspecting his toenails. Time to clip those fuckers. "You having fun in Cincinnati?"

"Why are you in Cuttersville? Is everything okay? Is your dad dead?"

He rolled his eyes for the benefit of the empty room. "As

far as I know, he's not dead, and if he was, I imagine you'd know before me. I just wanted to visit my family, that's all. I had some time off work." A lot of time. An indefinite amount of time.

"Well, how long are you staying? We won't be back until suppertime tomorrow."

Which was when he'd originally been intending to go back to Chicago. But he heard himself say firmly, "I'll be staying all week." And maybe longer.

"Good. Where are you staying?"

"Last night I stayed at your house. I came late, it was raining. I thought you'd be home. Fortunately, Piper let me in. Damn, Shel, that girl has grown up. She's beautiful." Brady winced at the sound of enthusiasm in his voice. He hadn't meant to be that obvious, but it just came spewing out, like corn from the thresher.

There was a long pause then Shelby said, "Brady Stritmeyer. You keep your hands off Piper, do you understand me?"

Oops. A little late for that. But he could lie with the best of them. "What? God, I just said she was beautiful and you're jumping to conclusions. You're beautiful, and I don't want to sleep with you." It was a lame argument and he knew it, but there was no way in hell he was going to admit that he had nailed Piper in Shelby's bed. Not only because he didn't want to hear it, but because some things were private between a man and a woman. Special.

He winced again. Jesus. Different, that's what he meant. Different. Not special, just not ordinary, not an everyday sort of one-night stand. Not a one-night stand at all. Not something selfish and crude, not about getting off and nothing else. About feeding the fire that had sprung up between them so immediate and so hot it was . . . special.

Holy crap on a cracker.

"I know you. You like women. But Piper isn't just any woman. She's Danny's daughter. She's special, you know that."

Oh, my fucking God. There was that word again.

He did know that Piper was special to her family. He also knew that Piper knew it. And he suspected Piper would rather just be considered normal. "She's also an adult. I can't get over how much she's changed."

"People change when you've been gone a dozen years."

There was condemnation in that, loud and clear. "Ouch. Point made. I should have come home once or twice, I admit it."

"You should have. Your sister's kids are in high school. When was the last time you saw them? When was the last time you saw your grandmother?"

Brady pressed the on button on the coffeemaker. If he was going to be lectured, he needed some coffee. "I'm here now."

"Why no warning? Are you in trouble?"

That made him snort. "No, I'm not pregnant."

"Very funny."

He kind of thought so. "So, do you happen to know the name of the fiancé who was killed in your house?"

"What?" That caught her off guard. "What are you talking about?"

Hopefully, it also prevented a tirade.

"You know, Rachel's cheating fiancé who did a head butt with a candlestick."

"No, I have no idea," she continued. "Why?"

"I can't believe no one bothered to ever ask at some point." That bothered him. A lot.

"It didn't seem important to the story. He was a dog, clearly."

"That dog has the same name as me."

"What, Brady? Really? That's a coincidence. How did you find that out?"

As the scent of the coffee filled the small kitchen, Brady looked around. He'd never felt unsafe in this house, ever. But suddenly he wished he could see what Piper saw. It was like walking around in a cemetery without headstones. He could be knocking into dead people left and right and he had no idea. "Piper and I found some papers in the basement, a photocopy of the original newspaper article."

"Why were you in the basement?"

"Why are you not focusing on the relevant facts of this conversation?" he asked, exasperated.

"You're staying with Gran tonight, right?"

So she was fixating on him being in her house with Piper. "I don't know. I haven't talked to her yet. Why?" He felt irritated with his cousin.

It was clear she felt the same way. "You really should have called and let me know you were coming to town."

"Oh, for Chrissakes. I'm sorry. Next time I won't call you at all," he said petulantly. "I'll talk to you later."

"Can I talk to Piper before you hang up on me?"

"She's not here. She took the girls to the farm."

"Oh. Well, that's good. That's great. What a wonderful idea."

Shelby couldn't be more transparent if she were glass. "Yeah, I get it. You don't want me around Piper. But if Gran doesn't have a bed for me, I'm staying here tonight and you can just suck it."

"You've always been a brat." But there was no heat to her voice, just a begrudging affection.

"And your favorite cousin." Brady grinned, jumping down so he could get himself a mug. "Admit it." He and Shelby had always been close, despite the distance.

"You're not so bad." There was a pause. "Brady. I'm glad you're home."

He smiled. "You know what? I am, too. Who would have thunk it?"

SHELBY HUNG UP HER CELL PHONE AND TURNED TO her husband, who was looking damn sexy in his jeans, the river behind him. "We have to go home."

He didn't react at all. "Is someone bleeding?"

"No."

"Broken bones?"

"No."

"Then we're not going home." He took a sip of his beer and shook his head. "Shelby, we never leave the kids. Ever. It's two nights total, and we've already managed one and nothing bad happened. In fact, we had some damn hot sex last night and I would like to repeat that tonight. There is no reason we need to go home early unless your grandmother died."

That shocked her enough to smack him on the arm. "Don't say that! Not even as a joke. You're borrowing death. God, Gran can't die."

"And you're borrowing trouble. What do you think is going to happen?"

"Brady is in our house with Piper. He's always had a way with girls."

"Piper is an adult. She's not stupid."

That was easy for him to say. He wasn't a girl. Shelby knew what happened when boys talked you out of your panties. You wound up married and pregnant at eighteen with bad hair. Wait. That was her. "I know she isn't. But I just have a bad feeling."

"Honey. We're at Oktoberfest. It's a beautiful day. The only thing you should be feeling is a buzz from the beer."

"I can't believe I'm drinking a beer at eleven in the morning." That did freak her out a little. She was having a hard time not being responsible. In fact, it hurt a little to loosen up.

"I think it's awesome." Boston leaned over and gave her a kiss that curled her toes.

Fifteen years and there was still toe curling. Shelby found herself relaxing.

"What do you think the girls are doing?" she asked, snuggling up close to her husband. She didn't have to guess what Zach was doing. It would involve headphones in his ears at the neighbor's house. But the girls were still so little. She worried.

"Getting dusty just like their mama did when she was a little girl. Lilly more so than Emily, but they'll both be filthy by noon."

"They do take after me, don't they?" she said ruefully. They attracted dirt like a Hoover. "It's too bad none of the kids are neat like you."

"But I love all of you anyway. Now come on. I want you drunk and going down on me in the hotel room by dinner."

Shelby sucked in her breath. Yep. Still toe curling. "I think that can be arranged."

PIPER SAT ON THE BACK PORCH OF HER PARENTS' house, a glass of iced tea in her hand, as Lilly and Emily were hanging out on the play set with her brothers, Logan and Jack. The sun felt good on her arms and she tried to feel and act normal, not like a woman with a big, old, dirty secret.

It had been disappointing that Brady was still sleeping when she left. But on the other hand, she wasn't sure she could face him in the light of day in front of the girls, his eyes slumberous, his feet bare. She wasn't a good actress, and she was a lousy liar.

Which was why she was rocking, rocking, rocking, anxiously waiting for someone—mostly her mother—to figure out that she had had sex the night before. Excellent, intense, orgasm-causing sex. The kind that made her want to do it all over again.

Her cheeks felt hot and it wasn't even that warm of a day. Piper took a sip of her tea and almost choked.

Lilly was dangling upside down on the trapeze bar. "Piper! Look at me!" She let one hand go to wave, before her shirt slipped down over her chin, baring her round belly.

"Great job," Piper said, waving back.

"I'm so glad you never did that," Amanda said, sitting in the wicker chair next to her, inspecting her manicure. Her dog Baby was at her feet, snoring gently. "All I can think is that she's going to fall on her head. It scares the crap out of me."

"She's a total monkey. She's not going to fall. And I wasn't much of a risk taker as a kid." Nor was she normally now. With one notable exception. Piper felt the burn of embarrassment when she thought of how she had dropped her robe for Brady in the hallway the night before.

"Well, thank you for that. I appreciate it. You never gave me a single gray hair." Piper's stepmother glanced out at her two boys. Logan was beating something in the yard with a stick and Jack was standing on the swing instead of sitting in it. "Your brothers on the other hand . . . What do you think Logan is hitting with that stick?"

"I think it's a garter snake." The scene was chaotic, dogs running all around, one of them tripping Emily and sending her down to the hard-packed dirt, Jack leaping off the swing in a superhero move that resulted in him accidentally kicking one of the other dogs, who darted away with a look of alarm.

"Eeeww. Why do boys like snakes so much? Is it Freudian?"

Piper had long ago given up trying to figure out boys, young or old. "If it is, that seems a little counterproductive to be slapping it with a stick."

Her mother was about to speak, then seemed to think better of it. She just crossed one long leg over the other, her tribal maxi skirt effortlessly stylish, her gold sandals and pedicure immaculate. Her hair was shorter now than it had been when Piper was a kid, but it was still just as blond as ever. As far as Piper knew, she'd yet to need to dye it to cover any gray.

When Piper had first come to live with her father, when Amanda was hired as her nanny, Piper had favored simple, tomboy clothes. She had wanted to downplay her looks, disappear into the background. Standing next to Amanda had made that easy, and Piper had taken comfort in holding her hand, knowing that Amanda would always command attention in any room they walked into, and people wouldn't see the little girl with the eyes too big for her head. They had been quite a pair, the expensively dressed heiress from the city and the bald, abandoned kid. But it had worked, and while her father had been falling in love with Amanda, Piper had as well. Amanda was truly the woman she thought of as her mother, and when she'd hit her awkward middle-school years, she'd tried to imitate Amanda's style, with disastrous results. A gawky thirteen-year-old wearing tangerine orange skinny jeans and big gold hoops with a suitcase of a handbag had been a sight to behold, especially since she had still been painfully shy. Fortunately, that phase had been short-lived and she had settled on a feminine style that suited her, consisting mostly of skirts and dresses and simple jewelry.

She wondered what kind of woman Brady was attracted to. She'd taken extra care with her hair and light makeup that morning, but she'd been forced to leave before he'd woken up because the girls had been restless. The note might have been a little wordy, now that she reflected on it, but she had wanted him to feel welcome.

Oh, yeah, she definitely wanted him to feel welcome. She supposed dropping her robe had accomplished that, all right.

"So, would you like to tell me who he is?" Amanda asked.

"What?" Piper glanced over at her mom, startled out of her thoughts. "Who who is?"

"The man who has you smiling that secret smile."

Yikes. Piper tried to look innocent. "I don't know what you're talking about." But she could feel her cheeks burn even hotter. She must look like she'd been slapped with a box of blush at this point.

"Oh, come on." Amanda wasn't known for her patience or gentle coaxing. "You know you can tell me. I hope he's hot. Is he hot?"

Piper laughed. "It's not what you're thinking." Actually, it was probably exactly what she was thinking. She hesitated, because saying his name out loud would surely give her away. But not saying anything about Brady would make it even worse when her parents did find out he was in town. Which they would, sooner than later.

"It's just that Brady Stritmeyer showed up at Shelby's last night and it was a shock to see him, that's all. I was thinking how weird it is that he came back after all these years." That hadn't precisely been what she was thinking, but it was close enough to the truth to sound legitimate. She was curious about his return. That was no lie. It just wasn't her primary concern at the moment. Things like how long he was staying and when she could kiss him again were occupying far more of her thoughts at the moment.

Amanda sat up straight in her chair. "What? Brady is in town? Why? And why do we still have these damn wicker chairs? It's like sitting on a bale of straw."

Piper chose the easier question to answer first. "We have the chairs because Grandma likes them." Her father's mother, Willie, and Amanda were as different as ants and elephants, but they had a deep respect for each other. "And I don't know why Brady is here."

"Curious."

"What, about the chairs? Not really." Even though Piper knew that wasn't what her mother was talking about.

"No, why the prodigal grandson has returned home. Talk about wasted potential, that one. It's depressing. And you know how I feel about depressing."

Oh, yes. She knew. It was one of Amanda's catchphrases whenever she didn't like something. If it was depressing, it didn't have the Amanda stamp of approval. Sometimes she was serious, sometimes she was exaggerating. Piper was used to her being slightly overdramatic. But her words reminded her of what Brady had told her about not painting anymore. "Why do you say that?"

"He could have been a successful artist, but he went off to art school in Chicago with all that swagger and bravado. It turns people off, makes it so no one wants to help you get ahead. It's a shame, because he's talented, but he was always a little insecure."

"You think he's insecure?" Piper asked in amazement. She wouldn't have said anything of the sort. "He seems pretty sure of himself to me." In bed and out.

Amanda swept her eyes over Piper. "I always thought you had a bit of a crush on Brady. But I'm sure you've out-grown that."

Maybe not. "Why does it matter? He's just here for a few days."

Piper didn't like the way she was being studied, like a butterfly pinned to a board.

"I like Brady," her mom said. "I always have. He's charming and funny. But he's the kind of man who is never satisfied."

Piper could disagree on that one. He'd seemed plenty satisfied the night before, but she couldn't exactly say that.

"He's restless," Amanda added.

"So?" Piper sounded petulant and she knew it. But she didn't want her fantasy squashed like that dead snake in the yard. Couldn't she pretend and indulge for a day or two before someone stomped on her head? She had known when she had gone into the hallway that there was no possibility of a relationship with Brady. But that didn't mean she wanted the bloom knocked off the rose quite so fast. She wanted to enjoy the memory for at least a day or two before reality kicked her in the teeth.

"He's not good enough for you," Amanda said in a soft voice. "You deserve the best. Someone with staying power."

Because she'd had a mother who died and a shitty stepfather. Because she'd been a bald little ragamuffin.

She got it.

She knew it.

She lived it.

Her parents wanted the best for her. She understood that and appreciated it. She loved them for it. But sometimes it was just damn frustrating to have them treat her differently. Like she was fragile. Never once in her childhood had she been spanked or grounded, even when she had acted up, which hadn't been that often, but still. Nor had she really taken any risks or made any mistakes because she hadn't wanted to scare them, cause them worry.

Her father had saved her from hell, so she shouldn't cause him any. That was how she'd lived her life.

But damn it, she was a grown-ass woman, and if she wanted to get naked with her childhood crush, that was her business. It might have been a huge mistake, but it was her right to make it.

"Thank you," was simply what she told her stepmother, because she wasn't going to argue with her. Piper didn't argue. She'd learned by three years old never to do that.

"I always thought you'd end up marrying Cameron," her mother said.

Which made Piper want to roll her eyes. "Cameron and I are best friends, that's it." Nor was her friend the kind of guy who dug in and committed himself to a lifetime, which was why Amanda's argument about Brady seemed doubly ridiculous. Piper heard the irritation in her voice and winced.

Fortunately, Logan chose that moment to serve as a distraction by whacking the dead snake so hard it flipped up and smacked a gawking Lilly in the eye with the tip of its tail, who burst into tears. Several of the dogs started barking, agitated.

"Daniel Logan!" Amanda said, bolting out of her chair and striding to the end of the porch. "That's it. You are as done as dinner, mister. Apologize to Lilly and then get in the house."

"It was an accident," Logan protested, with the irreverence only thirteen-year-olds seem to have.

"For real? I mean, did your arm holding a stick just happen to fall on a snake? If you're going to form an argument, make sure it's a solid one. I know you watch *Law and Order*. The end result was an accident, but your initial action caused it."

Piper got up herself to go and comfort Lilly, who was

putting up quite a fuss. "There's a snake in my eye!" she screamed, running towards the house.

Amanda snorted and shot Piper a grin behind her hand. "The kid has style. I like the drama of it all."

It certainly wasn't what Piper would have done at that age. But Lilly was a pint-sized drama queen. She flew up the porch steps and hurled herself at Piper, who hugged her.

"Let me see it," Piper said gently, coaxing Lilly to step back so she could see whether any damage had been done. "Okay, everything looks fine. It will feel better in a second."

"What's all the racket about?" Piper's father came out the back door onto the porch and adjusted his baseball hat to better shield him from the sun.

"Logan hit Lilly in the eye with a snake," Amanda told him. "And I would like a cocktail."

Logan was sullenly coming towards the house, his gym shoes kicking up dust. He'd gotten tall and lanky over the summer, his hair bleach blond like his mother's.

"Oh. That sounds about right for a Saturday." Piper's father moved to the end of the porch, ruffling Piper's hair on the way by as though she were still Lilly's age. "Daniel Logan, I think you're coming with me to clean out the chicken coop."

"Dad, it was an accident!" Logan looked appalled at the injustice.

"Coop still needs cleaning."

"Piper never has to clean out the chicken coop," was her brother's final protest, the stick still in his hand and striking the porch posts now.

Amanda stared down her son. "Really? Piper was cleaning the coop when you were in diapers."

"Man up," their father told him. "It's not that big of a deal."

Piper felt bad for Logan. It had been an accident. Sort of.

He certainly hadn't meant to hit Lilly in the eye, even if he had been smacking the crap out of a snake. But whereas she normally would offer to do the task herself, she bit her lip and resisted the urge. She spent far too much of her time trying to please other people instead of herself.

"Piper." Her brother turned big, brown, pleading eyes on her. He might be a sullen teen a lot of the time, but when she looked at him she still saw the toddler who'd snuggled up with her and followed her everywhere.

"I'll help him," she said.

Her parents protested. She knew she was undermining their intention, but truthfully she couldn't say no to her brothers. Given that Lilly was gasping with laughter from being swung around by her father, it seemed she was already over her injury, so there was no permanent damage.

Piper moved with Logan across the hard-packed dirt of the yard to the perky yellow coop. Her brother was as tall as she was now, and it was a little disturbing. He wasn't a little kid anymore. They both pulled on waders from the vintage cabinet sitting next to it and went inside. Logan reached for a rake while Piper shooed the hens up the plank to their nests.

"Sometimes I hate living on a farm," Logan commented.

"I've lived in a trailer, and trust me, this is a whole lot better," she told him. A farm was smelly and hard work, but Piper loved it. It was Tucker land and it would always be there. Like her father—consistent, reliable, steady. But Logan didn't appreciate that as much as she did, and why would he? He didn't know any better, hadn't experienced hardship. Their younger brother, Jack, was more likely the one to wind up running the farm someday. Not only did he look like their father, with a stockier build and caramel hair, he loved the farm, had been clamoring for tractor rides since he was a toddler.

"Why do you still live with us?" Logan asked, giving a halfhearted pull at the straw and the muck beneath it. Then he seemed to realize how that sounded. "I mean, not that I want you to leave, but I don't know why you'd want to stay. I'm not coming back home after college."

"Because I love you." Piper made kissy sounds in his direction, laughing at the look of discomfort on his face.

He stuck out his tongue. "Don't you want to have a boyfriend or anything? I mean, I would kill to be alone with Jasmine. Mom won't even let her over here to watch a movie."

Piper was a little startled by the vehemence in his voice. Oh, Lord, puberty had kicked in with a vengeance. "Yeah, I don't think Mom is going to let that happen anytime soon." Their mother didn't like Jasmine, and there had been under-the-breath comments about sluts sniffing around. She wasn't about to trust Logan and Jasmine in a dark room.

It brought to mind the challenge of dating even at her age, because she did live with her parents. Until now, it had never particularly bothered her. Now it suddenly seemed to matter. If she did want to pursue a flirtation with Brady, how was she even going to do that? Once she came back home from Shelby's the next day, they wouldn't have any opportunities to be alone. Then when Brady left town, she would regret it.

There was no guarantee that he'd want a repeat of the night before, but she certainly did. How many opportunities was she going to have for sex like that? Not a lot. She shouldn't have done it in Shelby's house. If she had her own place, she would at least have had a shot at knocking boots a second time. Without any ghosts around.

Maybe she was still living at home because it was safe. Easy. Maybe it meant she didn't have to date, to go out there and risk getting hurt. Or being lonely. She had never been alone, not since she was eight years old. Her stepfather had left her alone a lot, and it had scared her to the point she'd made up an imaginary friend to keep her company. Anita had moved to the farm with her but eventually had stopped turning up altogether.

But the fear of being alone was still there, deep down, in a dark, ugly spot.

She wasn't a kid anymore, and she wasn't fragile. But if she didn't move on, she couldn't really expect her parents to treat her any differently.

She didn't want to live her life making decisions based on fear. She wanted to be in control.

Maybe she hadn't gotten enough sleep the night before, what with Rachel staring at her half the night and memories of Brady's body over hers clouding her thoughts, and her judgment was impaired, but as the smell of chicken waste clogged her nostrils, she felt a swell of conviction. "You know, Logan, maybe it is time for me to get my own place."

BRADY'S GRANDMOTHER WAS EXACTLY WHERE HE would have expected her to be on a Saturday afternoon. She was on her front porch, rocking, a baseball cap on her head. Only whereas ten years ago she would have had a book in her hand, now she had an e-reader in front of her. As he came up the walk, she glanced up.

"Heard you were in town," was her dry greeting. "About goddamn time."

"Hi, Gran. It's good to see you, too. How are you doing?"

"Fine." She assessed him. "Well, your hair's not blue. That's a start."

Geez, you dyed your hair as a rebellious teen and you never lived it down. "My hair hasn't been blue in fifteen years." Though he couldn't be too annoyed. Seeing her face, he suddenly felt his gut clench. He had missed her. She looked older than he remembered. Her skin was thin and she'd lost weight. Her feet were a road map of blue veins and her hand shook a little. It shocked him. Scared him. Had a flood of guilt rushing over him.

"Thank God—that's all I can say about that." She patted the chair next to her. "Remember when you had that Mohawk? Your hair was jacked all the way to Jesus."

That made Brady grin. "It was a statement."

"You can call it what you want. Come sit down and tell me what's going on in your world." She held up the e-reader. "I'm just reading a novel I downloaded by that guy who writes those smaltzy books. It's crap, but at least on this thing I can make the print huge. Easier on the old eyes."

Brady kissed her on the cheek and sank into the chair next to her. "You think every book you read is crap, but you keep reading books. So I'm not sure I believe you."

"Smart-ass."

The weight of her stare fell on him hard. "So what's new in Cuttersville?" he asked.

"Just the usual. Your aunt has a new boyfriend she met on the Internet. She's all atwitter because he's five years younger than her, but I think she's lying. Or more likely he's lying. The man is sixty if he's a day. Nicole Platner got divorced. She was your age, right? Abigail Murphy is having a baby."

"Oh, yeah?" Abby had been his girlfriend his senior year in high school, and while it shouldn't surprise him that a peer was procreating, it was jarring.

"About time. She's been married seven years. We were all starting to think she was missing a uterus."

Brady laughed. "Maybe they just wanted to wait."

His grandmother made a sound of dismissal like that was the stupidest thing she'd ever heard. "So what's life in the big city like? Do you have a girlfriend?"

"No." Brady drummed his thumbs on his thighs. "And I got laid off from my job three days ago." He shrugged, wanting to give the impression it wasn't as big of a deal as it really was. "The economy, you know."

His grandmother gave a sharp nod. "Well, we all know the economy sucks donkey dicks, but I'm sorry to hear that. Did they give you a severance package?"

Leave it to Gran to say it like it was. He couldn't help but laugh. "Donkey dicks about sums it up. I just get what was left of my vacation and sick days. About three weeks' worth of pay." The thought had his ass cheeks forming a fist. He was fucked. "I'm thinking I'm going to have to break my lease because there's no way I can afford my rent, and jobs just aren't that easy to come by. Not in three weeks. Not in marketing."

"So you came home." Gran nodded, like this made complete sense to her. "You can look for a job in Chicago from here with no expenses. Makes sense."

That hadn't exactly been his plan. He hadn't really had one. But now that she said it, it did make sense. He could stay with family and look for a job. Most companies would be willing to do a first interview on the phone. Maybe he could even get a part-time job here while he was surfing online for a real job. "So can I stay with you? I don't think Shel has the room."

"Hell, no, you can't stay with me. I like my space." She crossed her ankles. "I haven't lived with anyone since Shelby moved out fifteen years ago, and I'm not about to start now. Besides, I host my book club here on Mondays and belly dance on Thursdays. Then Richard and I have a standing date on Saturdays."

Brady stared at her in disbelief. "Are you kidding me? You're letting your own grandson be homeless because you have some dude named Richard over for meat loaf? That

ain't right, Gran. I'm not going to cramp your style, I swear."
Nor was he going to reflect on the fact that his grandmother
had a more active social life than he did.

"Don't get your panties in a wad. I'm not going to let you
be homeless, though I should, given that you couldn't be
bothered to come home once in ten years. But I won't. I just
meant you can't live here with me. But you can stay in the
blue house I own over on Swallow Street. It's vacant
right now."

Brady sank back in his chair, relieved. He hasn't realized
how much he'd been wanting a bailout of some sort. His
grandmother had always owned a number of properties and
he was glad one was tenant free. "Okay, cool. Thanks. Does
it have furniture?"

"No."

Great. He was going to be living in an empty house while
he watched his bank account shrink. Well, it gave him three
weeks anyway. Three weeks to figure out what the hell he
was doing with his life. Because when the money ran out,
he was going to have to make some tough choices about his
apartment back in Chicago. He bit his fingernail, wondering
how long it would realistically take to find a job. Word on the
street was six to nine months. If that were the case, he might
just find himself back in Cuttersville for the duration. It was
really the most affordable option. Hell—only option. "Do
you think I can get a part-time job here? Maybe do those ghost
tours or something?" Even if he made a few hundred bucks
while he was there, it would help him pay for the gas back to
Chicago.

The seriousness of his situation started to dawn on him.
He had no savings to speak of and he still owed a year's
worth of payments on his car. Sweat broke out in his pits,
and his hands went clammy.

"Shelby hasn't run those tours in years. She's too busy

since the twins came along. And while there was a spike in business after Darius Damiano had the Murphy house on his TV show, the last few years haven't been very lucrative for tourism here. I guess every ghost gawker in the Midwest has already checked us out."

Well, shit. "Is there a cell phone store or something I can work at?"

"You should talk to Boston. He'd be more helpful with that than me."

Reality was definitely sinking in with *Titanic*-like speed, and it bit the big one. He was going to be living in his grandmother's vacant house on Swallow Street. This wasn't exactly where he had pictured himself at thirty-one years old.

"By the way, the house needs cleaning up. In exchange for free rent, you need to paint the main rooms on the first floor and redo the landscaping out front."

Seriously? He guessed it was only fair, but at the same time, he felt like he was being fleeced just a little by his own grandmother. "Fine. But you supply the paint."

"Of course. So Shelby says you're sniffing around Piper Tucker."

Brady sighed. Was this worth free rent? He wasn't sure. It didn't help that he *had* been sniffing around her. He'd sniffed *and* buried his bone. "I am not sniffing around Piper. She was at Shelby's last night babysitting. It was a coincidence." That he happily took advantage of. "But what would be the objection to me dating Piper, by the way? Shelby acted like I was a convicted child molester."

"Piper is Danny's daughter."

Well, that was stating the obvious. "It's kind of insulting, you know. I'm getting the message loud and clear that no one thinks I'm good enough for Piper. If I were interested. Which I'm not." He was offended. So maybe he was a thirty-one-year-old unemployed guy living at his grandmother's,

ERIN McCARTHY

but he wasn't a bad guy. He had charm. He was nice enough.
He worked hard. Sort of. And he had good biceps. Brady
reached for his gran's drink, suddenly feeling the need for
fortification. He took a big swallow and choked. "Holy shit,
Gran! That's whiskey."

"Of course it is. I'm diabetic. I can't have all that sugar
in lemonade anymore, so I water it down."

"Except whiskey isn't water." Brady coughed again. The
burn fed down into his lungs. "Christ. That's whiskey with
a shot of lemonade."

"Oh, don't be a wimp. And no one is saying you're not
good enough for Piper. But you have a life in Chicago, and
she deserves the right man for her."

"Who, Gandhi?" There was no man who could live up
to the ideal they all seemed to have. He suddenly felt sorry
for Piper on top of his personal irritation. She was going to
have a hard row to sow when it came to dating. There wasn't
going to be much approval for any man she chose.

"I thought he was dead."

"Speaking of dead people." Brady turned in his chair so
he was facing her better. "Did you know I have the same
name as the dude who was murdered in the white house?
Rachel's fiancé?"

"Sure, I knew that."

Of course she did. "And you never bothered to tell me?"

"Why does it matter?"

"Well, why do I have the same name? Was he a relative?
Was I actually named after him or was it just a coincidence?"

"He's like a great-great-great-great-uncle or something
like that. As for your first name, I don't know if it was
intentional or not. Your mother was a twit. It seems a little
too with it of her to be aware of ancestors' names, but there's
no telling. Ask her."

That figured. "I haven't talked to her in twenty years,

Gran. You know that." His mother had left her family when Brady was two years old for a man who had wound up in prison for the dumbest crime ever. He had robbed a bank after giving his license to the teller for a legitimate withdrawal. Brady's father had remarried, and while Brady got along just fine with his stepmother, he and his father had always butted heads. His contact with his mother had dwindled to nothing when he'd entered middle school, and Brady had no idea where she was at this point.

"Well, like I said, she was a twit. Your father was blinded by her boobs."

Ugh. Brady didn't want to think about it. "I could do without knowing that."

Gran shrugged. "She had a nice rack. It was the only thing she had going for her. I smelled loser from the minute I met her. But don't worry, you're nothing like her."

That was reassuring.

Chapter Six

❧

JESSIE STRITMEYER WATCHED HER GRANDSON LEAVE with a curious eye. So he'd been laid off from the so-called fancy job he'd been bragging about having for years. She was glad. He'd never been happy in that office, and she knew it. She could hear it in his voice every time she talked to him on the phone. He wasn't the kind of man who liked to be stuck in a cubicle like a chicken in the nesting coop. Brady had always been what his stepmother liked to call a free spirit. Jessie knew that was just code for someone who liked to make their own damn rules.

Brady wasn't meant to live in a congested city. He was meant to be back home, with his family, carving a living out of something artistic, something on his own terms. She knew this as surely as she knew the damn dog from next door would be in her yard later, plowing his paws through her dusty miller and mums. Little shit.

If losing his job was what it took to bring Brady home, Jessie was all for it. She just hoped his ego wasn't dented too deep. Men had fragile egos. She also knew what it would take to keep him home—a woman. There was a reason he was thirty-one and he'd never even come close to marriage. It was because he needed to meet a local girl, not those yoga-mat-carrying city girls.

Piper Tucker was actually perfect for him. She would ground him, make him want to stay put. That girl had eyes so huge that no one could resist wanting to help her, be kind to her. She was like a cocker spaniel begging for a treat. Plus, she wore her heart on her sleeve, and Brady needed to be hit over the head with it or he'd never notice it.

Shelby seemed to think Brady was intrigued by Piper. Jessie didn't know how the girl felt about it, but Piper didn't appear to get out much. Surely Brady would seem enticing to a girl who spent all her time with snotty five-year-olds.

Her cell phone, which was sitting on the wrought iron table next to her lemonade, rang. "Hello?"

"Mrs. Stritmeyer? This is Piper Tucker. How are you, ma'am?"

Well, well. How was that for a coincidence? "I'm just fine, Piper. How are you? Those great-grandkids of mine behaving themselves?"

"Oh, yeah, they're great. We've been out at the farm all day."

"Good, good." Jessie crossed her ankles and waited for Piper to cough it out. She wasn't calling out of the blue for her health.

"So, I've been thinking about getting a place of my own and my mom suggested I talk to you and see if you have any properties available."

Even better. "Sure. I have a two-bedroom house. Since you're family, in a manner of speaking, I'll give it to you for five hundred a month. How soon were you looking to move?"

"As soon as possible. It's time for my own space."

That was code for wanting to get laid on her own terms. Jessie understood that. It was exactly why she'd told Brady he couldn't live with her. She was used to her Saturday-night special with Richard and she didn't want to let go of it. "I understand, dear. You can move in October first. Or, if that's not soon enough, you can move in now, but just so you know, Brady is going to be staying there for a few weeks painting and cleaning up the yard. If sharing the place temporarily with him doesn't bother you, I'm fine with you moving in tomorrow. I won't charge you until the first of the month. Or if you want to skip the security deposit, you can help him with the painting."

Float the balloon, let them grab the string. That had been a strategy that had served her well over the years. And it would tell her loud and clear exactly how Piper Tucker felt about her grandson.

There was a pause that lasted about three heartbeats then Piper said, "I can help with the painting. That's no problem. And the yard work. But I can wait until Brady goes back to Chicago to move in. I don't want to . . ."

"What, dear?" Jessie smiled. The girl sounded like a Dickens urchin staring into a pastry case and saying she wasn't hungry. Her longing was palpable.

"Bother Brady. But I can certainly help with sprucing the house up. Thank you so much, Mrs. Stritmeyer. I really appreciate it."

Jessie smiled. She was right again. As usual. Piper Tucker wanted her grandson, and Brady was never one to pass up a pretty skirt.

If all went well, he'd have her knocked up by Christmas.

If Piper was maybe getting the raw end of the deal with Brady, well, Jessie wasn't going to worry about it. Her priority was her family, even when they were idiots. Well, except for Brady's mother. But she wasn't blood. And anyway, it wasn't like Brady was a bad catch. He just wasn't necessarily the freshest. But Piper could throw some breading on him and he'd grill up just as nice. There was a lot of potential there.

Jessie put her e-reader down. She was suddenly hungry for catfish. Maybe she could hit the Busy Bee Diner for lunch. Manipulation worked up an appetite in her.

AMANDA LAY IN BED WITH HER BIG, STRONG HUSBAND and pouted. Her leg draped over his, she said, "I can't believe Piper just decided to move out. Just like that. Sayonara, Mom and Dad. See ya. Wouldn't want to be ya."

She knew it was the right thing for her stepdaughter, to have her own space, her own social life, but it still sent a pang through her heart. She was going to miss her. Piper had made Amanda a mother, and she was used to her constant, quiet presence.

Danny sighed, his hand resting lightly on her backside. "It had to happen sooner or later, I reckon. But yeah, it caught me off guard. But we still have a couple of weeks before she moves out, and she'll be in town nice and close to Shel and Boston so they can keep an eye on her. Plus she won't have the drive to work in the winter. I do worry about that, and now she'll be five minutes from the school."

"What prompted it, do you think?" Amanda trailed her fingers over Danny's chest and worried. It had been so sudden, Piper just announcing she was moving out, that it made her feel like something was wrong.

"I don't know. She is twenty-four. Maybe Daniel Logan hitting puberty made her feel old. Or maybe it's the smell in his room. It's like wet dog and old cheese in there. It's disgusting."

It was. There was no denying it. Her sweet little baby boy had sprouted armpit hair and an attitude. "I don't think that's it."

"Well, you could ask her."

Amanda rolled her eyes in the dark. "Why are you always so damn logical?"

"One of us has to be."

She stuck her tongue out at him.

"I saw that."

"How could you see that? It's pitch-black in here."

"Because I have tiger eyes."

She laughed. It still amazed her how much she loved this man, and how content she was on the farm. They had traded houses with Danny's parents when Jack was born, to give them more room, and Amanda loved lying in the four-poster bed in their bedroom with the window seat, the soft breeze wafting in through the window, bringing with it the scent of her lavender plants. Danny had thought she'd gone overboard with them, but if three were pretty, wouldn't thirty be even prettier? It wasn't like they didn't have the space.

This was her home, the place she had found herself. So had Piper. Amanda just couldn't imagine the farm without her.

"I'm going to miss her," Danny said, his voice tight. "But this isn't about us, hon. It's about Piper. Maybe she just needs to spread her wings a little. I guess we should be proud we helped her regrow her wings, because when she came to me, they were clipped tight."

"I know." Amanda kissed his shoulder. "You're a good father."

"You're a good mother. And a hot one to boot." He smacked her ass.

Normally that was a good indicator that friskiness would

follow, but Amanda was still too distracted to take the bait. "I feel this huge emptiness inside me."

"I have something I can fill it with." He placed her hand on his erection.

Really? Not that she was surprised. He was a man, after all. "Pervert." As if she really minded. She had to say she was pretty pumped that after all these years and kids, they still couldn't keep their hands off of each other. "I'm having a moment and all you can think about is sex."

"That's because it's real simple. When women are stressed they want to talk about it for three days straight. A man wants to be distracted thoroughly so he can ignore his feelings. And what's a more thorough distraction than sex?"

He had a point. "Maybe I could use a distraction myself." Otherwise she might burst into tears.

"Really?"

He sounded so hopeful it was cute. "Really. Show me what you got."

Amanda knew her husband was the kind of man who liked to rise to a challenge. Literally.

"Oh, I've got it. And you're going to like it."

He was a man who always spoke the truth.

Amanda most definitely liked it.

PIPER SAT ON THE COUCH AT SHELBY AND BOSTON'S, a novel in her hand, and glanced at the clock on her cell phone for the sixth time in six minutes. It was almost ten and Brady wasn't there. She hadn't heard from him all day. Not a single peep, text, or appearance. Not that she had necessarily wanted him to show up at the farm. It would have been damn near impossible to pretend that nothing had happened between them, and her parents would have been closely watching her. It would have resulted in a very uncomfortable afternoon.

But that didn't mean she didn't want him to want to be where she was.

Or to at least acknowledge in some way that they had swapped spit and a whole lot more the night before.

Though how he was supposed to do that, she wasn't exactly sure. She wasn't a one-night-stand kind of girl and she wasn't sure what you did the day after, though if she had to puzzle it out, she supposed you didn't do anything the day after. Hence the phrase "one-night stand."

But she'd thought he would feel a bit obligated to see her again, even if it didn't involve more sex. He was staying at Shelby's house and they shared family. They weren't strangers who'd met in a bar.

Maybe he had found somewhere else to stay for the night, like the house on Swallow Street.

Which was highly disappointing. Or maybe he wanted to stay with his grandmother. She understood. But it would be nice if he told her, so that she didn't have to anticipate his key in the door every time she heard the slightest noise in the house. She could give up pretending to read her book, change out of her sundress into her pajamas, and cleanse her pores. Not that he owed her anything.

Yet at the same time, "It was nice to see you" went a long way. That was it. That was all she needed. Just some sort of acknowledgment of something. That was it.

Piper shifted on the couch, annoyed with herself. Her thoughts were running in a circle and it was completely pointless. She should just put the pj's on. She glanced at her phone. Two more minutes. At ten she would go change.

She wondered whether Jessie Stritmeyer had told Brady that she was the renter moving into the house on Swallow. Piper guessed that he was helping his grandmother out on his vacation time, which was very sweet of him. Most guys his age wouldn't devote all their free time to tearing out an old lady's weeds. It made her like him all the more. Not that she needed much help in being attracted to him. She did have to wonder if Jessie had told him that she was going to be at the house helping out as well, and how exactly he felt about that.

Truthfully, Piper wasn't sure how *she* felt about it. Calling Jessie had been impulsive, something she normally wasn't. Change wasn't something she ever sought out—in fact, she avoided it. But standing in chicken poo with her little brother, who was not so little anymore, Piper realized that change had to come sooner or later and she might as well be the one driving the truck towards it. At least then she was making her own decisions, not reacting to decisions made for her.

Plus it had definitely occurred to her that if she ever wanted to have a sex life again, she couldn't exactly do that while living with her parents. And she did. She really, really wanted a sex life, regardless of Brady going back to Chicago. Last night had proved that she had certain physical needs and that maybe it was time to start dating. Create a sex life for herself. Lord knew her parents had one. She had heard a thing or two she would have preferred missing many a night on her way to the bathroom.

She appreciated that until now, no one had suggested she move out. They had assumed, and rightly so, that when the time came, she would tell them. But her parents had been stunned to hear that she wanted to move out now. Not in three months, or after Christmas, or when her car was paid off. Just now, in a couple of weeks. Suddenly, with no real plan.

Yet she hadn't changed her mind, even hearing the words out loud, or when seeing her parents' astonishment.

A key turned in the front door. The relief she felt embarrassed her. She had put far too much stock into Brady coming back. Plus she'd been letting her imagination run away with her as she'd sat there picturing working on a house with him for three weeks, thinking things she had no business thinking.

Maybe she needed to keep her paintbrush and roller tucked away until Brady went back to Chicago, because she had a feeling that playing house with him wasn't going to be good for her state of mind. Or her libido, if he treated her like a casual friend.

Like someone he couldn't be bothered to call or text all day after they had sex.

Yeah. She was losing it. So probably, to keep her sanity, the less time she spent with Brady, the better. She had just learned a very valuable lesson. She sucked at casual sex. She may have gotten exactly what she wanted, a hot interlude with Brady Stritmeyer, but she was going to be flip-flopping between gratitude and regret for weeks.

"Hey," he said, giving her a smile as he appeared in the doorway of the parlor, wearing jeans and a T-shirt, a bottle of wine in his hand. "How was your day?"

The day before, Piper hadn't given any thought to Brady Stritmeyer. To moving out or dating or strolling into a man's bedroom to attempt to seduce him.

Now she was melting at his smile and picturing him as her boyfriend, husband, father of her children.

It made her completely annoyed. That she was still so vulnerable, so needy, that she would jump from A to Z without a pause at any letter along the way, even when she gave herself fair warning not to be ridiculous.

"Good. How about you?" To her own ears, she sounded clipped, but to anyone who didn't know her—and Brady most certainly didn't know her—she imagined she sounded perfectly fine.

"I spent some time with my grandmother and then my stepmom. The kids like the farm?" He moved into the room, sat down in the chair across from her, set the wine on the coffee table.

"Yes. They usually do. How is your grandmother?" And had she mentioned Piper's plans to him?

"She's good. Same as usual. Full of fire and whiskey." He shook his head with a laugh. "I asked to crash with her for a few days and she said no. It seems she has a standing Saturday-night date."

"I guess she's earned her right to privacy." Piper bit her fingernail. "So are you going back to Chicago tomorrow?" She knew he wasn't, of course, but she didn't want to come right out and ask him how he felt about them working on the house together. And she didn't know what else to talk about, anyway. She kept looking at him and picturing him over her, his erection pushing inside her, his eyes dark with desire.

"No. I'm actually going to stay a few weeks in my grandmother's rental house. She said it's empty but I can stay there for free if I do some work around the place."

Piper waited for him to elaborate but he didn't. She also thought it was strange that the work was in exchange for rent. Like Brady was the one in need, not his grandmother. "So . . ." She hesitated, but then just went ahead and asked, "Are you on vacation from work?"

"Nope. I got laid off. The economy sucks, you know." He stood up. "I brought us some wine. You like Pinot Grigio? I'll get us a couple of glasses."

"Oh!" Brady had lost his job and he'd brought them wine. She wasn't sure what to make of either one of those things.

So she started with the obvious. He must feel bad about losing his job. "I'm sorry about your job."

Though he didn't look particularly upset. In fact, he smiled as he moved past her and reached out to tug a piece of her hair. "Come into the kitchen. It's cozier in there. For the record, my job sucked. It's no great loss, but I will miss the paycheck."

"Are you moving back here for good?" The thought made her want to throw up, but in a good way. Piper stood up and smoothed the front of her sundress down as she followed him towards the kitchen.

"No, just until my vacation pay runs out. Three weeks. But then I'm going back and hopefully I'll have a job sooner than later."

Piper's gut fell back down to its approximate appropriate location. "That sounds like a good plan." She needed to break it to him. What had seemed like a perfect arrangement a few hours ago now seemed like the dumbest thing ever, right after eyelid lifters and pajama jeans. "So did your grandmother tell you she rented the house on Swallow to me?"

"What?" Brady blinked at her. "What do you mean?"

"I mean, I'm renting the blue house. I'm supposed to move in in a couple of weeks, after you and I finish the painting and the yard work."

"I thought you said you live with your parents." He set the wine on the kitchen counter. "And are you seriously saying that my grandmother conned you into working on the house, too?"

Piper nodded. "She isn't charging me a security deposit if I do the work. And I just thought that it's time to move out on my own. My brothers are coming up fast and things are changing. I'm an adult now."

His green eyes darkened and his gaze dropped to her

chest. "That you are," he told her. "Well, that sounds exciting for you. Just remember that my grandmother is a shark."

Piper smiled, relieved that he didn't seem to have any issue with them being around the house together. Or that he thought there was anything suspicious about the timing of her moving out, because frankly, it was not a coincidence. She wouldn't be taking this step if he hadn't showed up. "Will do."

Brady turned to find glasses for the wine in the cabinets and to hide his expression from Piper. She had no idea what she did to him. He had brought the wine because he'd wanted some way, however lame, to express his appreciation for her note, her thoughtfulness. For her body. Hell, he'd stood in the grocery and had actually debated buying a bouquet of wildflowers that had been in a bucket of water next to the register, because they reminded him of Piper. How ridiculous was that? You didn't give flowers to someone you weren't dating. You just didn't. It was creepy. It was a stalker-weirdo way to make a woman sorry she'd gotten naked with you.

So he had restrained himself, but now he wished he had them all over again. There was just something about Piper that got under his skin. She stood there, in a dress that showed her cleavage to major advantage, that glorious hair spilling over her shoulders, and told him so bravely that she was an adult, a woman. As if he needed reminding. Christ. It had been all he could do all day to not drift off into daydreams of motorboating her breasts. He hadn't wanted to do that since he was thirteen.

Now she was telling him that she was moving into the house he was temporarily staying at, that she was going to be around helping him patch drywall and pull weeds. Bending over. Reaching up. On all fours.

How was he supposed to resist that? And did he really

have to? He'd already had her once. Did it matter if he went there again? He didn't think so. Spending time with Piper while he was in town was a perfect distraction. He would just have to make it clear that he was going back, that it was casual, a satisfying way for both of them to pass their time. She understood that already, he was sure of it. But if he made it clear, then they could both enjoy what they both so clearly enjoyed—each other.

"So, are you willing to go to the cemetery with me?" he asked her as he pulled down two glasses. "I want to see old Brady Stritmeyer's headstone." The thought kept surfacing, so he figured that meant he should go for it.

"Are you serious?" Piper looked horrified by the thought. "That won't freak you out? It would me. Seeing my name on a grave." She shuddered.

He hadn't really thought of it that way. He just wanted to see if he felt any connection, any kinship to his long-lost bludgeoned relative. "Nah. I'm not dead, so what difference does it make?" He opened a drawer, searching for a corkscrew. "I just want to see it. We can go on Monday after Shelby gets home."

"I have to teach."

"Well, I know that." Brady reached out, because he couldn't resist, and gave her a soft kiss, maybe to test whether she would pull away or accept his touch. She stiffened slightly but didn't move away. "I meant after school."

"I can probably do that."

"Meet me on the playground," he murmured in her ear. "I'll bring beer and we can make out on the jungle gym." He was kidding, of course. But it sounded exactly like something he would have said at fifteen. Given that Piper made him feel like a horny teen, it seemed appropriate.

"I'm afraid I'll get caught. I've always been a good girl, you know," she said.

Brady almost groaned out loud. "Well, good girls usually like bad boys."

"I can't argue with that."

Her fingertips were making contact with his abs, right above his waist, a teasing touch that was all it took for an erection to spring up. He was about to kiss her, for real this time, thoroughly and with tongue, when suddenly she shrieked and stumbled backwards.

"What's wrong?" he asked, reaching out to stabilize her, his desire replaced with confusion.

"Something pulled my hair." She reached out, her hand visibly shaking, and rubbed the back of her head. "It was hard, like a yank."

Goose bumps rose on Brady's arms. Piper was not the kind to lie or exaggerate. She looked terrified and he didn't doubt that something had just happened to her. A protective instinct he hadn't even known he had kicked in. Brady reached out and pulled her into his arms without hesitation, like he could shield her from whatever had just dared to harm her. "Are you okay?"

"I'm fine. It just scared me." She looked up at him, her eyes huge with fear. "They've never touched me before."

Ghosts. She meant ghosts. It was the only thing that made sense, yet it was so bizarre to him that he couldn't formulate a response.

"Piper?" A shaky voice drifted down the stairs over top of them.

Piper jumped.

"They know you by name?" Brady joked, relieved to hear a normal child's voice. Somehow it shattered the tension of the moment.

She gave a shaky laugh. "That's Lilly, not a ghost." She added, "Though I guess they probably do know my name. If they can see me, they can hear me, right?"

"I don't know."

"Me either." She moved to the kitchen doorway. "Lilly, I'm down here in the kitchen. Are you alright, sweetie?"

Shelby's daughter appeared, wearing princess pajamas, her caramel-colored hair sticking up on the left side from sleep.

"I thought I heard you scream." She sounded clearly annoyed that she'd been woken up, her tone accusatory. "You scared the crap out of us. Emily's still upstairs hiding because we thought you got killed."

Brady snorted. "Yep. The kid's a Stritmeyer despite her last name," he murmured. She had the no-nonsense tone of Brady's grandmother and the looks of Shelby, particularly the crazy hair.

"I'm sorry. I saw a spider." Piper pulled Lilly into a hug.

"Who are you?" Lilly asked, eyeing him like she knew without a shadow of a doubt his intentions towards her baby-sitter were not pure.

"This is your cousin Brady," Piper said in a high-pitched voice he'd never heard her use. "He's visiting from Chicago. You remember Brady."

Brady had to say that he wouldn't recognize this kid on the street if she tripped him. She'd grown quite a bit since he'd seen her two, maybe three, years ago.

Lilly seemed to agree. "I don't remember him. But my mom talks about him all the time." Then she seemed done with the conversation and circled back to her original irritation. "I totally thought you got killed."

Little bloodthirsty, this one.

Piper pulled Lilly into a hug, kissing the top of her tousled head. "Nobody got killed or is ever going to get killed."

"Lots of people get killed. My mama said that the girl

who lived here, like, five million years ago killed her boyfriend. She beat the crap out of him."

Really? Brady wanted to reach out and hold Piper's hand. He was fairly certain she was the one who needed comforting at the moment, not Shelby's brazen offspring. Brady had a feeling he had sounded a lot like Lilly at eight, and he felt sorry for his stepmother. She'd had her hands full with him. Piper, on the other hand, had been a sweet kid. Everyone had said that. Never a cause for trouble.

She seemed to know how to handle Lilly. Instead of letting the conversation about beating the crap out of people continue, she shut it down with a few gentle but firm words.

Piper frowned at Lilly. "I happen to know for a fact that your father does not want you saying that particular word. I've heard him reprimand you for it, so I suggest you rethink your vocabulary."

"What? 'Crap'?" Lilly asked as she moved into the kitchen away from Piper, studiously checking out the open wine bottle and their two glasses on the counter. "Mommy says that all the time."

"No, she doesn't." Piper gave him a pointed look. "Does she, Brady?"

He just grinned at her, unwilling to get sucked into her obvious lie. "So you're Lilly, huh?" he asked his cousin, reaching out and ruffling her enormous and snarled hair. "Did anyone ever tell you you look just like your sister?"

Lilly giggled, pushing her loose front tooth back and forth with her tongue. "Duh. We're twins."

"How do you know?"

That stymied Lilly for a second. Piper rolled her eyes at Brady, but she looked amused.

"Because we have the same birthday. And Emily's face looks just like mine."

"Maybe Emily isn't real. Maybe she's just your shadow. Or your reflection. Or maybe you're the reflection."

"You're nuts," was Lilly's opinion. "There's pictures of us in the hospital together when we were born."

"Photoshop."

Lilly made a sound of delighted exasperation.

Piper looked like she was fighting a laugh, which pleased him. Seeing her scared had done terrible things to his gut. He much preferred her smile.

"I'm going upstairs to let your very real twin know that I am most certainly not dead. I'll let you two sort this out, but when I come back down, it's time for bed, Miss Lilly Macnamara. And you, Mr. Stritmeyer." She gave him her best teacher's look. "You need to stop filling this girl's head with nonsense or she'll never be able to sleep."

But Brady looked unrepentant. With the corner of his mouth turning up in a slow, sexy smile, Brady scratched his nails lightly across his chest. Piper felt that deep ache pulsing between her thighs again and she crossed her ankles. He was so damn charming. Lilly had been suspicious of him initially, but five minutes later she was already warming up to him. Piper knew how the girl felt. She had been bedazzled by Brady when she was Lilly's age.

Maybe even still was.

"A little nonsense now and then is relished by the wisest men."

She knew that quote. Gene Wilder as Willy Wonka had said it. For some reason, it tripped a switch inside her, one that caused her desire to burn even brighter. She had loved that movie when she was a kid, had desperately wanted to be Violet Beauregarde—well, before she blew up like a blueberry anyway. She had wanted her confidence, her smile. Her hair.

If the girls were in bed, would she and Brady have a

repeat of the night before? It wasn't appropriate. At all. She knew that. She needed to resist. Or discourage. Or not throw herself at him. But it was going to be hard given how unnerved she'd felt when something or someone had yanked her hair so hard she'd had tears spring up in her eyes. What she really wanted was to feel Brady's arms around her again.

She took a deep breath and gathered her resolve. "When you buy a chocolate factory, let me know. Otherwise, it's bedtime for the twins."

Brady laughed. "She's a tough one," he told Lilly.

"Nah," was Lilly's opinion. "Piper is the best babysitter on the planet."

Kids had always liked her. Piper smiled, genuinely touched. "Thanks."

"I babysat Piper once when she wasn't much older than you," Brady told her.

"Really? You must be *old*."

Too old for her. That was what Piper needed to remember. She needed to repeat to herself ten times in a row that a man like Brady, who dated sophisticated city women, was not going to be interested in a small-town girl like her, who had nothing of interest to say to the living or the dead.

But that wasn't exactly what she was thinking as she went up the narrow wood steps to the second floor of the creaky old Victorian house.

What she was thinking was that she wanted to indulge in a little nonsense herself. The naked kind. Again and again.

Emily was standing at the top of the stairs, looking a lot more terrified than her sister had. "What's going on?"

"Nothing, honey. Everything is fine." Piper swept her into a hug, enjoying the tight grip of Emily's warm arms around her middle. Family meant the world to her, even convoluted relations like these girls. "Your cousin Brady is here for a visit. It was a surprise for your mom and dad, only Brady didn't count on the surprise being that your parents aren't home."

When she paused to reflect on it again, it was interesting that Brady had chosen to come home after being laid off, given that he hadn't done so in a decade.

It wasn't Shelby's cooking that had drawn him back, that was for certain. Piper had tried her pot roast on more than one occasion and it never improved.

But it must have been something other than a deep desire to see cornfields and old women with perms.

"Oh. So why'd you scream?" Emily asked.

"I saw a spider." Which was mostly true. She had seen one the night before. A shiver crawled up her spine when she remembered standing there in front of Brady, knowing he was going to kiss her, desiring his lips on hers with a fervency that was palpable, alive, when suddenly her head had snapped back, her hair tugged so hard she'd felt the sting of all her nerve endings in her scalp.

"I hate spiders."

"Me, too. Now let's say hi to your cousin, then it's back to bed, little lady."

"We're coming up," Brady said, Lilly hoisted on his back. They bounded up the stairs, he making sure to give her as much bounce as possible, she squealing with delight as she sailed up, then smacked down onto him with each step. "Hey, Emily, how goes it?"

"What do you mean?" Emily gave him a suspicious look.

Brady laughed. "We have Piper Junior here. Emily, I just meant how are you?"

Piper turned away from Brady and Lilly, his words confusing her. She wasn't sure what he meant by that, but it sure didn't sound like any sort of compliment.

"I'm tired," Emily told him.

"Into bed." Piper ushered her back to her twin bed, her bedding a soft pale pink in contrast to Lilly's in-your-face electric purple with a zebra accent. Maybe Emily *was* like her. Piper worked hard to keep her life and her surroundings calm, peaceful. And maybe that was boring. In fact, she knew it was boring, but it was what it was and she couldn't change, not for anyone and certainly not for a man who wouldn't be content to stay put. He was restless. If you nailed Brady's foot to the floor, he would just run in circles.

His nature and her nature were two different things and there wasn't any point in listening to her body. It was like a dog who'd just sat up and started panting, but there wasn't any treat being offered. Not really. He might have caved the night before, and he might cave again, but it was pointless. Most likely he didn't really see her as much more than the weird little kid she'd been.

Maybe it wouldn't be as hard to resist sleeping with him again as she'd thought.

Brady dumped Lilly onto her bed and both girls crawled under the sheets, yawning.

"What do you think Mom and Dad are doing right now?" Emily asked innocently, obviously missing them just a little.

Brady snorted. "I can think of a thing or two."

Piper shot him a warning look. It figured his thoughts would go there. She didn't disagree with him. She was pretty darn sure that Shelby and Boston weren't in Cincinnati for the culture and food but for the hotel room with no small children interrupting them. But the kids didn't need to know about their parents knocking boots. "They're probably eating room service and watching TV in bed. And missing you."

Giving each of them a kiss on the forehead, she moved to the door, shooing Brady out into the hallway. Making sure the night-light was still on, she clicked off the overhead light and closed the door softly. Feeling the need to remind him what was appropriate in front of little girls who soaked up everything he said, she faced Brady in the dark hallway.

"I didn't say anything," he said, grinning, before she could even speak. "Don't give me that look."

"What look?" She knew exactly what he meant and it bothered her that she was so easy to read.

"That look of total disapproval." He rested his hands on her waist. "It's not going to prevent me from kissing you."

Be strong. "Why would you kiss me?" she asked, intending it to sound disapproving like he clearly expected. Instead, it sounded breathy and flirty.

"Because you taste delicious."

She tried to stand her ground, even as her body swayed towards his. "I shouldn't have done what I did last night. With the girls here . . . It was wrong. Way too risky."

"But we didn't get caught." He kissed her ear, his hot breath making her shiver. "Let's go make out on the sofa and not get caught tonight either."

Piper wanted to. She wanted to melt against him and have his lips make her forget everything around her, all her responsibilities, all her worries, all her fears. "Just kissing," she said, which was a lame attempt at standing her ground. Way to not be a slut.

His eyes danced with amusement. "Sure thing." He sounded like he thought that was about as likely as recreational space travel. "But if you start taking your clothes off, I won't be held accountable for my actions."

She would not blush. She just wouldn't. She did. Damn it. What was she supposed to say to that? So she just went with honesty. "I would love to take my clothes off for you again."

He made a sound in the back of his throat and he nipped her ear.

"But not here, not tonight." She wanted to ask, suggest, imply that the blue house on Swallow might be a better venue for their activities, but she couldn't force the words out. Not even in a dark hallway after she'd already had sex with him.

Moving away from him, she started down the stairs, annoyed with herself. Why couldn't she just say what she wanted? She'd already thrown it all out there. It wasn't like the man hadn't figured out she had the hots for him. Why was suggesting they do it again so shocking? He'd already suggested it himself.

It was because she had been trained from an early age not to ask for anything. She knew that. She'd worked to erase that particular remnant of her childhood but those fears and habits were like cobwebs that clung to your skin. You could shake and they didn't go anywhere. You could use your other hand to scrape them off and they would just transfer to the clean hand, an annoying sticky mess that might break into smaller pieces but was still there until you blasted it off under the faucet. Piper hadn't figured out how to turn the faucet on yet to wash off her childhood. Sometimes she wasn't even sure she should.

But then she found herself mute, unable to ask for what she wanted, needed, and it frustrated the hell out of her.

Asking or suggesting the rental house meant she had expectations beyond tonight, and she was afraid to have expectations.

"Well, there's always the blue house," Brady said as he followed her down the stairs, his voice a warm promise. "It will be empty except for you and me."

"True." Now that he had said it first, all her anxiety instantly disappeared, consumed by desire. What had she been worried about? He clearly wanted to have sex with her as much as she did with him. Last night proved it. Now proved it all over again. "Swallow Street." She darted a glance back at him on the stairs as she neared the bottom of the staircase. "Ironic-sounding name, don't you think?"

His jaw dropped. "Holy shit. You're going to kill me."

She wasn't sure where that bit of flirt had come from. But it had popped into her head, and so she'd said it. Not that she'd ever swallowed, but there was always a first time for everything. The look of astonishment on his face amused her.

Looking back at him, Piper never saw it coming. As she hit the landing at the bottom of the stairs, her body was facing the parlor, her head turned to Brady. So when something slammed into her head, the pain was so unexpected, she felt her knees buckle. The smell of blood filled her nostrils and she grabbed onto the railing, confused and woozy.

"What the fuck?" Brady asked.

Grabbing her temple, Piper fought back a wave of nausea and tried to figure out what had hit her.

It was a candlestick, now lying on the floor in two glass pieces.

Chapter Seven

THE DOG CAME RUSHING INTO THE ENTRYWAY, BARKING at the wall as Brady tried to retrieve his gut from his throat and wrap his arm around Piper, who looked like she was fighting the urge to faint dead away. Jesus Christ. A fucking candlestick had lobbed her in the head.

But while she was bleeding a bit above her left eye, it was a small cut. She was more scared than injured, so Brady pulled her against him in a lean, taking her weight. "It's okay. You're alright."

"She threw a candlestick at me." Piper's voice shook. "They've never thrown anything at me. Ever. And she pulled my hair earlier."

"Maybe they just don't like someone being here when Boston and Shelby aren't. Maybe they're trying to protect the girls. A warped sense of loyalty or something." Brady led her into the kitchen, where he sat her down in a chair and pressed her wineglass into her hands. But then immediately, he realized her hands were shaking too badly to hold it without sloshing liquid all over her sundress, so he took it back and held it to her lips. "Have a sip."

"My feelings are hurt," she said after obligingly taking a drink. "I know that sounds stupid, but I always thought that the ghosts liked me. That they wanted to show themselves, talk to me because I could understand them, have sympathy for them. You know, like an outcast kind of thing."

Brady pretty much sucked when it came to comforting anyone. He liked to be left the hell alone, or distracted with a workout or a trip to the microbrewery, when he was feeling bad. So he usually offered the same to someone when she was upset. Yet Piper wasn't the kind of girl who would pump iron to improve her mood. She was different, and Brady found himself sitting in a chair at the ancient kitchen table, pulling her out of hers and onto his lap, where she snuggled up against him without hesitation. Without thought or warning, his hand reached up and stroked that glorious hair.

"Maybe she meant to hit me, not you. Think about it. Didn't Rachel kill her fiancé with a candlestick? And he had my name, I might add. Plus I was flirting with you. Maybe it offended her." That actually made more sense than anything else. Why would a spirit suddenly take a hit out on Piper? From what he could tell, everyone liked Piper. People defended Piper. They didn't hit her.

"I didn't see anything both times tonight, no sign of her. Normally I see her. I can sense her. Last night, after you left my room, Rachel stood at the foot of the bed for hours."

Well, that was damn creepy. Brady wondered if Rachel had been there when they'd been getting busy. Ghosts seemed to have zero respect for privacy. Not that he could blame anyone for wanting to see Piper naked, dead or not. "She didn't say anything?"

"No."

"And you've been seeing her since you were a kid?"

"Yes."

Brady shifted, the weight of Piper in his lap oddly comforting. He wasn't even the one who needed comforting, yet there it was. A sense of contentment stealing over him. Like nights cuddling in a cozy kitchen weren't a bad thing. Not a bad thing at all. He wiped the little streak of blood that still marred her forehead, wanting its glaring color gone from her beautiful skin. The cut was tiny but it still twisted his gut to see it, and he wiped her blood on his jeans.

"I think maybe we need to look a little more deeply into what happened, Piper. I think Rachel is trying to tell you something."

"What—that she hates me?" Piper asked, her voice glum.

Brady laughed. "I don't think it's personal, honey. I just suspect she's pissed that she's stuck here. And hell, maybe she didn't kill old Brady. Maybe that's what she's trying to tell you."

"I didn't ask to be able to see ghosts."

"And I didn't ask to be laid off. It just is what it is."

Piper sat up and studied him so intently he fought the urge to look away. To crack a joke. Run for the nearest highway. His normal tactics when someone tried to ferret out his emotions or ask him for an honest answer. He forced himself to stay put, to keep his mouth shut, to wait to hear what Piper had to say.

"Why did you stop painting?" she asked.

Because it was Piper, and because she really wanted to know, Brady found himself telling her the truth. "Because it hurt too much. To see something in my head and then produce a pale, watery version of that vision. It was like being disappointed over and over again, like the Coyote always trying to catch the Road Runner. I got tired of smacking into a wall repeatedly."

"I understand," she said, and he knew she did. "But we're usually our harshest critics."

He was definitely hard on himself. But then again, his art professors hadn't exactly wrapped him in fluffy clouds of praise either. "Are you your harshest critic?" Though he honestly couldn't see what anyone could criticize about Piper Tucker, loyal daughter, lover of children and animals.

"Yes, I probably am. Though it would seem the spirits are none too pleased with me tonight."

"Maybe Rachel is just jealous that you're alive and she's dead." Brady imagined it would suck with a capital S to just have to float around and watch people living. He wouldn't be all that happy about it himself, especially if there were no erections in the afterlife.

He was also glad that she didn't ask him anything else, for a better explanation, or to urge him to take up a paintbrush again. Encouraging people got on his nerves. If he wanted to do something, he would, plain and simple, and no amount of lip from another person was going to change that.

"I feel really sad for her," Piper said. "Regardless of what she did or didn't do, no one is denying that her fiancé was unfaithful. That must have hurt."

"Yeah. Cheating sucks." He'd never understood it himself. "If you're not fully in a relationship, you should get out. It's the right thing to do. But people are selfish. They want everything. A loving spouse and a flirt buddy. It's all about ego." Which was why he'd never gotten married. He knew himself. He had a short attention span when it came to women and he never wanted to be that douche bag of a husband who was eyeing every big-breasted waitress who served him.

"I had a boyfriend whose ego needed its own zip code," Piper said softly. "It ruined my sophomore year in college."

"That's sucks. I'm sorry. At least it was only a year and not a lifetime." Though Brady kind of wanted to find the guy and punch him in the face for making Piper miserable.

Piper climbed off his lap and stood, disappointing him. He liked the way she felt all up against him, her ass resting on his thighs, her breasts pressing against his chest, her arms wrapped around his waist.

"At least he never cheated. Or not that I know of. But he was the kind who was so into himself, he had to tear down other people, including me. I'm surprised I found the nerve to break up with him," she said. "Sometimes I have a hard time saying what I want."

Brady reached out and took her small, delicate hand into his. "You didn't seem to have a problem last night." For which he was very grateful.

"But I still didn't use words. I wish I could figure out how to unstick my tongue."

He appreciated how honest she was being. It made him feel less of an ass for sharing his feelings about his art. "Tell me what you want right now." If she didn't want to talk, he could think of a thing or two to do with her tongue.

"I want . . ." She shook her head. "I don't know."

"Start with the first thing that comes to mind."

"I want to make out on the couch, like you suggested."

He could get on board with that. "Done."

She laughed, and it was the best thing he'd heard all day. "But you know we can't . . . you know, because of the girls."

Her inability to say "sex" amused him. "What—play loud music? Make popcorn? Watch a Disney movie marathon?"

She rolled her eyes. "You know what I mean. We can't. So maybe we shouldn't get started on something we, uh, can't finish."

"Are you questioning my self-control?" Which she probably had a good reason to, because he wasn't sure he wouldn't try to charm her out of her panties if he got started on kissing her and feeling those curves up against him.

"No. I'm questioning mine."

Brady watched her take a sip of her wine, leaning against the kitchen counter, her cleavage eye level with him, a hint at the glorious breasts he really wanted to worship in full detail. She had no idea what she did to him. That she was the most intriguing mix of innocent and direct, shy and sensual. She was the kind of woman who acted like what his stepmother would call a lady. She didn't slam other women or snarl at her parents or a boyfriend. She would never be rude to a sales associate or stiff the waitress. Yet she was clearly a woman who wanted to explore her sexuality, who was comfortable with her body.

It was a combination that appealed to him on some deep, intrinsic level, sent a rush of desire through him so aggressive that just that little glance at her chest bursting out of her sundress and hearing her words had his cock rising and ready to salute.

"Then there's no hope for me," he told her. "So why don't I walk you to your room before we both do something you'll regret."

The corner of her mouth turned up. "You wouldn't regret it?"

"I seriously doubt it. But I'm not as good of a person as you are."

"Says who?"

"Everyone, if you asked them, but I don't think that's necessary. Let's just say I'm not the most selfless guy you're going to meet, and you can bet the farm on that." He wasn't fishing for compliments. He was just being honest. He was no blue-ribbon prize. Maybe a consolation prize, but even more likely he was a participation prize. Thanks for showing up; you get a restless, selfish, jobless guy. What kept him from being a booby prize altogether was that he was good in bed. Everyone had at least one talent, and he supposed that was his.

Piper didn't argue with him. But neither did she agree. She just put the two-thirds-full bottle of wine on top of the refrigerator and drained her glass, which she then rinsed out, like she knew he wasn't the kind who could be convinced with a few words. "Are you done with your wine?"

He stood up. "Yes." There were just a few drops clinging to the bottom of the glass. Before he could blink, or think too long about how amazing it would taste to dribble that red wine on her nipples and suck them into tight peaks, Piper had both glasses washed and turned upside down on a dish towel.

"I think you have low self-esteem," she told him, surprising the crap out of him. "And that's unfortunate because I'm sure you have a lot to offer to the people in your life."

Brady stared at her for a second, wondering whether he should be offended. But he couldn't be. He just started laughing. "No one has ever accused me of having low self-esteem. I think that's a first. It doesn't sound nearly as sexy as being selfish does."

"I don't suppose so."

"I'm bringing sexy back, that's for sure. I'm unemployed and I have low self-esteem." God, that killed him. There was one thing he wasn't, and that was displeased with himself. Piper clearly couldn't believe that someone was just hardwired to be selfish, yet wasn't a total dick. But he figured that summed up the majority of people.

Piper tucked her hair behind her ear. "Now I have all these dumb slogans about being sexy running through my head."

"Like what? Selfish is the new sexy?"

"Sexy is saving a whale."

Now he really laughed. That was an awful slogan. He wouldn't have thought of Piper as being funny, necessarily, but she had a dry wit that entertained him. "That it is. Come on, you whale saver, let's go to bed." Before he kissed her and never wanted to stop.

At the top of the stairs, Brady stood in front of Shelby and Boston's room and tried to resist those big brown eyes staring at him. Piper had her hand on the knob but she didn't go in the bedroom, and it wasn't fair that he had to be a better man and walk away. It just seriously wasn't fair and he sucked at it.

But he forced himself to brush a kiss across her forehead and murmur, "Good night."

Then he walked across the hall, closed the door behind him, and locked it for his own protection.

What the hell was he doing?

He was starting to really like Piper Tucker—that was what.

Flopping down on Zach's twin bed, he tried to remember all the reasons why he couldn't date Piper.

The only one that even came to mind was her father's fist, and Brady was starting to think he'd risk a black eye for the chance to explore what there might be between them.

Brady groaned into his pillow. Nothing. That was what there was. He was going back to Chicago and she would marry a nice boy who farmed a neighboring plot of land.

That was reality.

The truth stank and so did Zach's sheets.

* * *

HER STEPFATHER, MARK, HAD HER BY THE ARM AND
was shoving her into the closet. Stay in there until I get
back, he said, his eyes bloodshot, his words slurred. Piper
fought the panic as the door slammed shut, leaving her in
darkness. It was okay. She'd be fine. Anita would keep her
company, and once Mark the Butthead left, she could open
the door a little. He was too drunk to remember to lock it.
She wouldn't leave the closet, because he could come home
at any time, and then she would get caught, and then he
would hit her in the face, hard, the way he had when he'd
knocked her baby tooth out and the Tooth Fairy never came.
When her mom was still alive, the Tooth Fairy came. But
now no one seemed to remember that Piper was here. Just
Anita.

And sometimes the man in the flannel shirt who sat under
the tree outside their trailer. He smiled at her and she knew
he was what her mom called 'good people.' But he couldn't
help her because he was dead. He still had the rope around
his neck.

He had never been in the trailer before, but today he was
in front of the closet when she cracked it open and peered
out. She gasped and fell back on her bottom but he just
stood there, smiling until he turned into a woman, with a
funny dress on and her hair wound on her head like the
women who passed out church flyers, the ones her mom
called 'those goddamn Christians.'

Who are you? Piper asked her.

It scared her that the man was gone. Did all men leave?
That's what Mama always said. They loved you and they
left you. Sometimes Piper wanted Mark to leave, but if he
left, then she'd really be all alone with this lady who was

*frowning at her, her mouth moving like the fish down at the
pet store. Her hands came out, bony and white, with torn
and bloody fingernails, and reached for Piper's neck. She
swallowed a scream and tried to slam the door but it
wouldn't close and the fingers came closer and closer . . .*

Piper sat up straight in bed, her heart racing. "Oh, my
God," she whispered out loud, sucking in air.

Rachel was standing at the foot of her bed again, and
Piper wondered if that was why she had seen her in her
dream, reaching for her. Curling her fingers around the sheet,
she used her other hand to brush her hair back. She was
covered in sweat, the fear still crawling over her skin like an
army of ants. Why the hell had she dreamed about Mark? It
had been years since he had invaded her nightmares.

Pushing back the sheet, she stood up on shaky legs, wondering what time it was. She'd been up late, wide-awake
while Rachel had stared at her again and Piper had wished
that Brady were in bed with her. She hadn't fallen asleep
until probably three in the morning. Normally she loved to
stay at Shelby and Boston's, but she was going to be happy
to go home to the farm where there was no Rachel. Glancing
at her phone, she saw it was after nine. The girls usually
were up and running by seven.

Unnerved that no one had woken her up, she skirted
Rachel without comment, yanked open the bedroom door,
and rushed into the hallway in her pj's. The smell of coffee
brought her up short. She turned around and looked at the
spirit, like she had any answers. Aware that she probably
looked like complete ass, Piper jogged down the steps, worry
clawing at her insides. The girls were her responsibility and
she couldn't believe she'd slept so late. The fear from her
dream still clinging to her, she burst into the kitchen and came
to a dead stop, stunned at what she saw.

Brady was in jeans and no shirt, flipping pancakes on

the skillet. Coffee was brewing. The girls were standing on chairs on either side of him, hanging on to his every word and action. The smell of bacon sizzling on the stove mingled with the coffee, and it was a warm, cozy smell. The smell of family and lazy Sundays.

"Alright, now drop those chocolate chips there and it makes a pair of eyes for our teddy bear pancakes."

Piper was speechless. Brady was making teddy bear pancakes for the girls. She'd swear she had never been so turned on by a man as she was right then, seeing his bare back and his tight butt, his voice sleepy, his words so cute and domestic.

"Sorry I slept so late," she said, her heart rate finally starting to slow down now that she saw the girls were okay and now that the dream was receding.

Brady turned and smiled. "Looks like the lazy bum is up. Want some coffee?"

"Piper!" Lilly shrieked and almost fell off her chair when she turned to wave. "We're making pancakes. And look— I'm taller than Brady." She did a cheerleading routine that involved a heart-stopping leg kick. Heart stopping for Piper, anyway, when she pictured all the broken bones that might result from that chair flipping out from under her. Lilly didn't seem concerned.

"Keep the cheers on the floor, okay?" Brady told her, expertly flipping a pancake. "No one wants to spend Sunday in the ER."

Piper came over to the counter and gave Emily a hug as she peered around her at the pancake cooking on the griddle. Emily had carefully dropped her chips in. Lilly's were crooked. But overall, they were quite adorable. "I'm impressed," she told Brady. "You have hidden skills."

"My stepmom used to make these all the time. You know, I think I owe her a big thank-you and maybe some flowers.

ERIN McCARTHY

She taught me everything I know about being decent, and I don't think I've always appreciated her enough." He pointed the spatula at Lilly. "Appreciate your mama."

She giggled. "Duh."

"I didn't realize you were raised by your stepmom. I guess we have that in common. I owe a ton to Amanda."

"Auntie Amanda isn't your real mom?" Emily looked horrified. "I didn't know that."

"Duh," Lilly said again. "She doesn't look anything like Auntie Amanda."

Well, that was true. She was no tall, willowy blonde. Trying not to be insulted by an eight-year-old, Piper said, "My mom died when I was seven. I was lucky that my dad married Amanda and she loved me just like I was hers."

"I'm sorry your mom died," Emily said, looking appropriately sad.

"Thanks."

"Did your mom die, too, Brady?" Lilly asked, not looking particularly broken up about the possibility, just curious. She was more interested in shaking her booty from side to side.

"No. She moved away when I was two."

The twins looked suitably horrified at the prospect. Piper hadn't realized that's what had happened, and she felt sympathy for Brady. "I'm sorry to hear that."

He just shrugged and plated the bears. "I don't even remember living with her. She popped in and out over the years, then disappeared altogether by the time I was ten. Her loss, not mine. Girls, grab the syrup and some forks. Food's up."

Piper pulled out two coffee mugs and filled them both, needing to feel useful. She just felt off from her lousy night's sleep. Maybe coffee would help.

As the girls ran around being busy, Brady leaned over

and murmured, "I would love to kiss you right now you know that?"

"I would like that myself," she said. She took a sip of her coffee and sighed.

"You okay? You look tired."

"Bad dream. And Rachel standing at the end of my bed all night," she told him in a low voice.

He frowned. "You should have let me know."

Piper shrugged. What was he going to do about it? "She's tenacious, I'll give her that."

"I wonder why she's suddenly so interested in you?"

"I have no idea." And at the moment she didn't really care. She just wanted her to go away. As it was, she found herself warily glancing towards the parlor, sure Rachel was going to appear in the doorway.

"I think we should do a little research on her, along with the original Brady Stritmeyer."

The thought made Piper uncomfortable and she wasn't sure why. Maybe it was because she just wanted the spirits to leave her alone so she could go back to pretending that she was a normal person who didn't see ghosts. Or maybe she was afraid of what she might find. Or what might be asked of her.

She was the first to admit she didn't like change. She'd had so much change in her early years that she liked stability, the same, reliable routine in her life. Yet in the past two days her world had been shaken like a snow globe. Some of it she had initiated herself, like going into Brady's room and calling Mrs. Stritmeyer about rentals, but Rachel suddenly getting aggressive was not her doing. Not in any conscious way. She didn't like it.

"I don't imagine we'll find a lot out," she said. "That article we found was probably all there really is." For some reason, she hoped that was all there was, and then she felt guilty for being so wimpy. What did she think was going to happen? She did want to help Rachel, but at the same time, she wanted to be left alone. It didn't make her feel particularly good about herself.

"Come eat!" Lilly demanded, a huge bite of pancake on her fork, her mouth already crammed full.

"We're getting our coffee," Brady told the girls mildly, but instead of reaching for his coffee mug on the counter, he moved closer to Piper. "What was your bad dream about?"

"I don't remember," she lied, not wanting to tell him about her stepfather.

"You're lying," he told her. "But I understand if you don't want to talk about it."

Piper stared into his green eyes and suddenly she thought maybe she could share her feelings. That he wouldn't think she was pathetic or weird or clinging to the past. That he could reassure her that it was normal to have a dream about ghosts when one was standing at the bottom of her bed.

But before she could open her mouth and say anything, a voice from the doorway had her whipping her head around.

"Well, isn't this a cozy Sunday morning," Shelby said breezily.

"Mom!" Emily yelled and shoved her chair back with a screech.

Lilly quickly followed and in seconds Shelby was getting squeezed by her pj-clad daughters.

Piper stepped away from Brady, conscious of how close they had been standing, and well aware of how lousy she felt about sleeping with him in Shelby's bed. She didn't do things like that. Ever. She wasn't impulsive. She wasn't selfish. She always put everyone else's feelings before her own, and she felt confused and off-kilter by her behavior, even more so now that Shelby and Boston were home. Piper knew she must look guilty, and, good gravy, she wasn't wearing a bra. She crossed her arms over her chest.

Brady didn't look uncomfortable. He casually put his hand on the small of her back as he reached around her for his own coffee. "Hey, Shel, how the heck are you? You're home early."

"Yes, we are," Boston said from behind his wife, sounding less than happy about the situation. "Hey, girls."

Shelby kissed the twins on the tops of their heads before they moved past her to hug their father. "I just missed home," she said defensively. Walking over to Brady, she gave him a hard hug. "And I wanted to see you before you disappeared again for a decade."

"It's good to see you," he said, tugging the back of her hair as he hugged her.

"Now put a shirt on for crying out loud," Shelby said as she stepped back and looked at him.

"When did you get all prude?" he asked, clearly unperturbed.

"Don't let her fool you. She's not prude," Boston said, cracking a grin.

"Honey!" Shelby didn't deny it, though. "How were the girls?" she asked, turning to Piper. "I hope they were okay for you."

"They were great, as always. We had fun on the farm yesterday." Piper crossed her ankles, self-conscious in her pajamas. "I'm going to run upstairs and get dressed and give you all some time to catch up."

"Did you eat? Sit down," Shelby said, gesturing for her to take a chair. "Good Lord, you made teddy bear pancakes? I'm impressed."

"Actually, Brady made them."

"He did?" Shelby looked at her cousin in utter amazement.

"I'll be back down in a second." Piper bolted from the kitchen, wanting at least the protection a bra offered. She couldn't shield herself entirely from prying eyes, but she could cover up her nipples.

As she headed for the stairs, she heard Lilly say, "Piper saw a spider and she screamed. We thought she was killed and we were *freaking* out."

Piper had to admit she was freaking out just a little herself, and it wasn't because of a hairy spider.

She felt like she had been playing house and Shelby had busted her.

Only once in her entire childhood had Piper taken more than she'd been told she could have. She had never been sneaky, had always been grateful for whatever she'd gotten. But her grandmother Willie was an excellent baker, and one time when Piper was about twelve, she had made a strawberry pie with the fruit from her garden. All morning Piper had been smelling the thick scent of ripe strawberries and sugar. When her grandmother told her she could have only one piece, Piper had inhaled it. Then sawed off a second sliver when Willie left the room to check on a napping Jack. When she had returned, Piper was caught with the piece halfway to her mouth.

She'd never felt so ashamed of herself, so ungrateful for everything she had, yet so mulish about it.

Until now.

BRADY DRANK HIS COFFEE, LEANING ON THE COUNTER, and waited for the assault he knew was coming his way the minute Piper was out of earshot.

"Are you insane?" Shelby hissed at him, after telling her daughters to sit back down and finish their breakfast.

"What?" he asked mildly. "Since when does making pancakes qualify you for insanity?"

"That's not what I'm talking about and you know it." Her eyes were flashing as she impatiently shoved her hair back off her forehead. "Why are you and Piper Tucker cuddling half-naked in my kitchen?"

Here they went. "You're being ridiculous. We were not cuddling. We were making breakfast for your kids." He, for one, was damn glad that Piper had come downstairs without a bra, though. It had been a hell of a view and made him all the more eager to get her alone in the house on Swallow Street. Though he'd just keep that thought to himself.

"Did you"—she made some frantic hand gesture— "with her?"

Brady smirked. "What? Play charades? No." What had happened between him and Piper was not Shelby's business.

"You know what I mean!"

Boston looked up from the table where he had sat down with the girls. "Leave it alone, Shel. This really isn't the time or place." His head tilted towards their daughters.

Shelby's lips pursed as she clearly struggled to control her irritation. "You have some explaining to do later," she told Brady.

There would be no conversation about any of this later. He didn't answer to his cousin or to anyone. "I lost my job. That's why I'm in town." Change the subject. Dodge and weave. He'd learned that as a mischievous kid who was frequently in trouble.

Shelby drew up short. "What? Oh, honey, I'm sorry."

Brady shrugged. "It was a crap job anyway. The only regret I have is that my rent isn't going to pay itself."

"I'm sure you can find another job right away." But she looked as doubtful as he felt.

"That's the hope. I'm staying here for a couple of weeks to help Gran clean up that blue house she has. Apparently she has rented it to Piper." He forced himself to say her name out loud. Be casual. Admit to nothing. Engage in whatever he wanted to engage in with Piper Tucker without the interference of his family—that was his plan.

Of course, he hadn't been home in a dozen years, so he'd forgotten how really impossible it was to keep his family out of his business. Hell, to keep the whole town out of his business.

"Oh, my Lord in heaven," was Shelby's opinion. "I swear, Brady Stritmeyer, if you hurt that girl there will be hell to pay."

"Hurt what girl?" Lilly asked, adding enough syrup to her plate to coat ten pancakes.

Boston sighed. "There is no girl being hurt. Your mother is just overreacting."

Brady had to agree. "Your mom thinks I'm a heart-breaker, Lil. Girls can't resist my charms." He reached over and snatched a piece of her bacon and crammed it in his mouth. "Yum."

She giggled.

Piper reappeared in the doorway, wearing another sundress and holding her overnight bag in her hand. "I'm going to head out since you're home, Shelby."

"Don't you want to eat breakfast?" Boston asked.

"No, I had some coffee. I'm good." Her nervousness was obvious. She wasn't making eye contact with anyone and she was bouncing on the heels of her feet.

Brady felt guilty for making her feel uncomfortable with his cousin. He was going home to Chicago, but Piper had to live here in Cuttersville.

"Well, thank you so much for staying with the girls,"

Shelby said, looking flustered. She went over and hugged Piper, as did the twins.

"My pleasure. You know I'm happy to help out anytime."

The thing was, Brady knew she meant that. She was sincere, and he found that really appealing. Frighteningly appealing.

"I'll call you later," he told her, when the hugging arms had cleared out and he could see her face.

She nodded.

Then before his cousin flipped her wig, Brady told Shelby, "Piper and I are going to do a little research on the original Brady Stritmeyer. I figured it can't hurt to know a little more about my namesake."

"I don't think he's your namesake. No one has ever said you were named for him." Shelby made a face. "I say just leave it alone."

"And I say I'm curious."

Brady faced off with his cousin. This wasn't about researching a dead guy, and they both knew it. It was about him spending time with Piper.

They were both stubborn, and chances were they would have stared each other down for an hour or two before either one of them caved. But Piper intervened.

"I'm sorry about the candlestick on the console table in the hall, Shelby. It seems to have fallen and broken."

"What?" Shelby looked away, at Piper. "Oh, that's okay. You know how clumsy I am."

"Maybe it was Rachel," Brady said, because he knew Piper would never say anything. "Didn't she used to throw plates and stuff?"

Shelby's eyebrows shot up. "Rachel? Geez, it's been a while since she tossed anything. And her target is usually Boston."

"I'm lucky that way," her husband said.

With a few more murmured words and good-byes, Piper and Shelby went to the front door and Piper headed out.

"I think Rachel wanted to nail me, actually," Brady commented when Shelby got back, not wanting his cousin to think Piper was to blame in any way.

"I don't think she's the only one who wants to do that," Shelby said wryly.

Brady went for his coffee, ignoring that comment.

No one needed to know that the nailing had already occurred.

PIPER STOPPED FIVE HOUSES DOWN FROM THE MAC-namaras and pulled out her cell phone. Dialing her best friend, Cameron, she bit her fingernail and glanced backwards, irrationally worried that someone might come out of the house and see her parked here for no apparent reason. But she didn't like to dial and drive. And she had to talk to someone before she exploded.

"Hello?" Cam sounded sleepy and annoyed.

"Hey. Are you busy?" It was an inane question but now she wasn't sure where to start.

"I was busy sleeping until thirty seconds ago. It's the crack of my ass on a Sunday. And I know you're not in trouble, because you're never in trouble, so please tell me no one has died or been diagnosed with cancer."

"No, no, it's nothing like that. It's just that, well, you know how Shelby has that cousin who lives in Chicago—Brady?"

Cameron hadn't moved to Cuttersville until seventh grade. By then, Piper had had hair and Anita had left town, but Piper still hadn't made any true friends. Cameron had strolled into middle school, fresh from the big city, his father transferred to the Samson Plastics plant in Cuttersville from New Jersey, a bridge ride from Manhattan. He had expensive and trendy sneakers and he was Jewish, which essentially made him an alien in rural Ohio. He and Piper had forged the bond of misfits, though Cameron had never lacked an ounce of confidence. He just had no interest in deer hunting.

"Yeah? The one who makes you cream when you mention him?"

Cameron was also incredibly straightforward. Piper grimaced. "That is not true."

"Oh, come on. The guy was like your childhood fantasy, admit it. He was probably who you were thinking about when you humped your stuffed animals."

That had her speechless for a second. It had never even occurred to her to hump her stuffed animals, and the fact that Cameron assumed that was commonplace was mildly disturbing. Not that she hadn't masturbated, but she had named her stuffed animals. It would have been far too weird to take advantage of them like that. It wasn't like they could give their consent.

"Anyways," she told him pointedly. "He's back in town. He showed up at Shelby's unannounced Friday night." In the rain. Then he'd taken his shirt off. Piper sighed in delight at the memory, goose bumps rising on her arms.

Cameron yawned. "Panty pudding time."

Ew. Piper started to question why she had called him. But she couldn't stop herself from blurting out, "I slept with him."

The laziness left Cameron's voice. "Really?" he asked in amazement.

"Yes. And I'm not sure what I should do now."

"Sleep with him again. Unless it sucked. Did it suck?"

"No." That, she could say most emphatically. "But it was

quick. And quiet, because the girls were home. I feel terrible about that. I mean, what if we were caught?"

"Where were you, the kitchen table?" Cameron sounded delighted by the prospect.

"No. In the bedroom. With the door locked."

"Then you wouldn't have gotten caught. And you didn't get caught. So don't get stressed after the fact. Is he going back to Chi-town today? That doesn't leave you much time to get another spread eagle in."

"He's actually staying for a couple of weeks. In the house that his grandmother is renovating. The house I just rented."

"What? You're moving out of your parents'?"

"Yes."

"Hallelujah." After they had both graduated from Ohio University, Cameron had moved to Cincinnati, which wasn't the same as being a stone's throw from Manhattan like his childhood, but it wasn't cornfields and bait shops either. He had access to Thai food and an apartment of his own to keep meticulously clean. Cam was a neat freak who liked his privacy, and he couldn't understand why Piper hadn't followed the same path as him. "What brought this on? I don't think it's a coincidence that your girlhood crush shows up and suddenly you want to move out."

"No, it's probably not a coincidence. But I feel weird inside, anxious. What am I doing?"

"Listening to your lust. I mean your gut. Come on, don't freak yourself out. Moving out will be good for you. You're still close to your family and yet you can live your own life. Sleep with a man without feeling guilty. You've never been good at taking something for yourself, so here's your chance."

He was right. She didn't take anything for herself. But giving was much more satisfying than taking. Unless it was Brady. She had definitely enjoyed taking him.

Piper glanced around the quiet street, forcing her shoulders to relax. Why was she so tense?

Because Shelby didn't approve. It had been written all over her face. It was clearly why she had come home early.

Approval was very important to Piper.

But she found that suddenly her need to please herself was almost equally as important.

"You're right."

"Duh."

She laughed. "And a bit of an egomaniac."

"I've never denied it."

It was on the tip of her tongue to tell Cameron about being plagued by Rachel all weekend, but Cameron was skeptical about spirits. He also had a deep-seated disdain for magician David Copperfield, but Piper wasn't sure if the two were related or not.

"Are you going home anytime soon?" she asked him instead.

"Not until Thanksgiving, unless my mother guilts me. They say Catholics can load the guilt on their kids, but my mother is the master of Jewish guilt. If I meet a hot girl between now and then, though, my mother can forget it."

Said the guy who had never once had to doubt his parents' love for him.

Piper, on the other hand, was never going to leave Cuttersville.

It was the way it was.

Chapter Eight

❧

"WHERE ARE YOU GOING?" SHELBY ASKED BRADY shrilly.

He paused in the foyer and turned back to see his cousin standing with her hands on her hips.

"Really? I am not one of your kids." He wouldn't care that she was inquiring except that she was acting nuts. Like she might ground him if she found condoms in his backpack. "And I'm thirty-one, in case you'd forgotten."

"What? I was just asking," she said begrudgingly. "If you're going to see Gran, I was going to see if you could give her some of the tomatoes from my garden."

Uh-huh. "I'm not going to see Gran."

"No? Alright, then."

She was dying of curiosity, he could tell, but Brady wasn't about to oblige her. "See you later. I won't be back for dinner."

With that, he left Shelby writhing in agony as to what he was doing, and he hopped in his car and backed out of the drive, the gravel crunching beneath the tires a reminder of his childhood. He had the windows open to the beautiful September weather, and the air smelled clean, fragrant. Like freshly cut grass and wood baking in the sun. It wasn't a bad thing to grow up in a small town. He'd had a lot of freedom to roam about and he'd spent a lot of time outdoors. When had he started to feel so discontent?

He wasn't sure. Had it just been teen angst or had it been something else? A desire to escape family? Prove something?

It was too hard to step back into the battered Converse shoes of his teen years and come up with any legitimate answers. All he knew was that when the letter arrived with his acceptance into the School of the Art Institute of Chicago, he had never felt so excited about anything in his whole life. Even nailing Joelle for the first time hadn't brought quite the same heady buzz, and that was saying a lot because he'd been finessing entrance into her pants for months. When he'd been given the green light, he'd thought he'd died and gone to heaven. But not even that first full sexual experience had felt as good as knowing he was going somewhere. Getting out.

Now where was he? He drummed his fingers on his steering wheel.

Nowhere.

Right back where he started, equally as broke, and with the same piss-poor attitude. Only now he had failure weighing him down. Not only had his art ambitions come to a whole lot of nothing, but his post-art compromise career had ended as well. That left him wearing the label of big old loser, in his opinion.

Which was why he should not be spending any more time

with Piper Tucker. She deserved better than what he had to offer.

But that hadn't stopped him from calling her and making arrangements to meet her in the cemetery. As he pulled up to the Lakeview Cemetery, with nary a lake in sight, now or at any time in the past, Brady saw that Piper was already there. Of course. She was punctual. Reliable. Considerate.

No, he didn't have anything to offer her in terms of a future or a relationship. He knew that. Had already established that in his head. So why did he keep circling that stupid thought? Because it was stupid.

But the truth was, he had something to offer her now. He had charm and skill in satisfying women. It was going to give him a great deal of satisfaction to satisfy her, something Brady suspected had never really been offered Piper. She was a giver, not a taker. Obviously he had his selfish reasons for wanting to have sex with her, but he could at least justify to himself that he was giving something to her. Regular good Samaritan, that was him.

He snorted at his own thoughts.

Piper was leaning against the weathered fence posts, wearing a flowy pink skirt that was shorter than what she had left Shelby's in that morning. It gave a nice view of her legs, though he was disappointed to see that her cleavage was covered with a tight white T-shirt. But then he thought about how that particular shirt would look wet, like how she had looked Friday night after taking the dog out, and he was instantly hard and appeased. He didn't always have to see the cleavage. Sometimes a little mystery was good for the soul. Since his soul needed some help, clearly picturing Piper with her breasts pushing through wet cotton was a good thing.

It was messed-up logic and he knew it, but hey, he wasn't hurting anyone.

Parking next to her truck, he shook his head at her choice in vehicles. He supposed it made sense for a girl raised on a farm, but Piper looked too small, too feminine, to drive such a large, utilitarian car.

"That's quite a truck there," he told her when he stepped out of his own car, which looked small and pathetic next to hers. It felt like his nuts had shrunk, and he didn't like it.

She smiled. "My dad chose it. He figured if I was the biggest thing on the road I'd win in a collision."

That didn't surprise him at all. Danny Tucker was a practical man. But it made Piper look like a kid driving her dad's truck without his permission. Brady was smart enough not to mention that thought out loud, however. "I always wanted a truck when I was a teenager," he told her honestly.

"Why? So you could do doughnuts in the snow?" She peeled herself off the fence as he came closer, her hand nervously going up to her neck, in a gesture he was starting to recognize.

"No. So I could park it in a cornfield somewhere and convince a girl to do it in the truck bed with me, under the stars." It had seemed wildly romantic and sexy to him at the time.

Now that he thought about it, it still did. He hadn't done the dirty outside since he'd left home. It was hard to get it on in public when the only outdoor space you had was the stoop to the intercom buzzer of your apartment building. Cops tended to object to pulling out body parts on a sidewalk.

"Oh, yeah?" Piper brushed past him, giving him a flirtatious smile. "I guess that never worked out for you."

"There's still time," he said, following her like a tail-wagging mutt.

"You in the market for a truck?"

"No. But I figure yours would work just fine for us." Now

that the idea had popped into his head, he was kind of liking the thought of tossing some blankets into the back of Piper's truck and climbing in with her.

She laughed. "That's presumptuous, you know."

"You're the one who dropped your robe," he teased, reaching out and snagging her hand, because, well, it was there, and he wanted to hold it.

God, he acted like a sixteen-year-old around her. Silly and greedy and intent on showing off. But he had to say, he was definitely enjoying himself.

"I don't think you minded at the time."

"I most definitely did not mind. But it would lead me to believe that you're willing to have some fun with me in the back of a truck." Now that the idea had taken hold, he glanced around, wondering where they could find some privacy right now. Too bad it was the middle of the day and they were on the edge of town with no natural barriers. The church next to them was empty, abandoned a couple of decades earlier, but they weren't that far from the hardware store and the diner, so this wasn't the ideal location. Not to mention, you know, the whole dead people thing. Probably a bit of a mood killer.

"Maybe. You'll have to do a lot of convincing, though. Despite my earlier behavior, I'm not much of a risk taker. Getting caught scares me."

They walked into the cemetery, which was moderately neglected. The grass needed to be cut and there were weeds infiltrating the paths, but the headstones looked tended to.

"I guess I can't say anything about that. It's been a while since I took any risks." The thought made him feel a little glum. "Though I never cared much about getting caught. Shelby will vouch for me on that."

"I don't know. I'm not sure there's anything admirable about intentional disdain."

His eyebrow shot up and he dropped her hand. Was she reprimanding him? Because that was not hot. "I don't think not worrying about others' opinions is the same as disdain."

"Maybe not." Piper looked around at the headstones. "I don't think I've ever been in here. That's a good thing, I suppose."

Not sure why she had dropped that line of conversation so suddenly, Brady decided not to worry about it. He was probably imagining judgment because he was feeling a little defensive. Failure tended to do that to a guy. "My grandfather's buried here but he died long before I was born."

"I don't like cemeteries. I tend to see things other people don't see."

Brady hadn't even thought about that. While Piper had originally downplayed her interaction with ghosts, claiming she hadn't really seen them since she was a kid, it was clear now that wasn't true. At all. She had seen enough that she'd chosen the route of avoiding any circumstances that might increase her odds of encounters. It explained the wariness she was wearing on her face.

"What's the craziest thing you've ever seen?" he asked. "You have to have some good stories."

"The worst was the time I tried to pet a cow that wasn't there. God, I was so embarrassed. We were on a school trip and I tried to pretend I'd done it on purpose. But the girls in my class weren't buying it. It gave them one more reason to make fun of me."

The thought of little Piper, the way Brady remembered, solemn and wise beyond her years, enduring the taunts of her classmates, gave him a pit in his gut. "Jealous bitches."

Piper laughed. "I don't think a single one of them was jealous of me, but that's sweet of you to say."

"I don't understand bullying. Why does anyone enjoy

making someone else feel so terrible?" Brady had been well liked in school and he had moved easily between groups of students, despite his penchant for rebellious hairstyles. He had never really understood what the big deal was—why a jock couldn't be friends with a brainiac or an emo kid. "There was this one kid in school . . . He was really small and had these thick glasses. You know what it's like here. Not every family can afford those freaking featherweight lenses, so these glasses were thick. And one time a couple of football players were harassing him on the bus. They were punching him, and I stepped in between and took a hit to the side of the head. Got back up and nailed the asshole in the gut." Brady dropped Piper's hand and squatted down beside a headstone to read it. He shrugged up at her. "I felt like a superhero defending the weak."

Come to think of it, he might have been more selfless in his youth.

"I got my ass kicked but it was worth it. Then my dad grounded me for fighting. When I tried to explain what had happened, he told me I shouldn't have interfered." Brady hadn't really remembered that until right that very second. "That the little loser needed to learn to stand up for himself." He furrowed his eyebrows, the pit in his stomach growing, a hot bile rising up in his mouth. No wonder he hadn't gotten along with his father. "Good advice, huh?"

Piper stood there, her hair trailing down towards him like an aggressive vine, tendrils swaying and reaching for him, the sun behind her head. "That's terrible advice. Your father should be ashamed of himself. Everyone deserves compassion."

As she squatted down beside him, Brady thought that it would be a very wonderful thing to be loved by a woman as compassionate as Piper. What would it feel like to see that face on the end of every day, to see a love that would never bend or break, never demand or accuse? Needing to look away, or she would see his confusion, Brady stared at the headstone. *Edith Pearl Magnus, Beloved Wife and Mother.* Not what he was looking for. Or who, rather. Or was he looking for something else entirely? Beloved wife and mother . . .

"You were a nice guy, Brady, defender of small boys on the bus and a butterfly painter for bald girls."

He'd forgotten about the butterfly mural. He'd taken a fair amount of pride in that job. "Your dad paid me to paint those," he said, feeling melancholy. He didn't want credit where none was due.

"I know," she said. "But you were nice to me, and that was natural. No one paid for that. Kindness always has an impact."

Brady was no hero, so he just smiled. "So do butterflies, apparently. I should have taken a picture of that wall."

"Oh, it's still there. My grandparents live in that house, but the room was never painted."

"Really?" Though he shouldn't be surprised. Things didn't change here for no reason. There was an attitude that you didn't fix something unless it was broken.

"Really." She smiled at him. "What you're looking for isn't this close to the entrance to the cemetery."

"How do you know?" Brady looked around. It wasn't a big cemetery, but given that he had no clue where Brady was buried, the task to find his headstone seemed a little daunting.

"Because there's a ghost over there, the one we call the Blond Man, from Shelby and Boston's house. He's waving to me. I think that must be the first Brady Stritmeyer."

The hairs on the back of Brady's neck stood straight up and did the tango. Holy crap. "He's here? In the cemetery?" He studied her face. Piper looked scared, but like she was trying to cover up that fact. "Have you ever seen him outside of the house before?"

"No. I didn't know the spirits could travel like that. But this is a cemetery, so I guess it's not surprising that he could be here, too." She stood up. "Should we go see?"

Her voice was a little shaky.

"You can stay here if you want," Brady told her. "Just point me in the right direction." Though with his luck he would walk straight through the dead dude.

"No, I'm okay." Piper was lying to Brady. She wasn't okay. Something about the fact that a ghost had traveled, well, it felt like he was following her. Which was more than unnerving. She also felt weird that throughout her whole life she had heard Shelby tell stories about the Blond Man, a ghost who wore a suit and smiled and waved at everyone. No one had ever associated him with the fiancé who had been murdered, and that such a cheerful spirit had been bludgeoned to death, and was a cheater, felt strange. It also seemed horrible that Rachel and Brady were trapped in the afterlife together, though Piper had never seen the two of them at the same time.

What would it be like to be stuck here, on earth, unable to communicate with living humans? Unable to touch or eat or feel? It sounded horrible.

"What direction are we going in here?"

"Over there. Second row. About five in from the fence." Was it her imagination or did the man start waving more enthusiastically?

"How do you know they're ghosts? What do they look like to you? Are they translucent or something?" Brady asked her curiously as they walked through the bushy grass.

Piper pondered the question. "I just know they're dead. It's obvious to me the second I see them. There is a . . . wispy quality to them. And a coldness. There is no body heat, no breathing, nothing that indicates they're alive. I guess it's like a reflection in a mirror. You just know the difference."

She thought about the man who had appeared in her dream that morning, the older guy in plaid who had a rope around his neck. She hadn't remembered him at all until the dream, but now she couldn't shake the memory. She had seen him half a dozen times outside her trailer as a kid, sitting under the big oak tree, his knees up to his chest. Had he hung himself in that tree? Had he been a victim of a sinister crime? So many people, so many stories, so much pain and loss . . . Why did they show themselves to her?

It was a burden she didn't understand.

"Let me know if I get too close to him, okay? I don't want to be the douche bag who walks into a spirit."

"You did punch him a couple of days ago."

Brady stopped scanning headstones as they walked and gave her a sheepish look. "I guess until that very second I didn't actually believe you were seeing anything."

She couldn't blame him for that. She probably wouldn't believe it either if she wasn't the one seeing it. Reaching out, she touched Brady's arm. "It's this one." The man, who she had a hard time thinking of as Brady, was pointing to a small, weathered stone. It had fallen over at some point and was partially sunken into the hard red clay soil.

The Blond Man smiled at her and nodded.

"Oh, my God, that's freaky as hell," Brady said, his face losing some of its color as he knelt down and ran his fingers over the headstone. "Brady Stritmeyer, January 7, 1860 to August 12, 1887. Talk about feeling someone walk on your grave. Staring at my own name on a headstone is a little disturbing, as you predicted."

Piper squatted down beside him. "There's a quote there, a long one. What does it say?"

Brady read carefully, " 'When he shall die, Take him and cut him out in little stars, And he will make the face of heaven so fine, That all the world will be in love with night, And pay no worship to the garish sun."

Piper felt the goose bumps start at her fingertips and gallop up her arms. She shivered in the warm sun, reaching out, needing to touch the stone herself. "It's Shakespeare. From *Romeo and Juliet*." She had been romantic enough as a teenager to remember such an overblown assessment of a man. But here, in death, it had a poignancy she hadn't understood before.

"Really? I guess someone was really grieving for him when he died. That sucks." Brady sat back. "I feel like we should have brought flowers or something."

Piper watched the bliss on the man's face as he hovered near them, watching their actions. "I don't think it matters so much. I think he's just happy someone is here to see him." She tried to make eye contact, emboldened by his serene nature. He wasn't frightening at all. "Did you love her?" she asked in a whisper. "Like Romeo and Juliet loved one another? Too much passion, too much rashness?"

But his eyes wouldn't meet hers. Instead he stared down at his headstone, his smile drifting off his face, like he had remembered death was no cause for joy.

Piper followed his gaze, and what she saw made her start, falling out of her crouched position when she lost her balance. "Oh, my God."

"What?" Brady took her arm, trying to help her back up, but she just sat on the grass, drawing her legs in towards her, away from the headstone.

The bleeding headstone. The name of Brady Stritmeyer was leaching blood from the bottom of each letter, like fat red tears trailing down over the pain-filled words of loss, running faster and faster.

"Do you see that?" she whispered. Of course he didn't see it. No one ever saw any of it but her.

"See what? Are you okay?"

She shook her head. No. She wasn't okay. Because the blood was forming a word as it rolled towards the end of the headstone, one lone, horrible word . . . "MURDER."

Swallowing hard, feeling like she needed to scream, but keeping it in, she pulled her hands in, too, not wanting to touch any of what she was seeing. Was the blood real? Would it dampen her fingers? She wasn't brave enough to test it.

When she looked up, the Blond Man pointed to the stone, to that heinous word, then to himself.

"I know," she whispered. "I'm so sorry. I'm very, very sorry."

There was a pause, like he was considering this. Piper didn't know what else to say.

Then he pointed to the word again. Then to Brady. Her Brady. Living, breathing Brady.

Piper said, "No!" Even though she knew it didn't mean anything, she couldn't help but blurt out the dispute, because Brady was much too alive to think of as dead. And who would want to murder him anyway?

But the man in front of her just nodded. Then he smiled, like it was fine. All was fine.

Then, like an electric lightbulb dispelling darkness with a switch flip, he was gone. Like he had never been there.

The headstone was dirty and worn, a grimy layer of age coating it, but there was no blood. No "murder" on it.

"Are you okay?" Brady asked. "Is he talking to you?"

She shook her head, her heart pounding at a rate that could not be healthy. "He's gone." Bracing herself on the grass, she stood up so quickly her head swam. "We need to leave."

"What the hell just happened?" Brady scrambled to his feet.

"I don't want to talk about it." Which was the understatement of the decade. She felt like she'd fallen into a B-grade horror film. Was she insane? There was no way that headstone had read "murder." That was just not possible.

Yet she'd seen it. And she knew it was real. Or as real as the spirit world could be. Maybe not real in the sense that you could reach out and touch it, but real in that there had been a message for her. She just didn't know what to make of it. Obviously, the ghost wanted her to acknowledge that he had been murdered. She imagined any spirit who had been taken from this world so brutally would want people to know that.

But why had he pointed to Brady? Did he know they shared a name?

Or was it a warning?

"Piper. Sweetheart." Brady reached for her hand again, but Piper just walked faster.

She wanted out of this cemetery. "I never should have come here. It's not the kind of place a freak like me should hang out in." Immediately she hated how juvenile she sounded, but damn it, she hated being different. Abnormal. She wanted to belong, to fit in. She wanted to not be afraid.

The Blond Man had just terrified her.

Because he had communicated with her in a way that felt threatening. Yes, he was smiling, and yes, he seemed benevolent, but the warning felt frightening, personal. Her interactions with ghosts had never been personal before.

And she couldn't imagine something happening to Brady.

"You're not a freak. Don't say that. Please talk to me."

Once she had rushed past the front gate and was next to her truck, Piper finally felt like she could breathe again. "The headstone was bleeding," she told him, patting the pocket of her skirt to make sure her keys were there. The truck wasn't locked, but she needed reassurance that she could get away. She didn't want to stay for another minute.

"Bleeding?" Brady looked at her blankly.

"Yes. Bleeding. I think he was warning me." It seemed obvious to her now. "I don't want to do any research on Rachel or the original Brady Stritmeyer. I think we need to let the past lie."

"But how do you know that's what that meant? Maybe he wants you to investigate his murder."

"There's nothing to investigate." If Rachel hadn't killed Brady or Brady hadn't flirted with the maid, well, Piper didn't see how they were ever going to find that out a hundred and twenty years after the fact. "We're not going to find anything other than biased newspaper articles."

"But you don't know that."

Piper yanked open her truck door and climbed in. Anxiety was boiling up inside her and she needed to leave. "I'm not doing it."

"Hey." Brady stepped into the door, preventing her from closing it behind her. "I'm not trying to push you. Don't run away."

Run away? That was a little insulting. She wasn't running away. She was just quickly exiting a situation that made her uncomfortable.

If he didn't understand the difference, that was his problem.

"I'm sorry. I don't want to be here. I can't." There wasn't any way to say it any clearer, and if she had to stick around and spell it out for him, she was terrified she was going to start screaming.

"Okay. I understand." He reached out and tugged a curl. "Drive home safely. Can I call you?" With a smile he added, "Say I can call you."

There really wasn't a whole lot of hope that she could tell him no. She wanted to hear from him. She wanted to know that he was interested in her. And she wanted to steal whatever time with him she could before he left town. "You can call me."

"Good." Brady kissed her forehead and then shut her door.

It made her feel like she was sixteen and her dad was sending her off for her first solo driving adventure.

That wasn't how she wanted to feel around Brady. At all.

Coupled with the burbling anxiety creating pressure in her chest, it made her just want to go home.

Which made her feel that maybe she wasn't as grown-up as she liked to think she was.

BRADY WATCHED PIPER PULL AWAY, THE TENSION ON her face evident as she swung her truck around. What the hell had she seen in the cemetery? She'd said blood, but he was sure there was more to it than that. Though seeing blood on a headstone would be disturbing enough, he imagined. Yet her reaction had been so strong, it seemed there was more to it. Then again, from what she'd said, Piper normally just saw spirits. A bleeding headstone sounded like something different altogether, something more . . . sinister.

He didn't like it. Glancing back at the cemetery, wishing he could see what she did, he found himself frowning. He wanted answers but he wasn't sure where to start.

A sandwich was in order.

Then he supposed he needed to stop up at the hardware store and get the painting supplies for Gran's house. He'd been over there to assess what was needed and had discovered a previous tenant had been fond of L bracket shelves. There were about a thousand holes that needed patching.

Food first, though. It was a two-minute drive to the Busy Bee Diner, a restaurant that had been around longer than he had. Brady didn't recognize the hostess, since she was in her late teens, but the waitress who approached him with a glass of water was as much a staple of his childhood as Frosted Flakes. "Hey, Marge," he said with a grin. "How goes it?"

The older woman's eyes narrowed, causing all her wrinkles to undulate. Her orange lips pursed. "Do I know you? Or are you just reading my name badge and being a smart-ass?"

"It's Brady Stritmeyer. Jessie's grandson."

Her eyes widened in recognition and she gave him what could pass for a smile. "Well, I'll be dipped. Didn't know you were back in town. How are you doing?"

"I'm good enough, I guess." He figured that was the truth. He wasn't exactly thrilled with his life, but he didn't have cancer either, so he was sort of in neutral. "I got laid off so I'm visiting my gran and my cousins."

"Sorry to hear that, but the economy does suck." Marge nodded in sympathy. "I have arthritis from waitressing for forty years, but this diner paid my rent and helped me raise four kids when that worthless piece of shit ran off on me with the tart from the bowling alley, so I can't complain. People always want a two-dollar breakfast even when jobs are scarce."

"That is true." He gave her a smile. "They hiring here?"

She laughed. "No. And even if the answer was yes, I'd tell you no. You'd be bad for business. We'd have all those young girls in here nursing a coffee for two hours mooning at you. You're too good-looking for your own good, always have been."

"Thanks," he said, rolling his eyes. He was not too good-looking. There was no such thing. He didn't fall out of an ugly tree, but he was no underwear model either.

"Please, false modesty doesn't suit you. I'm guessing before you leave town you'll have frosted a few cupcakes."

Brady's eyebrows shot up. Good God. He was speechless and trying hard not to examine that phrasing too carefully. Did she mean . . .

"Brady Stritmeyer! What the hell!"

He was saved from having to reply to Marge by a woman swooping down on him and enveloping him in a hug, smothering him in dark hair, dangling earrings, and a strong scent of patchouli. "When did you get to town?" she demanded, pulling back so he could actually see her face.

"Abby." He smiled, genuinely pleased to see his high school girlfriend. Unlike his first big romance, Joelle, who had been a cautious girl, Abby had been far too much like him for either of their own good. They had gotten into quite a bit of trouble together. "How are you?"

Her hands fell onto her stomach and she grinned. "Pregnant. That's how I am."

"I heard that from Gran. Congratulations." She looked good, her cheeks rosy, her hair glossy, her body unchanged except for the rounded tummy, defined clearly by a black T-shirt. She wore lots of noisy jewelry and there was a tall, dark-haired man behind her.

Marge hit Brady with her ticket pad. "I'll be back in a sec, hon. Going to get Mrs. Johnson her egg salad before she births a cow."

"No problem. Thanks." Brady stood up so that he could reach out and shake the hand of the man who was clearly her husband, his hand on the small of her back. "Brady Stritmeyer. Abby and I went to school together."

"Darius Damiano, Abby's husband. Nice to meet you."

The guy who was a millionaire. Abby had done well for herself, especially given the protective and awed way her husband looked at her.

Abby was the same as ever. "My husband's hot, isn't he?" she said with a grin.

"Absolutely," Brady assured her with a grin.

Darius rolled his eyes. "Thanks, babe. So what brings you to town, Brady?"

"I'm visiting my family."

"We should have you and Piper over for cocktails. Well, no cocktails for me. But for you three."

Brady started. How did she know anything about Piper?

Her hand flew over her mouth and she realized his reaction. "Oh, shit, I shouldn't have said that."

"Said what?" Darius asked.

"About him and Piper. It just came out. But it's too soon yet. I jumped the gun."

"How do you know anything about me and Piper? Not that there is a me and Piper." Brady felt thoroughly pissed. Had Shelby been talking? He looked around the diner, suddenly wondering who knew what about his personal business. That was something he definitely didn't miss about small-town life.

"Are you talking about Bree and Charlotte's babysitter? Isn't she kind of young?" Darius asked.

That was helpful. Not. Brady scowled at Abby's husband.

"No, she's in her early twenties and she's been out of college for a few years. She's a teacher, and she's about the same age I was when I met you," Abby said. "And you're ten years older than me, so that's not the issue here."

"I'm eight years older than you," Darius corrected.

Brady didn't care if Abby was pulling an Anna Nicole Smith. He just wanted to know why people were discussing his sex life. "Who told you about Piper?" he insisted.

"No one." She gave him a sheepish look. "I'm psychic, remember?"

What? "I don't remember anything of the sort." He never would have dated her if he'd thought for one second that she could read his thoughts.

"It's true. In high school it wasn't fine-tuned. But now I have fairly good control over it, but pregnancy has made me scattered. I blurt out stuff I shouldn't. Sorry."

Darius nodded slowly, like he was a man who had endured a lot. "It's been . . . interesting."

Abby smacked him. "Oh, stop. It hasn't been that bad."

Brady wouldn't have ever thought he would believe in psychics, but he certainly had come around on the ghost issue. Who was to say that someone didn't have insight into the future? And if Abby had some kind of telescope to tomorrow, he had to admit, he was curious. "So you saw Piper? With me?"

The idea made him feel a little hot inside, in all the good spots.

She nodded, studying him, like she was weighing what she should say. "Don't be afraid."

"Afraid?" He snorted. "What the hell would I be afraid of? Her father kicking my ass? I think I can handle Danny. His daughter is an adult, after all." Not that Danny would see it that way.

"No. I meant don't be afraid of your feelings."

Brady recoiled. Was she fucking kidding him? He stared at her, trying to see the seventeen-year-old smart-ass he'd known. All he saw now was earnestness. It made him uncomfortable. "Abby, I think you have me confused with someone else. The baby has clearly thrown your radar off."

There was an exaggerated silence before Darius spoke up, clearly trying to gloss over the sudden tension. "So how long are you in town?"

"A few weeks."

"Good, great—we'll have to get together. It was nice

meeting you. Abby, let's head out before Marge goes off on us for blocking the tables."

She nodded. "I'm glad you're home, Brady. And my sister has the information you're looking for. Go see Bree at the library. She can help you with your research."

Goose bumps rose on his arms. How could she know he was looking for answers about Brady and Rachel? God, he didn't remember Abby being this out there. He had no idea what to say, so he just nodded. "Good luck with the baby."

"Thanks." She smiled and reached out and squeezed his hand. "See you soon."

He supposed she would know.

Brady sat back down and stared at the menu, the words blurring. Suddenly he wanted a beer way more than he wanted a sandwich. Maybe he should swing around to his gran's for some of her special lemonade before hitting the hardware store.

"OH, MY GOD, I'LL CALL A CLEANING SERVICE FIRST thing tomorrow."

Piper sighed, wishing her mother had let her come to the house on Swallow by herself. But after dinner, when Piper had mentioned she wanted to see the house and take some measurements, Amanda had insisted on accompanying her. Now her mother was standing in the living room frowning, her designer handbag in fuchsia held in front of her like a dust shield.

"I can clean it. It's just a little dusty." The house had the musty smell of one that had been sitting empty for a while, and the dust motes danced in the fading sunlight from the grimy windows. But the floor looked like it was in decent shape and a glance into the kitchen showed it was the original fifties style, which Piper preferred over an eighties reno gone bad. It was kitschy and suited her. A sense of relief washed over her, and some of the anxiety she had been feeling since she'd opened that door to Brady on Friday eased.

It had been crazy impulsive to verbally agree to a rental she'd never seen, though she doubted Jessie would have held her to it if she had changed her mind. But she didn't want to change her mind. She wanted to make decisions for herself, move out and move forward with her life. The house gave her a good vibe.

Best of all? There was no hint of ghosts.

"So I talked to Jessie and she said we can choose whatever color we want for paint as long as it's not obnoxious. Given that she usually looks like a bedazzled produce bin, I think we'll be safe with whatever we choose." Amanda pulled a color swatch book out of her purse and fanned it out. "I was thinking a light gray with purple undertones."

The fact that her mother had paint samples in her purse did not surprise Piper. She had everything but miniature ponies in her handbag. It had been like falling into Narnia when she was a kid and had been allowed to look into it. There were sweets and beauty products and weaponry in it.

"I was thinking yellow. Or pink."

Acrylic nails paused in the blue family. "Pink? Are you serious?"

"Yes. I like soft colors. I want it to be like . . . a teacup." The rooms were small and demanded delicate furniture. The cottage details should be highlighted, not ignored, and Piper envisioned lots of plump pillows and fresh flowers, crisp whites, and soft, aged fabrics.

"When you were little, I had to beg you to dress like a girl. Now you never see a floral you don't like."

It was probably because when she'd been really little, she

had thought girly was the same as trashy. It had taken a few years to sort that out. "I guess I had to grow into it."

Her mother immediately started sniffling. "I can't believe you're moving out. I'm going to miss you." But then she shifted colors resolutely, holding up a swatch like she was determined not to cry. "How about a white backdrop? Fresh and clean, and then you can go to town with the florals. It will be beautiful, like you."

Oh, dear. Piper gave her a wan smile. "Thank you." If her mother started crying, she would start crying, and then they'd be a blubbering mess together.

But Amanda suddenly lifted her head and snapped her fingers. "Oh, my God, I have the best idea ever. You know what goes perfectly with this look you have in mind? Wicker! We'll give you the porch furniture and you can use it in the living room. You need furniture, right? We'll just freshen it up with some new pillows for you. There's a sofa and two big chairs. It will be perfect."

Piper also wanted to laugh. Her mother hated that wicker and she'd been looking for an excuse to get rid of it for years. "I thought Grandma bought that furniture."

"Oh, she might have." She waved her arm around. "But you're her only granddaughter."

Like somehow that explained everything. "You don't have to go to all that trouble. I don't really need anything other than my bed for a while."

"Oh, I want to. I really, really want to do this for you."

That was code for she wanted the wicker gone.

"And good grief, Piper, do you seriously think your father and I would let you live in an empty house?"

"No." They would offer and she would protest, and in the end, they would give her way more than she had ever expected. That was the way it always went. "Thank you, I really appreciate it. Especially since I didn't really plan for this very well. I do have a lot of money saved, though, so I'll take a little of it and get my kitchenware."

"We'll go to Walmart, my favorite place after the Prada flagship store in New York." Amanda winked at her.

Piper laughed. "Yes, your favorite place in the whole world. Daddy always says you should buy stock in it."

"Let's write down everything you need." A tablet came out of the handbag and her mother started muttering and typing. "Twelve bath towels, hand towels, washcloths . . . shower curtain, cotton ball container."

Even if she didn't do laundry for nearly two weeks, Piper didn't need twelve towels, but she didn't say anything. In the end, she would have to downsize whatever list her mother came up with by about 90 percent. But it would give her a jumping-off point. Hugging herself, she wandered into the bedroom. It was perfect for a full bed. Anything bigger would be a squeeze. There was a bedroom upstairs that ran the length of the house, but Piper wanted to be downstairs, by the bathroom, and with the big window overlooking the backyard. She didn't want to be stuffed in the attic.

"Which dog are you taking?" Amanda called from the other room.

"Huh?" She stepped back into the small hallway. "What do you mean?"

"You should take one of the dogs for security purposes. Angel will be heartbroken when you move out anyways. She's really more your dog than mine."

Sometimes her mother was exhausting. There was no other word for it. But after that afternoon, when she had seen blood trail down a headstone, at least this was normal. Wearying, yes, but well-meaning and loving and very, very normal. "I don't think there's really a security issue here, and I don't want to do that to Angel. She's used to the freedom of the farm. This is a small house with a small yard and I'm at work all day. She'll miss the boys and the other dogs."

"That's probably true. Maybe we should get you a puppy."

How that made any sense was beyond her. If a well-trained and low-energy older dog wouldn't like being cooped up all day, why on earth would that be fair to do to a bouncy puppy? She decided to change the subject. It was a strategy that always worked. "So do you think Dad could bring my bed over here in the next couple of days?"

"Your bed? Why?"

"Well, Brady is going to be staying here while he's painting, and it seems a little ridiculous that he's going to be sleeping on the floor."

"Why isn't he staying at Shelby's?"

"She doesn't have the room."

"That house is poky," Amanda agreed. "What about Jessie's house? She has room."

"She has a gentleman friend and she doesn't want Brady there."

"Oooh. I see." Amanda grinned. "Well, I say more power to her. But Piper, I don't know how appropriate it is to have Brady sleeping in your bed."

"Even if I'm not in it?" she asked. She shouldn't have asked. She should have just told her mother this was what was happening. She should have just sent Brady to go get the bed. That would have really raised an eyebrow or two. But no, she had asked, and now she was going to be questioned and eventually worn down to where she agreed not to proceed with the idea.

"It just seems weird to have him sleeping in your bed. I mean, you're not a Hilton hotel, for crying out loud. Why can't he get his own bed?"

"Why does he need a bed here if I can provide him with

one? It just seems like an easy thing to do," she said stubbornly. "It's only for a week or two. I'll wash the sheets." After she tussled in them with him, if all went according to plan.

"Ew. Okay, you know what? This is getting weird. I don't want to think about Brady snoring on your mattress."

It was on the tip of her tongue to blurt it out, to tell her the truth. That while yes, she was being kind and considerate and didn't want Brady to sleep on the floor, she also had an ulterior motive in that she wanted to have sex with him again without getting a butt splinter.

But she didn't.

Because her mother would tell her father and they would both disapprove and they would be disappointed in her, and she didn't want to think that they felt that way about her.

So instead she just said, "I'll have Brady call Dad so he can help him carry in the mattress and box spring."

If there was going to be an opinion offered to this statement, it was cut off by the sound of the front door opening.

"Is that Jessie?" Amanda asked. "I wonder if she has a preferred cleaning service."

Piper sighed. She loved her mother, but she didn't always listen. Amanda had a whirling-dervish quality to her, and she strode through a room confidently, problem solving in high heels.

But sometimes she surprised Piper. As they walked into the living room, she amended, "Oh, wait, you said we don't need a cleaning service. But I will drop off some cleaning supplies tomorrow."

"Thank you," she said, genuinely pleased. Leaving her parents wasn't going to be as easy as she'd thought, and she had to appreciate the way they were handling it. They were letting her go and helping her in every way they could, like they always did. She was struck again by how fortunate she was, the great gift that been given to her inadvertently by her stepfather when he had dumped her in Danny Tucker's driveway. His goal had just been to get rid of her, but he had changed the course of her life in ways that she could never fully articulate.

Sometimes she tried to visualize who and where she would be if she had stayed with Mark, and it wasn't a pretty picture. Contacting her younger half brother Marcus had confirmed that. He was a crystal meth addict at eighteen, with sallow skin and dead eyes. It had been devastating to see him like that.

She felt a rush of emotion and was going to hug her mom when she realized it wasn't Jessie in the front entry.

It was Brady.

He was carrying a yoga mat and a blanket. "Hey," he said to them with a smile.

"You going to bust into a downward dog?" Amanda asked him.

"No. This is my bed for the next few weeks. Shelby didn't mind giving it up. She said yoga is for people who can sit still, which is not her. The mat has been collecting dust in her basement."

"You're going to sleep on hardwood floors on a yoga mat?" Amanda looked horrified. "What is this— *Survivor*?"

Brady snorted. Piper laughed at the comparison.

"Well, that's just ridiculous, and Piper had a great solution," her mother continued. "There's no reason we can't just bring Piper's bed over here in the next day or two. It needs to come over anyway in a couple weeks, so why not now? That way you won't damage your back."

While her mother explained, Piper watched Brady's face. His nostrils flared, like he was picturing exactly what they could be doing on that bed.

"Where is Piper going to sleep?" he asked, his eyes trained on her, dark and seductive.

Piper felt her nipples harden and she crossed her arms over her chest so it wasn't noticeable. But he noticed. He glanced right down at them.

Where was she going to sleep? With him. That was where she wanted to sleep. Among other things.

"In the guest room at our house, of course," Amanda said.

Piper could feel the weight of her stare as she watched them, evaluating what she was seeing. Her mother was not stupid. She had to be able to see the sexual tension that stretched between them.

"That's really nice of you to offer," Brady said. "I can't tell you how much I appreciate your generosity."

If he only knew how generous Piper was feeling.

Then again, maybe he did.

"And I'm more than happy to help you get the bed here, plus anything else you're moving. Feel free to put me to work."

More than anything, she would love to put him to work between her thighs. Piper felt flushed in the small room, both aroused and embarrassed that she was so easily turned on, and in front of her mother.

Her mother who had clearly lost patience. "Well, I think we're done here for the night, Piper, so we'll let you get to settling your yoga mat, Brady. Though if I were you I'd get a hotel room."

"Why doesn't he come out to the farm and use the guest room tonight?" Piper said, surprising herself at how normal and innocent her voice sounded. "We have plenty of room and we can't just leave him here on the floor, can we?"

It was a question that effectively backed her mother into a social corner. She couldn't refuse.

"Of course not. Brady, you're welcome to stay with us." Amanda's face was carefully neutral.

Not that Piper necessarily wanted the torment of knowing he was sleeping a room away from her and she couldn't do a damn thing about it, but it felt phenomenally rude to not at least offer. She wouldn't want to sleep on the floor.

There was a lengthy pause then he said, "Why, thank you, ladies. I would really appreciate it."

And Piper felt both excitement and fear explode inside her.

It seemed like it was going to be another sleepless night for her.

Chapter Nine

WHAT THE FUCK WAS HE THINKING? TALK ABOUT GOING into the lion's den. Brady pulled up in front of the Tuckers' Victorian farmhouse and shook his head at himself. So he hadn't wanted to sleep on the floor. Big deal. He could have sucked it up for one night. So the house was empty and smelled a little like old lady. He would have been fine.

It would have been smarter, and possibly safer, than staying in the Tucker guest bedroom, a door or two away from Piper. And her parents. He hoped they'd had ample time to warn Danny he was showing up, but then again, Danny probably had no idea that he and Piper had, um, expressed an interest in each other. He would after tonight. It had taken Amanda about sixty seconds in the company of the two of them to figure out the score. Much like it had Shelby. Hell, Shelby had read it in his voice on the phone.

He couldn't help it. He smoldered when Piper was in front of him. Like a slow-burning coal fire, red-hot in the center.

Any man with a lick of sense would run. He should turn his wimpy car around and head back to Chicago, where his life was . . . what? What was his life in Chicago? Boring? Nothing like he had intended? Surrounded by casual friends and nothing more?

No, he was staying in Cuttersville. He wanted to know what had happened to the old Brady Stritmeyer, Rachel's fiancé.

And he wanted to know what had happened to the new Brady Stritmeyer. He'd lost the spunky kid he'd been somewhere along the way. He wanted to feel alive again, to feel excited about something.

So he got out of the car, leaving the yoga mat behind, and climbed the solid wood steps of their impressive front porch, right up to Piper, who was waiting for him in front of the back door.

"Thank you," he told her. "You're very sweet." Because he couldn't resist, he stroked his thumb across her bottom lip. "Like sugar."

Her eyes darkened in the porch light, but she just shrugged. "I wouldn't want to sleep on a floor in an empty house."

"I really, really want to kiss you," he murmured, cupping her cheek and moving closer, the floorboards creaking as he shifted. "But I suppose that's not a good idea."

"We're alone," she said, tilting her head into his touch. "If you're quick about it."

He was starting to think being quick about it with Piper was not going to work. He was starting to think that there weren't enough days in three weeks to satisfy his need to be with her, both sexually and otherwise.

But he was damn sure going to try, because the other option was to walk away right now, and he just couldn't do that.

So he leaned forward, closing the distance between them, and brushed her lips with his. It was fascinating to him that the most innocent action, a simple kiss, could have that kind of impact on him. But it did. It was soft and teasing, and it triggered a whole range of feelings in him from lust to impatience to awe.

Her fingers trailed across his chest, and down even lower, as he kissed her, and Brady forgot where they were. The kiss turned hot, frantic, and he buried his hands in her hair, grinding his hips against hers. Her breathing was hot and quick on his mouth and she made a sound, a little gasp of delight that nearly undid him.

He wasn't sure where he would have gone next, but he was pretty sure it involved his teeth on her nipple through her T-shirt, but he'd never know because the front door opened.

"Hey, uh—oh!" Danny cleared his throat. "Piper?"

She broke the kiss and spun around so fast her hair smacked him in the face. "Dad!"

Awkward. Brady put his hand on the small of her back and stepped in line beside her, reaching his hand out to shake Danny's. "Hey, Danny, long time, no see. How are you doing?"

Fortunately, Danny had always been a good guy, reasonable, polite. So even though he clearly wanted to snatch his daughter away from Brady and lock her in a convent, he shook the hand offered. "I'm good, Brady. How are you?"

"Aside from being unemployed, I can't complain. Thanks for letting me stay here tonight. I'm sure it's a bit unexpected."

The wheels were turning hard in Danny's head. "Not a

problem," he said carefully. "Happy to have you. Even if you were just making out with my daughter."

"Dad!" Piper's cheeks were the color of a ripe tomato.

"What?" Danny held his hands out. "I don't see any point in beating around the bush. So here's the deal—no funny business in my house, you understand? So Brady, that means remove your hand from my daughter's backside before you go in the house."

"Oh, my God," Piper whispered. "His hand is on my *back*."

"As far as I can figure, he hasn't known you long enough for his hand to be anywhere on you, but you're an adult. I don't have a say in who you date. But I do have a say in what goes on in my house."

"It's not what you think," she said.

Brady tried not to laugh. It was clearly everything Danny thought it was.

"Why don't you head in and help your mother set up the guest room? I'd like to speak to Brady alone for a minute."

"No," she said, surprising both her father and Brady. "I'm not going to let you threaten him."

"Who said anything about threatening him? We're just going to have a talk."

"It's okay," Brady reassured her, because this conversation had to happen sooner or later. He'd rather do it now and clear the air. He'd walked into this and he was man enough to own up to it. "I'll be fine. Danny and I go way back."

She hesitated, but then she pursed her lips and went into the house, closing the door firmly behind her.

Danny stared at it for a second. "I can't believe she told me no. Geez, she never tells me no."

"She's a very giving woman, Danny. You should be proud of how Piper has turned out."

"I am. Trust me, I am. She's special."

There it was again. *Special.* He wondered if any of them really understood what he was starting to—that Piper didn't want to be special. She wanted to be like everyone else.

"Yes, she is," he agreed, because it was true. Piper was a better person than 99 percent of those he'd met.

"Sit down, Brady," Danny said, taking a seat on a wicker chair. He grimaced. "God, I hate these damn chairs. Wicker sticks to the back of my legs."

"I kind of like them." The furniture reminded him of folks sitting on the porch shooting the shit while kids ran around like dust-covered heathens. Brady took a seat next to him and stared out at the inky-black evening sky. Damn, it was dark out here. He'd forgotten what the country was like, how still the air was, how quiet. It settled inside his shoulders, relaxed them, the knots of tension riding around in there for a week loosening.

"Sorry you lost your job. That's tough."

"Thanks." Brady watched a firefly shoot off its tiny glow. "It wasn't a great job, but it did pay the bills."

"I understand that. It isn't always profitable to run a farm. But if you love something, you just keep going."

"I don't love advertising." That wasn't even something he had to think about. "It was just a job I did because I didn't know what else to do."

"Then maybe this is an opportunity for you."

"Maybe." Brady waited, because he knew what was coming next. It had been a long time, but back in the day, he'd gotten The Talk from more than one father.

"I've always liked you, Brady. I have."

Here it came. "Thanks." Brady breathed deep, regretting that he had quit smoking. The sweet country air was perfect for a cigarette. It was a good thing the store was too far to go back to. He didn't want to start up such a deadly habit again after four years clean.

But it would taste amazing.

"But you're a little old for Piper, you know. She hasn't had a lot of experience with men. She falls hard and doesn't always understand a man isn't necessarily in it for the right reasons—you know what I'm saying?"

"Yeah." Because he couldn't deny it. While he didn't know any of it for fact, he could imagine that would be true about Piper. And he *was* too old for her.

"I'm sure there are women you work with, in your circle of friends in Chicago, who understand the game. They know if you're just looking to get your feet wet and nothing more. They're not going to get hurt when they realize all you want is sex."

Brady swallowed hard. He had told Piper he would be fine, but now he wasn't so sure. Danny was right. What the fuck was he doing? Piper was not the kind of woman you played with and walked away from. She was not the type who had a contact list of friends with benefits like half the women he dated in Chicago. Brady wondered when the last time he'd actually had a real relationship was. He'd settled into a routine of random sex with several women he had fun hanging out with, and that was it.

None of that felt appropriate here. Then suddenly he knew the truth of it. "Maybe I'm not just looking for sex. I can have sex with anyone." If it had just been about sex, he would have been able to resist her, ironically enough, because sex was easy to come by and he got it regularly. He wouldn't have risked the ire of family and friends if he hadn't been looking for something more.

But that wasn't fair to Piper either, and he knew it. He couldn't give her anything beyond a couple of weeks.

"Oh, my God." Danny put his fist to his chest like he had heartburn, and his face looked pained. "That might actually be worse. Are you telling me you're sticking around?"

"No." He couldn't. That was preposterous. "Look, Danny, I don't want to hurt her. That's the last thing I want. I'll talk to her, okay? Make sure she truly understands I'm going back to Chicago and that this is it." He was sympathizing with Danny's chest pain. His was feeling a little tight as well.

Danny sighed. "I guess I can't ask for much more than that. She's a grown woman. Almost." He reached out and clapped Brady on the shoulder. "I told you, I always liked you." He grinned. "Just not with my daughter."

Brady laughed. "Story of my life, man. I haven't met a father yet who wanted me around his daughter. It's tough on the old ego."

"Bullshit. You always liked being a ladies' man. Did you hear Abby Murphy's pregnant?"

"I didn't do it."

They both laughed. Danny leaned forward, his hands between his knees. "You know, when Piper was a teenager I worried that boys could take advantage of her, that they would sense that need she has to belong, and would use it to get in her pants. I worried she'd end up pregnant at sixteen like her mother. And I wouldn't be able to hate them or blame them because I was one of those boys. I wasn't thinking about anything other than how good it felt. But Piper was smarter than I gave her credit for—she didn't fall for any of those lines."

"Maybe she's not as insecure as you think. Guilt does funny things to perception, you know." Brady imagined Danny felt a crapload of it, given Piper's first eight years of life.

"Yeah. I can't argue with that." Danny fidgeted. "But she's older now. Old enough to go out on her own, do whatever she wants. Get married. Be a mother."

"So what are you so worried about, then? She seems like a very happy person, Danny."

"I'm worried some man will change that. And then I'll have to kill him."

The words were spoken with a lightness, but there was enough of a seriousness there that Brady's shoulders tensed again. Great. Just what he needed. Death threats.

"I thought you told Piper you weren't going to threaten me." Not that he was particularly offended. Danny was well within his rights to be concerned.

"That wasn't a threat. It was a warning." Danny stood up. "I'm getting a beer. You want one?"

"No, thanks. But maybe you can send Piper out here and I can talk to her. Make sure everyone is on the same page." Brady didn't want to spell it out, but it was the right thing to do. "But just so you know, you've done a fine job raising her. That's why I . . ." How did he say that he couldn't resist her because she was unlike anyone he'd ever met?

"You can stop there. I get it. And thanks. I think she's pretty amazing myself." Danny opened the front door and retreated into the house. Brady stared out at the stars and tried to decipher his restlessness. He was agitated and he wasn't sure why.

Piper appeared a second later. "Well, no punches were thrown. That's a plus."

"It's fine." He smiled up at her. "Want to go for a walk?"

She frowned, but then shrugged. "Sure."

"Do you want to get a sweater? It's cooling down out here." It was a completely dorky suggestion and Brady mentally kicked himself for sounding more like her nanny than her . . . what? What did he want to be? That was the question he kept coming around to.

"I'm fine, thanks." She smiled softly at him. "Where are we walking to? The farm isn't exactly a walking path."

"Don't you all have a pond?" Funny how he'd slipped so easily back into the speech patterns of his childhood.

"It's just an irrigation pond. No dock or anything. And it smells like algae." She turned back towards the door. "Come on, I'll get my keys and we can drive into the apple orchard. It's my favorite place this time of the year."

Was he supposed to follow her into the house? Brady supposed it was only polite he go say hello to Amanda. Trying not to feel intrusive, he followed her into the house. The rooms were large and airy, with comfortable furniture. The living and dining rooms were dark but as they passed the stairs to the kitchen and family room, warm lighting illuminated the back of the house. The kitchen had been remodeled at some point, but it was a classic farmhouse look, with distressed white cabinetry, and a deep copper farmhouse sink. It all spoke of Amanda's touch and, frankly, Amanda's money. While nothing was over-the-top, there was no way the Tuckers could have turned this house into the magazine showpiece it was without the bank account of the heiress. Brady wondered how that sat with Danny.

But given that he was pulling a beer from a Kegerator hidden behind a cabinet door, he didn't look too worried about it.

Two boys—one lanky and white-blond the other stocky and dirty blond—were lounging on the sofa watching TV. "Hey," Brady said to them when they glanced his way.

"Wassup?" the older one said, reminding Brady a lot of Amanda, with his carefully cultivated expression of boredom.

Amanda, who was holding a glass of wine, made a face. "Boys, this is Brady Stritmeyer, Shelby's cousin."

The younger one sat up and stuck his hand out over the back of the couch. "I'm Jack Tucker."

Brady grinned. This one was the spitting image of Danny. "Nice to meet you, Jack. Brady." He shook the kid's hand.

"You, too. This is my brother, Daniel Logan." Jack shot

a thumb at the teen lounging next to him. Then to the three dogs cuddled up between the two of them. "This is Daisy, and that's Duke, and the black one with the white ear is Prada. And my sister, Piper, is in the kitchen."

"Wow, full house. I've actually met Piper before. I even babysat her when she was a kid."

"Oh, really?" Jack seemed to find this intriguing. "Hmm."

Brady waited in amusement for an explanation but none seemed forthcoming.

Piper came over and ruffled Jack's hair. "Brady and I are going for a walk, Jack-Jack. Good night. Night, Logan."

Jack's eyes were shining at her words. Even Logan seemed to find this information curious, and for the first time he really studied Brady. Feeling as vulnerable as a stripper on her first night on the job, Brady refused to show it. He stared the kid down with a smile. Logan looked away first.

"You're going for a walk?" Amanda asked, like this was the most insane idea she'd ever heard in her life. "Why?"

Danny said, "Amanda."

She looked at her husband. "What?"

He gave her a slight shake of his head. Instantly she seemed to understand what he was trying to say. Brady found the silent communication between married couples fascinating. What would it be like to know someone so well that you could anticipate their actions and know what they were thinking without using words? He'd never even come close to that kind of connection with a woman.

"Take a sweater," Amanda said instead to Piper. "It's getting cold out there."

Piper laughed. "Since you're the second person to suggest that, maybe I'll get a sweater and make you and Brady happy."

She ran up the stairs, her gait light and graceful. He

imagined she got mothered a lot. There was just something about Piper's eyes that made you want to take care of her. But she seemed to understand and appreciate the sentiment behind it, and didn't reject it. Not that Brady wanted to mother her. There were a whole lot of things he wanted to do to her, and none of them should be considered standing in her parents' kitchen.

"You're freaking me out," Amanda told him.

"Why? What did I do?"

"You know why," she said cryptically, draining her wineglass.

"Actually, I really don't."

"Ready," Piper said breathlessly, tumbling off the stairs and into the kitchen. She grabbed her keys off a hook by the back door. "We're going for a drive, technically, then a walk. We'll see you later."

With that, Piper opened the door and rushed out into the driveway, clearly in a hurry. Whether he could flatter himself that she wanted to be with him, he wasn't sure. It was just as likely she wanted to get away from her parents as any burning desire for his company.

He kind of wanted to get away from her parents, too. The whole situation was a tad awkward.

She paused next to her truck and held her keys up for him.

"What—you want me to drive?"

"I know enough about men to know they prefer to be the one behind the wheel. My mother hasn't ever driven my father, to my knowledge. My dad is afraid he will lose a testicle and all his chest hair if he lets her chauffeur him."

Brady gave Piper a long, assessing look. "My masculinity isn't threatened by anything. Certainly not by having a woman drive her own car. You're welcome to drive. Unless you prefer to have a big strong man handle your truck."

The truth was, he wanted to see her driving that big old

four-wheel-drive pickup. It was just one more curious facet of Piper's personality. She was something of an enigma that he wanted to solve.

"Then I'll drive." She didn't hesitate. Going around the driver's side, she hopped into her truck in one smooth motion.

Brady climbed in the passenger side, noting that her truck was straight as a pin, no trash anywhere or miscellaneous items lying around. He barely had the door shut when she shot the truck into reverse and peeled around to head down the driveway. Whoa. Piper was a bit of a lead foot. It didn't fit his idea of her—hesitant and unassuming. But then again, hadn't he just thought she was multifaceted?

Gravel churned under her tires and Brady shot her a grin of appreciation. "Damn, girl, you know how to handle this truck just fine."

She was going at least fifty, and the speed had her bouncing around on her seat, her hair flowing over her shoulders. She shot him a quick grin. "I like the power of driving a big vehicle. I think my dad underestimated how much I would enjoy it. But hey, it makes sense for a farmer's daughter, right? I started out on a tractor and graduated to a pickup."

Brady hit the button to let down his window and he breathed in the night air. It was clean and sharp, but with the underlying earthy scent of animal and freshly threshed crops. It wasn't a bad way to grow up. "I'm impressed."

After a minute or two, Piper took a turnoff and started driving down between two rows of apple trees. The orchard went on as far as Brady could see in the dark, and after a dozen trees or so, Piper put her truck in park and turned it off. "Come on."

Where they were going he wasn't sure, but he got out of his side and realized that Piper was climbing into the bed of her truck. Once in, she nimbly jumped onto the top of the cab, reached out her hand, and plucked a ripe apple off the tree closest to her, all in her pretty little skirt.

Brady laughed. "That's handy."

She winked and took a bite, a loud crunch reverberating in the still air.

It was like a punch to his gut, that wink. She was by far the sexiest thing he'd ever seen in his entire life. He'd had strippers gyrate in front of him with practiced moves, he'd had gorgeous women drop their cocktail dresses to the floor, leaving them in nothing but heels, and yet not one had ever been as flat-out hot as Piper Tucker winking at him over an apple, perched on the top of her truck, legs a tad apart in her skirt. The sweater she'd grabbed was nowhere to be seen and her hair shifted in the soft breeze, all that bare skin and swagger driving him insane. He wasn't ashamed to admit that he attempted to look up her skirt, but the angle wasn't right.

"It's good," she said. "Juicy."

He knew another thing or two that was bound to be juicy. "How good is your balance?"

Chewing, she asked, "Why?"

"I'm coming up, so brace yourself."

Brady put his palms on the side of the truck bed and hauled himself up. The car rocked slightly but not enough to give Piper any trouble, though she had grabbed onto a tree branch for stability. He moved towards her. "Give me a bite."

"Get your own. There's a thousand apples."

"I want a bite of yours." Brady eliminated the gap between them, standing right in front of her, but enough below her that he was facing the apex of her thighs behind that cotton skirt. He couldn't have asked for anything more tempting. Her apple dangled just below her waist, so he took her wrist and raised it to his lips. She didn't stop him when he buried his teeth in the crunchy sweetness. "Thank you," he said with a full mouth, the juice sliding down his throat. "Now come back down here please, before I lift your skirt."

She laughed. "Here." She pressed the apple into his hand, and before he could process what she was about, she was gone. A few well-placed maneuvers and Piper had put herself in a tree, one leg on either side of the branch, her nimble fingers reaching out to pluck another apple for herself.

Brady took her spot on the truck cab, sitting down with his feet dangling over the edge so he could comfortably talk to her. He reached out and stroked her bare leg. "You're a regular monkey. I wouldn't have guessed that."

"I used to come out here as a kid to be alone. I found out I'm good at climbing trees, which was a happy discovery because there weren't a ton of things I was good at."

She didn't say it with any malice or bitterness or disappointment. Just a matter of acceptance that seemed to envelope her. About everything but seeing ghosts, that was.

"I was in Boy Scouts for one year in the second grade. I got pissed that we weren't going camping with army knives in like the first month, so I quit. That was kind of my childhood—searching for instant gratification and never getting good at anything." He bit her apple and chewed, reflecting. He'd never realized that until now.

"Why did you want to go camping with an army knife?"

"I don't know. That's what I thought you were supposed to do in Scouts. And I was hot to have a knife and start fires. It seemed like that would be cool." By sixth grade he'd been a damn good shot with a BB gun, could start a fire in thirty seconds, and had butchered a rabbit for stew, all self-taught. Because he'd been curious and had taken risks. So maybe he hadn't stuck with anything for very long, but as a kid he'd been tenacious and spirited. He wondered what the fuck had happened to that attitude.

"I'm sure it was cool. I was never in Scouts." Piper nicked at the bark of the branch she was on. "So I have a sleeping bag in my truck bed, you know."

Instant erection. That's what he had. Like instant oatmeal. Done in sixty seconds, hot and ready to serve. "And exactly why would I need to know that piece of information?" he asked teasingly, moving his fingers higher up on her leg.

"Because I believe you had a teen fantasy about the back of a truck bed. I'm offering to help you out."

Her boldness towards sex with him had surprised him initially, but now it just served to turn him on. There was no point in dissecting it. He'd leave that to the shrinks that neither one of them would ever go to. Therapy wasn't a Cuttersville kind of thing. If people in this town had a problem, they usually just tried to drink it away.

But he was off track. Focus, Stritmeyer. A beautiful woman was offering to get it on in her truck in an apple orchard. With him. He glanced up. Under the stars. Check.

"I thought you'd never ask," he told her. "Get on down here."

Putting her apple in her teeth, she came down off the branch and lightly dropped down next to him.

Brady smiled at her, feeling sort of strange inside. "Hi," he said.

She removed the apple from her mouth. "Hi," she said shyly.

He wasn't sure how she did that, navigating so easily between bold and demure, but it appealed to him in a way he didn't really understand. "So how long do you think we have before Danny comes looking for you?"

She shrugged. "He'll probably text me before he comes looking for me. Don't let that worry you."

"Okay." Because he didn't want to worry about anything. He just wanted to get naked in the moonlight with Piper.

He tossed his apple to the ground and reached for her. It was meant to be a slow seduction, a teasing lean that brought their lips together in a soft, enticing kiss.

But there was no slow because Piper more than met him halfway. In fact, she got to him first, her arms sliding around his neck, her teeth nipping at his bottom lip. Did she seriously just bite him? Brady almost fell off the truck from lack of oxygen in his brain.

"What was that for?" he asked, wrapping his arms around her and yanking her up against his chest. He wanted to feel her soft body against his hardness. He wanted to bite her back. He wanted to eat her.

"You bit mine, so I bit yours."

Oh, really? Brady kissed her ferociously, with an urgency he hadn't felt in God only knew how long. "That was an apple. I don't think it's the same thing. I think you're just a dirty girl who likes to bite."

She pulled back, panting, her eyes enormous as they floated above the pale skin of her face in the dark, her lips so tantalizingly close and moist. "I don't know if I am or not. I never have before. It just felt right . . . like I had to bite you."

"Do whatever feels right," he told her, cupping her cheeks with his hands, suddenly aware that he was in by far the deepest shit he had ever fallen into. There were no waders high enough to navigate this without getting dirty.

If it was at all possible for a thirty-one-year-old cynic to fall head over ass for an unsophisticated woman altogether too young for him, Brady was fairly certain it had just happened. If anyone had told him this would occur in whole or in part, he would have snorted in derision at the ridiculousness of the possibility.

But here he was, making out with a fervor he hadn't felt since he'd been sixteen, his fingers making inroads into her inner thigh like his very life depended on getting inside those panties. He wanted her and nothing else right now.

PIPER WASN'T EVEN SURE WHAT WAS HAPPENING TO her. She felt insane, like someone else had stepped inside her skin and was directing her actions. After carelessly dropping her apple into the dirt, she groped, she clawed, she nipped at Brady like he was the only thing standing between her and satisfaction, which she supposed, in a way, he was. She didn't act like this—she didn't. She was coming at him like she would die if she didn't have sex in the next ten minutes, and it was so not her. But it clearly was her. And she clearly was going to die if she didn't get to have sex with Brady in the next ten minutes.

When he pushed her away, panting hard, she gave a whimper, wanting his tongue back inside her mouth, plunging firmly, wetly, rhythmically. But he kept her at arm's length, like he needed the space. "Where's that sleeping bag?"

She had forgotten about the sleeping bag. Heck, she had forgotten her middle name. It was a good thing he was still coherent. "In that bag in the corner."

"Excellent. Good. Very good. But damn it, I have to talk to you about something first." He looked agonized.

Uh-oh. She didn't like the sound of that. If he had a girlfriend, she was going to shove him off this truck into the dirt. With trepidation she said, "Yes?"

He raked his hands through his hair in a way that made him even more appealing to her. Piper had never, ever been as attracted to a man as she was to him. And he was a man, she made no mistake about that. Not a boy like the others she'd been involved with.

Taking a deep breath, he looked up from his jeans and

met her expectant gaze. "I just want to make sure you understand that I'm going back to Chicago."

That was it? Piper let out a whoosh of air in relief. "Of
course I know that." He had said it, hadn't he? His grandmother had said it. It was a given that a man like Brady
would not want to stay put in a town like Cuttersville, which
he had run away from at eighteen. "I know."

She did, and if she had indulged in a fantasy or two that
he would stay longer, well, that was her problem. But she'd
never gone so far as to fantasize about them being together
long-term. She wouldn't allow herself to do that.

"So what are we doing, then?" he asked.

Piper didn't think a man generally asked that type of
question. She raised her eyebrows. "Having fun?"

His brow furrowed. "Yeah. We are."

"So is there a problem?" She didn't have one other than
the fact that she really, really wished he had waited until
after she'd had an orgasm to have this conversation.

"No." He jumped down into the truck bed and walked
over to the bag she'd pointed out to him.

Piper waited, sure the conversation wasn't over. There
was something else he wanted to say.

She was right. As she dangled her feet over the edge of
the cab, watching him, he dug into the nylon encasing and
pulled out the sleeping bag.

"Piper?"

"Yes?"

"Have you ever wanted to move out of Cuttersville? Live
in the city? See something of the world?"

"No." She didn't even need to think about it. The branches
of the apple trees stretched out towards her as she sat on her
truck, on Tucker land.

"Why?" He sounded frustrated, and she wasn't sure why.
It wasn't like he was considering a future with her.

Was he? She wouldn't dare to let herself even consider the possibility. Wanting him to want that was disastrous, because he never would, and she couldn't go to Chicago anyway.

"Because my family is here. Sure, I'd love to travel and see some of the world, but I don't want to live anywhere else."

"But the city has excellent food, museums, shopping."

He sounded like the Chamber of Commerce. "High rent, crime, pollution." She laughed, still unsure what he was getting at. "None of which would bother me if my family were with me."

"Really? You don't want the experience of living somewhere else?"

"I don't want the experience of being lonely. I want to know that I'm never more than a couple of miles from someone who loves me."

There was a heartbeat when he just stared at her, then Brady stretched his hand out to take hers. "I can understand that."

Did he really? He would never know what it felt like to have no one else in the world, no one who cared whether you lived or died. That's what Piper had lived with as a kid, and once she'd found her family, she had no reason to ever want to leave again. She put her hand in his larger one. "I'm happy here," she said. "It's where I belong. What about you? Did you find that sense of belonging in Chicago? The place you know you're meant to be?"

She expected him to say yes. To say that he had to go back because it was where he belonged.

Instead, he just said, "No."

Piper slid down into the bed and stood in front of him, looking up into his handsome face. "No? I'm sorry."

He gave a soft laugh. "You're very sweet, which is why

I can't resist you. I should, you know. I should walk away from you. Hell, I should get in my car and drive back to Chicago tomorrow."

"To the place you don't belong?" she asked, because it seemed so utterly illogical to her.

"Yes. Because I'm being selfish with you."

So that's what was bothering him. Piper was oddly flattered. "How are you being selfish?" She wanted to hear him spell it out.

"By doing this with you and then going home."

"I think they call *this* an affair. People have them all the time. We both understand it won't be more than a few weeks." Piper squeezed his hand. She wasn't going to be denied this because he was having a moral pang, probably brought about by her father's threats. "And if you remember, I'm the one who threw myself at you, so I don't think you need to feel guilt over loving and leaving me." She didn't really want to be having this conversation, but she wasn't one to be anything other than perfectly honest and direct.

Brady studied her, and the intensity of his scrutiny almost had her asking him what else was wrong, but she didn't want to be that girl, the kind who questions a guy every five minutes. Are you okay? What's wrong? Why are you quiet? Are you mad at me?

Piper would stab herself in the heart with a butter knife before she ever became that pathetic around Brady. She'd done that in college, and she would rather be alone for the rest of her life than let someone, or let herself, be reduced to a level-five clinger.

Her words seemed to have the effect she wanted. Brady shook his head a little. "Damn, you're right. You're totally right. You did throw yourself at me." Brady grinned at her. "As long as we're on the same page, hussy, I guess I shouldn't be worrying."

She supposed she'd walked right into that tease. "Ha-ha. Yes, we're on the same page. Though right now it's kind of a blank page."

Brady gave her a smile that had probably charmed many a resolute woman right out of her underwear. "So let's fill it up."

That worked for her. "With what?"

"Nothing you'd write home to your mother. But something that will set your diary on fire."

"I don't have a diary."

"Tomorrow you just might start."

Piper suspected he just might be right.

Chapter Ten

✿

HOW WAS IT THAT THIS WOMAN COULD DISARM HIM THE way no other could? Brady had fully expected her to go ballistic on him when he reminded her that he was going back to Chicago. Or to try to talk him out of it. Or suggest she come with him. All responses he would have gotten from other women. Or the most likely one—defiant disinterest. The who fucking cares? You're just a notch, baby—the attitude of a lot of women he'd dated. The attitude that he was never really sure was legit. Like was it that they really didn't give a shit or were they just trying to make it seem that they didn't?

But Piper didn't react in any of those ways. She just shrugged and smiled and told him they were having an affair.

My God. They were having an affair. He wasn't sure he'd ever done that. It was like traveling to Italy and meeting a local and spending two weeks sightseeing with her and making love and eating gelato, then going home. A wonderful and passionate interruption of life with a person you really connected with. That was exactly what he was doing, and now that she'd spelled it out for him, he was going to stop feeling guilty about it and dive right in and eat some gelato.

He spread out the sleeping bag and stripped off his T-shirt and bunched it up at the top of the bag like a pillow. Only a country girl would agree to do this, and he was feeling a whole new appreciation for farmers' daughters. Kicking his boots off, he sent them sailing into the corner so they wouldn't trip on them. Taking his cue, Piper stepped out of her sandals.

"Come here," he murmured, then didn't wait for her to follow his instructions. He couldn't let another minute go by before he felt her skin against his, had her in his arms. Burying his head in her hair, he said, "You feel good."

"Better than smelling bad."

"When did you get so sassy?" He nibbled at her ear, enjoying the warmth of her skin, the soft sigh she gave at contact.

"I don't think I am. I'm just matter-of-fact. I don't know how to flirt."

Was she kidding him? "Oh, I think you do just fine." He felt flirted with. Or maybe she was right. Maybe her just-the-facts-sir attitude was actually the real turn-on. Because she wasn't game playing. If she wanted him, she said it. "I find myself a bit turned around by you, Piper. I don't know what to do with you."

"I think you know what to do with me," she said, taking his hand and lowering it from her waist to her inner thigh. Not quite on her sex, but damn close.

Brady groaned. "You're right. I do know what to do with you. I'm going to start with kissing you again."

Her lips were soft, sweet from the apple, open for him. He kissed her with a tenderness he didn't know he possessed, kissed her with something like reverence. They were all right. Piper was special. She did things to him that he didn't understand, made him want to be a better man. Plunging his tongue inside her, he was determined to give her the same pleasure that she brought to him, wanting to make the most of the limited time they had, absorb her into him in a way, so that when he went home, she would still be with him.

Stroking across the front of her skirt, pressing against her clitoris when he found it, Brady tried to form a game plan, a calculated seduction. But all he could think was that he wanted her and he wanted her now. Everything he'd learned about taking his time and teasing a woman seemed to have evaporated. He was just overcome with the pure greedy need to take, take, take. So he stepped back and forced himself to drag in some fresh air and get a grip on his hormones. He was not going to just drive inside her again like the first time.

Reaching out, he drew her T-shirt off her head, slowly, easily, putting a lid on the frantic nature of his desire. He was in control. He was going to make this worth her time and the ire of her father. When the shirt popped off her head and her hair tumbled back down, he placed it on the side of the truck so it wouldn't get dirty. Or not too dirty, anyway. Then he took in the sight of her in the moonlight, her breasts firm and full, spilling out of the top of a white lace bra, her waist tapered, her arms slim and delicate, her neck graceful. "God, you're so beautiful," he told her, and he meant it. She was ethereal in her beauty. The portrait of feminine perfection, her hair shiny and healthy, her lips plump and rosy.

It was a compliment that drew a blush to her cheeks and stained the flesh above her breasts a pale pink. "Thank you."

"May I?" he asked, taking the waistband of her skirt and readying to shove it to the floor.

"Yes."

Brady kissed her while he pushed the skirt past her hips, letting it drop with a soft thump. Brushing his hands over her nipples, straining against her bra, he took his time kissing her, exploring the contours of her body, the dip of her waist, the curve of her hips, the heaviness of her breasts, the delicate bone underlining her shoulder. He couldn't place the scent she wore. It wasn't a heavy perfume, it wasn't floral. There was something fresh about the way she smiled. Like the outdoors. Like youth. Like soft, ripe fruit ready to be eaten.

Popping the fastener of her bra, Brady toyed with the top of her panties, hinting at where he would like to go next, even as her breasts spilled out of the open bra. She made a sound in the back of her throat that had his mouth hot and his boxers stretched to capacity. Her fingers were doing their own traveling, sliding up and down his chest, tracing all the lines of his muscles and squeezing here and there before coming to a rest on his waist. He bent over and pulled her bra off with his teeth, grabbing it right in the middle and drawing it away from her body before letting it fall down onto her skirt. Which left his mouth deliciously close to the breasts he'd been dying to taste. Flicking his tongue on the underside of one, he moved his feet apart, bracing for some serious playtime. The fingers on his waist tightened reflexively.

Her nipples were hard, a dusty rose, the perfect size to draw into his mouth and suck. When he did, she gave a low, soft moan that had him throbbing harder, something he wouldn't have thought possible.

Then he bit her. Just gently, but a definite nip.

"Oh, God," she said, her head falling back, her hands moving up to his head, to hold him tightly against her.

"Turnabout's fair play," he told her.

"I didn't bite your boob."

He laughed. Sometimes the things she said just killed him. "That's not your boob. It's your nipple."

"Yes, sir."

That deference, fake or not, made his blood surge south, hot tendrils of desire flickering along his body, consuming him. It was near impossible to maintain his composure, but somehow he managed it. She seemed to realize the impact her words had on him because when he said, "Can I take your panties off?" she gave the same response.

"Yes, sir."

"You're killing me," he breathed, closing his eyes for a second to grasp for the thin strands of his control. "That should sound so wrong, but Jesus, Piper, it's turning me on like nothing else."

"It's turning me on, too. Tell me what to do."

This couldn't be happening. It was just too amazingly perfect. He was in the back of a pickup under the stars with a beautiful woman who wanted him to tell her what to do. This more than made up for losing his job. He'd stay unemployed and broke for the next six months rather than give this up right now.

What he really wanted to tell her to do was to go down on her knees and suck his dick, but he wasn't there yet with Piper. It seemed like the first time for her giving him head should be entirely on her terms, not his. So instead he said, "I'm going to take off your panties, and then I want you to lay down for me."

She nodded, the pulse point in her throat jumping, her eyes dark with desire, goose bumps rushing across her chest.

Her panties matched her bra, just a simple white lace that glowed in the dark orchard, low cut but covering everything. Brady knew what he was going to find behind that triangle of lace and cotton as he peeled it down inch by agonizing inch. Soft dewy curls, not a bald eagle. While waxing everything had its own appeal, it didn't suit Piper. It was too . . . maintained. He liked to think of her as freer, untamed, feminine. It made more sense to him than anything else. This was Bush country, after all.

When the panties passed over her pelvis, soft downy curls the same caramel color as her hair emerged. It was neat and tidy, but for the most part was as nature had intended it, and he dipped his finger into the center of her curls, swallowing hard when he immediately slid into hot moisture. She was more than ready to take him inside her. But he pulled his finger back and put it into his mouth, tasting the sweetness of her body. She made a strangled sound, her chest rising and falling faster.

The panties weren't down all the way, but she dropped down to the sleeping bag anyway, like her legs could no longer hold her. Brady took in the sight of her, sprawled out for him, hair a riot of waves around her head and on the bag, her arms out to her sides, legs trying to spread, but still contained in her shocking white panties. There was something very pure about the way she looked, or maybe it was the purity of her soul that he saw, which sounded corny even in his own head, but he knew was true. And he was never more humbled and aroused in his life. This was more than he deserved. This was more than he knew what to do with.

But he'd be damned if he'd walk away. He didn't always finish what he started, but this, he was going to finish.

He was going to have this affair, for lack of a better word, for the time he was in Cuttersville. And he was going to give her as much pleasure as he possibly could.

Divesting himself of his jeans, Brady knelt down before her.

PIPER SHOULD CARE ABOUT HOW SHE LOOKED— whether she was posed awkwardly, whether her thighs looked big, whether she had a goofy look on her face—but she didn't. She couldn't bring herself to care about anything except the way Brady was looking at her, like she was the tastiest thing he'd ever seen.

There were no voices in her head for the first time ever except for Brady's telling her she was beautiful. She felt beautiful, appreciated. Not pitied.

Her skin felt alive, like every nerve she possessed had been sleeping until now, and Brady had awoken them. She gave a sharp intake of breath when he dropped between her feet, only in his boxers, and peeled her panties the rest of the way down. He stroked along the insides of her knees, then her thighs, casually spreading her legs, moving between them like he belonged there. When his mouth made contact with her aching sex, she allowed herself to release the moan she'd been withholding.

Then he used his fingers to massage her inner lips while he kissed her clitoris, sliding his tongue down deep inside her, and Piper knew that she had just crossed a line and couldn't go back. This was what a man with experience could do, with just a few touches here and there. There was hesitating, no overenthusiasm or tepid strokes, no constant changing of the rhythm or continual fussing with her curls, which she knew were probably in need of some grooming. But she wasn't dating anyone, so she hadn't bothered. And no one she had ever dated had known how to do this—this casual but earnest and confident approach to eating her out.

She had never felt anything as awesomely, amazingly

delightful as what Brady was doing to her. She wasn't even sure she was in her body anymore. It was like she had been reduced to nothing more than her clitoris, her tight nipples, and her aching vagina. Turning her head to the side, she stared at the ridges on the sides of her truck, needing to focus, to concentrate on something as a tightness built inside her. Gripping the sleeping bag with a viselike grip, she panted and moaned and squirmed, trying to back away from him. It was too much, the sensations overwhelming her, the realization of where she was and with who and what incredible things he was doing to her with his tongue and his fingers.

Brady stopped tickling the insides of her thighs with his fingers long enough to grip them firmly, holding her in place. "Stay still," he commanded. "No squirming."

It should have embarrassed her, the effect his orders had on her. She immediately stilled, a rush of hot fluid greeting his fingers when he returned with a thumb sinking into her and hooking to stroke her G-spot.

She wasn't embarrassed at all. She was beyond any care or concern for social boundaries. She knew what she wanted, and it was Brady. And she knew what he wanted, so as she stopped moving, she said, "Yes, sir."

Her obedience was rewarded with him sucking on her clitoris, his thumb deep inside her, his beard stubble tickling her inner thighs. Everything in her was tight and tense, poised to explode. She wanted to orgasm, knew she was seconds from coming. But some instinct compelled her to ask him for permission. She may not have a ton of experience with men, but she had learned to read people out of necessity. Her gut told her to ask him.

"Can I come?" she asked, struggling to hold herself still, wanting to grab his head and buck her hips. The sweet torture of it all sent another gush of moisture trickling over his tongue. She'd never been this wet for another man.

"Mmm," he said, lapping at her before he pulled back and looked up at her over the length of her body, his eyes narrowed, lips shiny. "Can you have an orgasm? Is that what you're asking?"

She nodded.

"Of course, sweetheart. You can come whenever you want." He nuzzled his nose against her inner thigh. "In fact, I wish you would. I want to taste your cum."

Whoa. She'd never had anyone say anything like that to her before. It sounded so dirty, yet so exciting. Like instead of him doing her a favor by giving her oral sex, he was enjoying it just as much as she was. It was that thought that had her whole body relaxing, her head lolling back onto his shirt, thighs dropping open farther.

Piper stared at the inky sky through the branches of the apple trees, stars burning as intensely as her passion as Brady stroked over her with his tongue.

It was surreal, so unbelievable, yet so intently real that Piper didn't think she had ever been quite so much in the moment as she was right then. She was at one with her body, and she was building towards an amazing release. Forcing her fingers to let go of the blanket, she sucked in a breath, then felt her body explode in a powerful orgasm that had her lungs tightening and her teeth sinking into her bottom lip to prevent a raucous cry out. Since her body was lax, her shoulders relaxed, she felt the waves of pleasure even more acutely, the breeze drifting over her skin like soft fingers, teasing her nipples and bringing on a shiver in the midst of her shudders of release.

As the undulations stopped, she finally remembered to breathe, sucking in a huge lungful of air, the shock of what she had just experienced robbing her of any speech. She didn't know what to say. She didn't even know what to think. But she didn't need to. Brady looked up.

"Delicious," he said. "That's how your cum tastes."

She nodded, which was probably an odd response, because how would she know, but she was just giving an automatic polite reply. Polite to her addled brain, anyway. Brady moved up beside her and kissed her, a deep, musky embrace that was her and him mixed together. Then he lay back, pulling her onto him.

"Ride me."

She hesitated, knowing she wasn't the best at establishing the rhythm required to make it work for the man. So he sat up, moving her legs to either side of his, holding her in his lap, her breasts pressed to his warm chest. The night air was cooler than she had expected and she was feeling the chill, but not pressed against him like that. Not with his muscular arms wrapped around her, making her feel protected and very feminine.

"I love your hair," he said, burying his face in her curls. "It's so soft and shiny . . . like a magical mystery tour."

She laughed softly, very aware of his erection pressing against her still-damp sex. "Are you comparing my hair to a Beatles album?"

"I think I am."

"Thank you." Piper started to move her hips, bumping against him, wanting more. Her ache had resumed, and had increased to a deep throb, and he was so close to being inside her, yet wasn't attempting to take her.

"Take it if you want it," he murmured, kissing along her jaw, nipping at the corner of her mouth. "Or maybe I'll just give it to you."

Shifting slightly, he pushed inside her. Their moans burst out simultaneously, his jagged and raw, hers high-pitched and shocked.

"Oh, Brady," she said, because there didn't seem to be anything else to say.

His eyes locked on hers. "Piper."

There was something about the way he said her name that threw her. Was it supposed to sound like that? So focused, so intense, so reverent? Was that how a man who was having a casual affair sounded? She didn't know. She couldn't, wouldn't, read anything into what he was feeling.

But she knew what she was feeling, and it wasn't casual. It was so far from casual it needed more than six degrees of separation. At least seven, maybe eight.

Brady thrust up into her once, twice, then he wrapped his arms around her and brought her down on top of him. Her breasts splayed on his chest, her hair fell over his shoulders and face. Her hips were forced to spread in a way that brought her body in intimate connection with his, her clitoris rubbing on him, his cock buried deep inside her. She reached up to pull her hair back, force it back over her shoulder. He helped her, tucking it behind her ears, then pulled her mouth to his for a soft kiss.

His expression when their kiss ended was so searing, Piper had to close her eyes. She couldn't see those green eyes, couldn't imagine that he was as fascinated by her as she was by him. She couldn't do that to herself, so she closed her eyes and sat up, bracing herself on his chest. Moving her hips, she rode him, like he'd requested, enjoying the full length of him in a way she wouldn't have thought possible. He was big, he filled her, but it was a delicious stretching and she picked up the pace, feeling a little desperate, the aching in her sex moving upwards to invade her heart.

Letting go of his chest, she dug her fingers into her hair, dragging it back off her face, wanting to feel the air on her face, cool her heated skin, cool her heated emotions.

"Can I come?" he asked, gripping her hips tightly, grinding up inside her.

Piper opened her eyes. The urgency on his face sent a

shiver through her. "Of course you can, sweetheart," she said, mimicking his earlier words.

"I need to come." He gritted his teeth.

"So do I." It was amazing, but she did. The position tripped off little ripples of pleasure all up and down her moist channel, and she was going to come with him.

"Holy shit." Brady closed his eyes briefly, then held her hard enough to bruise her, thrusting with a fierceness that took her breath away.

The hot throb inside her had her squeezing her muscles onto his erection, and her orgasm blended with his, their cries puncturing the still night air. It went on and on and she was amazed her body was capable of such intensity, such depth. She let it express the emotion she couldn't, the acute pleasure she felt when she was with Brady.

Piper collapsed onto his chest, sweaty and out of breath, a cool shiver trailing over her skin, her heart thumping, her thoughts both awed and frightened.

Brady stroked her back and played with her hair. "Damn, girl. You nearly killed me."

"You feel pretty alive to me." Piper listened to the rapid thump of his heart in his chest. Her hips ached from the position but she didn't want to move. She wanted to hold on to this moment, to memorize it, to take it with her.

But the goose bumps on her flesh had him rolling her onto her side. "You're cold."

"I'm not sure I care."

Brady pulled the sleeping bag around them like a hot dog bun and kissed her cheek. "Thanks for fulfilling my teenage fantasy. Look, there's the big dipper." He pointed to the sky.

"I think you already showed me that," she told him, grinning as she snuggled up against him. He was big and strong and warm.

He let out a bark of laughter. "True that." He gave a yawn. "If this were a camping trip we could sleep like this."

She didn't say anything, not sure what point he was making. Or trying to make. Not wanting to think about how it would feel to wake up with Brady.

"I guess we should go back to the house."

"Guess so."

Neither one of them moved. The truck bed wasn't particularly comfortable but she didn't care. She was warm, her body satisfied. The moment lingered, and she wanted it to.

But with a groan, Brady sat up and crawled around the truck, collecting his discarded clothes, and the moment was over. Trying not to sigh, Piper did the same, grateful her panties were white. It was easier to find them in the dark. She lay back down on the sleeping bag to pull them on. A few more seconds, more fumbling with clothes and zippers and shoes, and they were dressed.

Like nothing had happened. But it didn't feel that way. When she jumped down off the truck into Brady's arms, she felt light-headed, and it had nothing to do with dropping four feet to the ground.

She was glad to be driving. It gave her something to do with her hands. Even though she was very aware of him next to her, she could pretend she had to keep her eyes on the road. At one point he brushed her hair off her shoulder, but otherwise he was as quiet as a church mouse, something she did not normally associate with him. What was he thinking? Was he as stunned as she was?

When they got to the house, he did stop her at the back door. "How about dinner one night this week?"

"Sure."

He kissed her. "Good night, then. Since I don't really want to kiss you in there."

She smiled, her complacent mood shifting to anxious. It was one thing to throw caution to the wind when no one was around to see it. It was another thing to face her parents with rumpled clothes. Hopefully they'd be in bed.

They went into the house, and she kicked her sandals off in the mudroom and moved into the kitchen. The room was empty, a single light left on for her. Silently they moved up the stairs, and she was opening the door to the guest room when the hall light came on, stark and harsh. Brady squinted like she did. Her parents appeared and there were words exchanged, crap about sheets and extra pillows and coffee, and she didn't hear a damn thing because she felt as awkward as she had the day she'd gotten her first period and her grandmother had baked her a cake in celebration of her womanhood.

Then Brady was in the guest room, the door firmly closing behind him, and she said, "Good night," to her parents, or more accurately the floor, then she went into her room. Leaning against the closed door, she took a deep, shuddering breath. What the hell was she doing? She was in way over her head. Like she was at the ocean floor with sunken ships and weird eyeless fish and no hope of getting to the surface kind of over her head.

Her parents' voices rose in the bedroom next to hers. If she went into her walk-in closet, she could hear them. It was a trick she had learned at fourteen, but one she had rarely used. She didn't like to spoil surprises like Christmas gifts, and she didn't want to hear them arguing or having sex. So if she heard them, it was usually an accident of her actually needing something in her closet. But tonight she went in and put her forehead to the wall so she could hear as clearly as possible.

"I should throw his ass out of here," her dad said, sounding very, very angry.

"Danny, you can't do that."

"Why the hell not? This is my house, isn't it? He said he was going to talk to her, the little prick. He told me he would tell her that he isn't staying here, that she shouldn't expect anything."

He had told her that. Brady couldn't be blamed for this. Piper crossed her arms over her chest.

"You don't know what they talked about," her mom said soothingly.

"I know they didn't do any talking at all. They come tumbling in here, all wrinkled and smelling like sex. That's not like her, Amanda, you know that."

Embarrassment crashed over her. They smelled like sex? It made sense, but she hadn't thought about it, and the realization that her dad could not only guess what they'd done but smell it . . . God, she wanted to crawl into a hole and die. After being beaten unconscious.

"She's entitled to a social life."

Her dad snorted. "If she wants to date, I'm good with that. A guy her own age. Who doesn't just want a quick lay in a pickup truck. I'm sorry, I just don't approve of what I saw tonight."

Piper pulled herself off the wall like she'd been slapped. Never in the sixteen years she had lived with him had her father said he disapproved of her.

It stung.

She stripped off her sex-soiled clothes in the closet and pulled on a clean T-shirt. Out of her dresser she yanked a pair of panties and stepped into them. In bed, she tried to close her eyes and sleep, but they immediately popped back open. All she could see in front of her was the deep green of Brady's eyes as he stared at her, their bodies entwined in the most intimate way possible.

And over that image she could hear her father's voice, ringing with anger and disdain.

One man had a passing interest in her.

The other would always be there for her.

The choice was obvious.

But that didn't make it hurt any less.

Chapter Eleven

BRADY PAUSED IN THE ENTRANCE OF THE CUTTERS-
ville Public Library and marveled that while the world at
large changed daily, life in Cuttersville remained very much
the same. There were new books featured on the New
Release wall, and the computers had been upgraded, but
otherwise the library looked exactly the same as it had when
he was a kid, rolling his way across the carpet through story
hour with his stepmom. He hadn't exactly ever learned to sit
still for a book, either to listen or to read one himself.

Yet he remembered this room, the main entrance with
its curved circulation desk, and the children's area with a
caterpillar mural painted on the wall, now faded and chipped.
There were a couple of old guys using the computers and
three mothers knitting while their kids flipped through picture books. He supposed a library was the sign of an elevated

society, but the Cuttersville one looked like a place where the budget had taken a crap. It was mildly depressing to him.

Then again, maybe he was just having a moody moment. He'd missed Piper that morning, getting up after she left for work, and he'd had to endure the cold, barely contained fury of Danny Tucker, who clearly had no doubts whatsoever that Brady had bounced his only daughter. Which he had. Quite thoroughly.

Just remembering the way she had rocked onto his cock had him wishing he were wearing looser pants.

His only defense was that no guy in his right mind would turn down what Piper was offering.

He'd talked to her. They were clear on what they were doing. It was a thing they were having for three weeks.

So why did he feel like he'd drunk too much apple juice? His chest burned. It wasn't good.

Something really weird was happening to him and he had a sneaking suspicion it was something he'd been avoiding for years.

Intent on getting away from Danny and his rather large fists, Brady had driven to his grandmother's to get her paint preferences, but was told to consult Piper on them. Then he'd gone to the hardware store for spackle and painting supplies but was told by the clerk that Piper had already purchased all of that for the house on Swallow, if that's what he was doing, and was that what he was doing? Annoyed by that point, he'd gone to visit his stepmother, who had enveloped him in a hug, then asked him whether he was aware that gossips were suggesting he had an interest in Piper Tucker.

There was nothing left to do with his day but come to the library and see Bree Murphy-Carrington, Abby's sister. He spotted her after a quick sweep of the whole room. There was no mistaking her black hair and long, dangling pewter earrings. She hadn't changed one bit, and as he walked towards her, she looked up from her desk. "Hey, Brady, how are you? Abby said you might stop by."

"I'm great, how are you?" "Great" might be putting a bit of a positive spin on it, but that was his story and he was sticking with it.

"Good." She stood up, and he saw her black lace shirt was covering a very pregnant stomach. "I'm having another baby, which is ridiculous. My son, Alistair, is ten. But this little girl decided she wanted to wait to be born. I guess she didn't want to share with her brother."

"Wow, congrats. Both you and Abby having babies at the same time—that's great. Cousins to play with are cool." Like him and Shelby, even though there was a gap between their ages.

"That is the upside. Alistair always had Charlotte's girls to hang with, so now these two have each other." She smiled. "But you don't really want to talk about my fertility, do you? I hear you want some details on the original Brady Stritmeyer and good old Rachel."

"If you have them, yes, that would be awesome."

"We have the old newspaper articles on microfiche, which is archaic, I know, but this isn't exactly tech central here. Then if you want to read about Rachel, we have the records from the Lunatic Asylum."

"That would be fantastic, thanks."

He followed Bree, whose gait could best be described as a rapid waddle. He'd bet dollars to doughnuts that she was due to give birth in the next thirty minutes. He patted his pocket for his cell phone, ready to dial 911 if necessary.

"So how's Piper?" she asked, glancing back over her shoulder at him.

What the fuck?

"Abby told me you two were an item. She's always been

our babysitter, you know. One of the sweetest girls I've ever met."

Brady fought the urge to roll his eyes. "I wouldn't say that we're an item. But yes, she is a sweet girl."

Unbidden, the image of her riding him, her hair tumbling everywhere, leaped into his head, and he cleared his throat. She was a sweet girl with a very sexy side.

Bree gave him a searching, knowing look. "There are certain things you shouldn't fight. Do you want me to read your tarot?"

He'd rather have a pelican peck his nuts repeatedly. "No, thanks."

If memory served, the Murphy sisters had always been a little odd. His recent encounters with Abby and Bree were confirming that. It was time for him to steer the conversation. "So do you know anything about Brady Stritmeyer?"

"Just what I've heard from the ghost stories. Here's our microfiche machine. I pulled the relevant films for you." Bree ushered him into a nook to the left of the main librarian's desk. "Just scroll up and down."

He smiled at her. "Thanks, Bree." He did appreciate the help, if not the advice.

There was a funny look on her face. "This baby is kicking the stuffing out of me." She grabbed his hand before he realized what she was doing and placed it on her stomach.

Brady's first instinct was to yank it away, but he knew how rude that would be. But it felt incredibly bizarre to have his hand on a woman's pregnant belly, and more than a little awkward. Yet discomfort was replaced by fascination bordering on horror when he felt the baby move. "Holy crap."

"I know. It's like a freak show, isn't it? Not exactly comfortable either."

"I can imagine." He really couldn't, though. The rippling motion beneath his hand continued, and he contemplated feeling his child move inside his wife. It was the first time he had ever actually thought that maybe he might be ready for such an awesome responsibility. A lot of work, yes, but there was something awe-inspiring about what he was feeling, and he could see how having a child could give a certain amount of meaning to an otherwise average life.

"If you need helping searching online job sites, I can help you with that, too."

"Thanks." Brady had almost forgotten to remember that he was unemployed. Reality came crashing back down on him. Hell, he couldn't even take care of himself. There was no hope for being able to have a child. Of course, there was no hope of marriage anytime soon, so why he would think about it was beyond him. Who was stupid enough to agree to be with him for any length of time?

Scowling at the screen as he sat down, Brady suddenly felt resentful. Of his own choices. Of certain people who seemed to think he wasn't good enough for a certain someone.

He could be good enough.

It was a dead-end thought, so as Bree moved on to other librarian duties, Brady resolutely read the three newspaper articles about the murder of Brady Stritmeyer. He also read a blurb from 1885 that mentioned the original Brady had been promoted to branch manager at the Ohio Savings and Trust Bank. Great. Even his dead namesake had been more successful than him, and the guy had been dead by twenty-five.

Other than that, there was nothing of particular interest or any new information. Brady lived in a boardinghouse. His parents were referred to as esteemed members of Cuttersville society. Rachel's parents were equally praised and they seemed to have the sympathy of the town post-murder, but they still moved to Marietta for a fresh start.

Rubbing his neck, Brady sat back in his chair. He wasn't sure what he was expecting to find, but this wasn't it. Pulling out his phone, he texted Piper, asking her if the next night was good for dinner. He wanted to see her. He wanted to kiss her, far away from her family, where he could let his tongue linger on hers.

Shutting off the machine, he went in search of Bree.

"No luck, huh?" she asked. "I can tell by the look on your face."

"Yeah, I'm not sure what I'm looking for, but maybe more details, I guess."

"If you want, I can search the storage room for the records from the asylum. They all got dumped here when the hospital closed in the sixties. There might be patient records on Rachel."

"That would be awesome."

"It might take me a couple of days to dig through the boxes."

"Sure, no problem. Let me know if you need help. I'm not sure how much digging in boxes you should be doing." He gestured to her belly.

"Oh, please, I still do yoga every day and have sex with my husband every night." She laughed. "Not that you need to know that."

He didn't. But he couldn't help but ask, "Every night? Really?" He was more than a little jealous of Ian Carrington, Bree's husband. Not that he wanted Bree, but he would like sex every night. "I thought marriage killed your sex life."

She snorted. "Don't let anyone tell you that. Married people have three times as much sex as single people. It's the convenience factor. Think about it."

Brady definitely wanted to think about that. Sex every night. With Piper. Screw the forty virgins in the afterlife. If he could have Piper in bed night after night, he'd die a very happy man.

He massaged his temples. He was getting a headache from all the fucked-up thoughts he was having. It was like he had too much time on his hands so his brain was circling around finding shit to think about since he wasn't working. Or something like that.

"I don't think I can have this conversation," he told her truthfully. "It's leaving me hopeless."

She rolled her eyes. "Wake up and smell the inevitable."

What did that even mean? "I would much rather smell coffee, if you don't mind."

His phone buzzed. Knowing it was rude, he still couldn't resist looking at the text. It had to be Piper. It was.

Won't be able to go to dinner tomorrow. Open house at school.

Why that had him feeling like a girl without a date for the prom, he couldn't say. Nor did he want to.

AFTER SHE HAD LOCKED UP HER CLASSROOM, PIPER headed over to Shelby's, who had called and left a message that she had something for her. Piper was distracted when she pulled in to the driveway of Shelby's gray house. It had been a long day and she was tired. It took a lot of energy to continually shove images of Brady out of her head. Brady smiling at her. Brady taking a bite of her apple. Brady between her thighs.

It was both a disappointment and a relief that she couldn't go to dinner with him. She didn't want to face her father's disapproval. But she didn't want to give Brady up either. So she was left with churning emotions and a tension headache.

Her phone chimed. Glancing down, she saw it was a text from her half brother, Marcus. Frowning, she opened it.

Need 2 tlk 2 u. Holla.

She sighed. Rarely did she hear from him. Usually if she did, he was asking for something. Money. To borrow her car. Trying to sell her electronics. It made her sad to see what his life had come to, and part of her loved the little boy he had been, but the adult he was now was a stranger to her. She wanted to love him, and she did care about his welfare, but it was hard to establish a relationship with someone she no longer had anything in common with. She wasn't even exactly sure what "holla" meant.

The hardest thing was realizing that he didn't really have any emotional attachment to her at all. He saw her as someone he could benefit from financially.

Not sure if she had it in her to deal with Marcus today, Piper knocked on the front door and entered.

"Hey." Shelby was in the hallway with a basket of laundry. "How are you, sweetie?"

"Fine. What's up? Did I forget something?" It was possible she'd left half her suitcase here given how quickly she'd been determined to dash away from Brady and the curious stares of Shelby and Boston.

"No, not that I noticed. I just wanted to give you a little something for watching the kids."

"You don't have to do that. You know I enjoy their company."

"I want to." Shelby plucked at the front of her oversized T-shirt. "Come on in the kitchen. Also, do you mind taking some things over to the house for Brady? I figured the least I can do since I can't house him is give him some food and some basic household items."

Wonderful. Piper followed Shelby into the kitchen. "I wasn't planning on going over there today."

"No?" Shelby looked overly innocent. "Do you mind stopping on your way home anyway? I need to be here when the girls get off the bus."

Actually, she kind of did. "I can take them tomorrow." Today she just couldn't deal with it. She knew that her father was planning on taking her bed over to the house today, and the last place she wanted to be was in a house with Brady, her father, and her bed.

"Thanks, I appreciate it." Shelby handed her a pink envelope off the counter. It probably contained a check or, more likely, a gift card for babysitting. "So, can I ask what is going on with you and Brady?"

That did it. Piper felt tears well up in her eyes and she bit her lip in mortification. She wasn't even sure why she was on the verge of crying, but she was.

Shelby's eyes widened. "Oh, baby Jesus in the cradle. I'm sorry. What's wrong? Did my idiot cousin hurt you?"

She shook her head, fighting back the tears, feeling incredibly stupid. "Of course not. I just . . . I don't know."

"Sit." Shelby gestured to a chair. "Tell me what is going on."

"Nothing. It's fine." This wasn't something she could talk to Shelby about, for obvious reasons. She was mortified that she was crying. Or almost crying. She wasn't really crying. And she had no reason to cry. About anything. She had a wonderful life, with a wonderful family.

"Well, you're not just crying to wet your cheeks. Something must be wrong." Shelby scrutinized her, concern on her face. "He's not worth crying over, honey. Honestly. I mean, I love Brady, don't get me wrong. He's a lot of fun and there's just something about him that makes a person smile, but he isn't worth the price of Kleenex when it comes right down to it. No man is."

That was a mixed message if Piper ever heard one. She

wasn't really sure what to say to that. "Brady didn't do anything wrong, Shelby." He hadn't. He had been honest and up-front with her. She had pursued him even when he had suggested that maybe it wasn't the best idea.

The problem was not that Brady was an idiot. It was that she was an idiot. Because now she had to give him up because she could not stomach disappointing her father. "But . . . I think that my dad thinks that Brady and I . . ." Which they had. "And he's disappointed in me." Shelby's sympathetic look almost undid her entirely. Piper propped her chin up with her palm on the well-worn table and felt miserable.

"Hon, your dad really has no say in what you do in your private time. Whether he wants to admit it or not, you're a grown woman. He and I had already been married for four years and divorced by the time I was your age."

Sometimes it was hard to remember that Shelby and her dad had been married. They seemed so much more like brother and sister to her. It was weird to think of them as passionate about each other.

"Your dad just doesn't want you to get hurt, that's all."

She wasn't going to get hurt living in a bubble, but she wasn't going to experience life that way either. "I know. But it just seems like he's angry with me. Like he thinks I'm—"

Piper suddenly felt a shove, her head catapulting forward and her chin falling off her arm. The force was so powerful, she almost hit her nose on the table. When her shock wore off, she glanced over her shoulder and saw Rachel. There were none of her customary tears. Rachel was angry.

Rage distorted her shadowy features. Her eyes were narrowed, her eyebrows arched, her forehead furrowed beneath her severe hairstyle. Her mouth was twisted into a sneer, and Piper sucked in a breath. It made her feel a profound sense of sorrow, and she wasn't sure why. More likely she should be afraid, but she wasn't. She just felt like a huge weight had descended on her, like a wet blanket, like she was taking Rachel's rage as tangibly as the blow she'd just been given.

"What's wrong?"

"Nothing," she told Shelby, standing up and sliding to the left away from Rachel's reach, her anxiety crawling up her throat. This wasn't good. She wasn't sure what had changed so rapidly, why Rachel was suddenly so aware of her and determined to hurt her.

Was the spirit of a murderess retaining the same rage she'd felt when she had found her fiancé cheating on her? Was she furious that she was forced to stay here, in this house, with him?

"Are you sure?" Shelby looked like she wasn't buying the load of crap Piper was trying to sell.

"Yes, I just lost my balance and when my head fell I bit my tongue." Piper couldn't bring herself to tell her about Rachel. She didn't want to be fussed over. Pitied. Questioned. She didn't want to hear the suggestion that she should look into the history of her haunt. It was hard enough to know that Brady was off digging into the fiancé's past.

She just wanted to pretend that none of it was happening. That really wasn't so much to ask for.

"You look as nervous as a whore in church."

"Well, my dad is upset with me. That upsets me."

Shelby stood up and came around the table. Piper had managed to inch her way closer to the doorway, putting a good four feet between her and Rachel, who was watching them with a look of resentment. For a split second Piper thought Shelby was going to walk right through Rachel, but she just missed her.

"There's a draft in here all of sudden." Shelby glanced around her. Then it suddenly seemed to occur to her what might be happening and she opened her mouth to speak.

Which Piper was determined to avoid. "Where's the stuff you wanted me to take to the house? I need to get going. I have open house at school tomorrow night and I still have some prep work to do." The start of a school year was always an exciting time. It was only her third year teaching, but Piper didn't think she was ever going to get tired of that fresh start a new year brought, a crop of nervous and excited little ones starting off on their big kindergarten adventure. Frankly, all the new parents with a thousand questions would be a welcome distraction. "How do the girls like their new teacher? Mrs. Lucas is really great."

"Oh, they like her a lot. Lilly isn't the reader that Emily is, so I might see about some reading intervention."

"I can work with her if you'd like."

With that, Shelby was off and running in the direction Piper had guided her to, discussing the pros and cons of various reading materials and what would be best for Lilly and whether there was really any cause for concern.

By the time Piper walked out the door ten minutes later, Shelby seemed to have forgotten entirely that Piper had almost cried and that the kitchen had a cold spot.

It was a definite talent to be able to remove all attention from herself at any given moment. There wasn't a whole lot to thank her stepfather for, but she supposed she owed the bastard for this one.

That night when Piper took the sheets her mother handed her and went into the guest bedroom, she hesitated, then set them on the dresser, leaving the sheets Brady had used on the bed.

When she crawled into her new temporary quarters, she buried her head into the pillow and drew in a deep breath, the masculine scent of Brady still lingering on the linen.

Lame. Totally lame. That's what she was.

Or was it possible to fall in love with someone she barely knew?

Or had she always loved him, from the first time she'd met him and he'd treated her as any other eight-year-old? Like she wasn't weird or different.

Piper rolled onto her bed and stared at the ceiling. Being in love with Brady would be really, incredibly stupid. She liked to think she wasn't that dumb.

But she was having a hard time convincing herself of her intelligence at the moment as she snuggled in the sheets hoping for a lingering scent of him.

Lame.

Piper sighed.

Chapter Twelve

BRADY TAPED OFF THE BASEBOARDS IN THE LIVING room of the house on Swallow Street and tried not to feel frustrated. It wasn't working. He hadn't seen Piper in four days. Not since they had done some serious pleasure seeking in the back of her truck. They had succeeded. Then nothing. He hadn't seen her even for a minute.

It was deflating. When you shared something like that with someone, you wanted to see them again, share the secret of what you had done together, what just the two of you had shared, and no one else would ever have knowledge of. You wanted to laugh with them, kiss them. Do it again.

Piper had said they were having an affair. But as far as he could tell, they were having a whole lot of nothing. It was making him nuts.

When he pursued a woman, usually she let herself be caught right away, or she gave chase with lots of flirtation and games. Piper wasn't doing any of those things. She wasn't avoiding him, exactly, since she did answer his texts, and she did have reasonable explanations for why she couldn't see him, but it still felt like a brush-off.

Why that made him so aggravated, he wasn't exactly sure. But damn it, if half the town was talking about him and Piper, he wanted there to actually *be* a him and Piper.

Brady paused, blue painter's tape stretched out between his arms. A him and Piper? Was that what he wanted?

He slapped the tape on the baseboard, disgusted with himself. That wasn't going to happen. He had to go back to Chicago. She'd made her feelings on moving out of Cuttersville perfectly clear. Her father wanted to kill him. Plus his own family didn't think he was good enough for her. Nothing about that said happy relationship.

Relationship.

God, he was out of mind. Too much fresh air out here in the sticks. He needed to get back to Wrigleyville, hit an exciting new restaurant and a bar for drinks.

He had music cranked, intense heavy metal that felt like there was a drummer banging away on his kit inside Brady's skull. It was perfect for his mood. Maybe the high volume would drown out his thoughts.

Having spent the day sanding and scraping and prepping, he was ready to paint, and he had to admit, the no-brainer work was satisfying. He didn't have it in him to think, which might explain why he had yet to update his resume and send it out. It wasn't good to ignore his unemployment status, but at the moment he didn't particularly care.

Doing a little head banging, he moved on down the wall, singing along with the screamer lyrics. Standing up to move to the window, he even did a little air guitar since there was no one there to see him.

ERIN McCARTHY

Spinning around, he suddenly stopped strumming. No one there to see him except Piper.

Jesus. Really? He'd been hot to see her for days and this was their first post-mind-blowing-sex encounter? He in dusty jeans and an old T-shirt he'd found in his dresser from high school to paint in that stated, PROFESSIONAL MUFF DIVER. While doing air guitar. He'd picked the shirt because he knew it was going to get trashed painting and he didn't share the opinion of his fifteen-year-old self that this was a funny statement. It was just stupid, and now it felt even more stupid given that someone else was seeing it. A someone whose respect he actually wanted.

"Hi," he blurted out, feeling like a douche bag tool idiot moron.

She was smiling. "Hi."

Or at least that was what he thought she said, since the music was blaring and making conversation impossible. Brady hit the volume button repeatedly until the music went down to something other than earsplitting.

For the first time in a very long time, he was unsure of himself with a woman. He didn't like it. So he mentally pulled his balls back out of his body and got a grip. He crossed the room and gave her a kiss. "I'm glad to see you."

He was. Ridiculously so, despite his offensive shirt. Which he felt compelled to explain. "This is an old shirt. Found it in my old drawer at my parents' to paint in. And I was never a pro."

Fortunately, she laughed. "There's still time."

Brady loved that she had a sense of humor behind her quiet exterior. "Well, I am unemployed. Maybe I should check out the pay scale."

"I can give a letter of recommendation."

Oh, yeah. She was remembering the other night. He liked the sound of that. "Thanks. But truthfully I'd rather keep my services exclusive to one woman. And by that, I mean you, so don't ask me who."

Her eyes darted to the floor. "Brady, I want to spend time with you. I do."

His throat closed. Jesus, was he getting dumped? That definitely sounded like he was getting dumped.

"But my family's opinion is very important to me, and they don't understand why I would get involved with you knowing you're going back to Chicago. They have concerns."

A small curse slid out before he could stop it. "What it really means is they don't think you should be involved with me. Hey, I can't say I blame them. I would feel the same way if I were Danny. But what happened to us having fun? Us having an affair?" He wanted her to remember that. Even as he knew he never wanted to jeopardize her relationship with her family, he still wanted what he wanted.

And what he wanted was her.

Her eyes were agonized. "I want to do that. More than anything. But . . ."

"But you have to live here after I leave." Brady sighed. "I get it." He hated it. But he got it. "I have to say, I'm more than a little disappointed, Piper. I enjoy spending time with you." He took her hand in a move that could probably be classified as manipulative. Rubbing his thumb across her palm, he said coaxingly, "I want to spend more time with you."

She was caving, he could tell. Her eyes were soft and wide, her lips parting. "I . . . I have to think about it."

"Thank you," he told her in all sincerity. He was being a total selfish prick, but if she chose to see him, then he didn't have to feel guilty about that, right? "So did you just stop by to tell me that?"

"I have bags from Shelby. She sent some food for you. But I figured it's about time for me to make good on my bargain to your grandmother to help you paint. It looks like I'm right on time."

He was down with that. "Sounds good to me. Let me take care of these bags and then we can get started."

When he picked up the shopping bags and headed for the kitchen, Piper burst out laughing. "What?" He liked to think his ass was cause for groping, not laughing.

"The back of your shirt is even better than the front."

Uh-oh. He hadn't looked at the back. "What does it say? Or do I even want to know?"

"It says, 'I yodel in the Valley.'"

"I don't even know what that means," he told her, trying not to wince at his total lack of game. He was not pulling out a stellar seduction in Piper's case. He did know what it meant, but for some reason he felt compelled to act innocent. Frankly, it was a look that didn't work on him.

"I'm not sure either. It's like it could be a double entendre, right?"

"I'm fairly certain it is, come to think of it." He waggled his tongue at her to demonstrate.

Her eyes widened in understanding. "Oooh."

Brady peeked in the bags before setting them on the counter. Yay. He had cookies. "By the way, I much prefer sleeping in your bed than sleeping on the floor. Thank you."

When he turned she was in the doorway. He just realized it was the first time he'd ever seen her wearing jeans. They seemed to be work jeans of some kind. There was a paint smear on the thigh and the cuffs were frayed. Her little navy tank top said OHIO across it, and she was painfully cute. He wanted to lick her from head to toe. He wanted to lock her in the bedroom. His bedroom, soon to be her bedroom, but not their bedroom. It was so damn frustrating.

"You're welcome. It's my pleasure."

"No. I think 'pleasure' would be a good description if

you were sharing the bed with me." Just to drive his point home.

Her cheeks tinged with color. "I imagine so."

He figured that was enough laying the seeds for the moment. "Do you want a drink or anything before we start painting? It seems I have cookies now."

"I'm fine, thanks. So do you want to cut in or roll?"

Neither. But he didn't want to sound like a lazy shit so he told her, "You pick. I'm fine with either one."

"Okay. I'll roll." She went over to the paint can and pried the lid off.

Brady went back to taping off the window. "Do you want me to turn the music off?"

"No, I love metal."

Say what? How many ways could this woman surprise him? "For real?"

"Yeah. I'm dying to go see the Big Three—Slayer, Metallica, and Megadeth—but they never come anywhere around here."

Brady was amused. Piper was his kind of chick.

"Plus, I'm not sure I could talk Cameron into going with me anyway."

Hold up. "Who is Cameron?"

"My best friend. He lives in Cincinnati now. Other than my family and work friends, he's really the only one I would want to do something like that with." Piper poured the paint into the tray.

There was a stabbing pain in his chest that Brady suspected was jealousy. It scared the hell out of him. "Your best friend's a guy? Did you two ever date?" He meant it to sound casual, but it just sounded annoyed.

"No. I would never date Cam, and he does not want to date me. We're totally different. But our friendship works well. He moved here in middle school and he's Jewish, and while this isn't exactly the Bible Belt, a Jew is a rarity. So we were a couple of misfits who found each other."

Brady felt better about the whole thing. Not that Piper and Cameron had been outcasts by mean kids' stupid parameters, but because it didn't sound like he had competition. "It's good to have someone in your life who has known you a long time. I didn't really stay in touch with anyone." Nor was he sure why. Maybe because as the years had ticked by, Brady hadn't wanted anyone back home to know he was an art school failure.

Picking up a brush, he dipped it in the paint. It wasn't the same as painting as an artist. The brush was huge, the paint quantity enormous, but just the smell, the sound of his brush moving on the wall, raised a fair amount of melancholy in him. It was a raw deal to get just enough talent to have a dream, but not enough to be successful at it.

It also sucked that he couldn't offer to take Piper to see the Big Three. But he'd need to rob a bank to take her on a trip. That was seriously depressing.

"My mom always says she thought Cam and I would end up together, but she just doesn't get that if there isn't an attraction, there isn't an attraction. You can't create that, and we've had enough time now to see it's not going to just appear like magic." Piper was rolling away and wasn't looking at him.

Which was good because Brady suspected he looked like a bratty kid. He was jealous. It was insane. Nothing that she was saying was anything other than what it was—she telling him that her friendship was strictly platonic. Yet all he could think was that he wouldn't mind if Cameron fell off a bridge.

"Attraction is a funny thing." He went back for more paint. "Like for example, the fact that I'm attracted to you even though it's not a good idea. I can't seem to stop it." Brady told himself to shut up but he couldn't stop the flood of words. He wanted—no, needed—to hear that she was just as interested in him as he was in her. "I know I should let you end this because this is your home and I don't want to cause trouble for you, but damn it, Piper, I can't."

Oh, God, what was he doing? Brady dropped his brush in anger. Now he was just being an ass. He was disgusted with himself. She was trying to do the right thing and he was pressuring her.

When Piper turned, her face was stricken. "I know. I can't really stop it either. I don't want to disappoint my parents, but I . . ."

The light from the living room window streamed over her face and her eyes were enormous, filled with an emotion he couldn't quite place. She looked beautiful. The most beautiful woman he'd ever met, her beauty so real and here and now, yet at the same time so otherworldly. Dust motes danced in the sunbeam, her skin fresh and pink, her shadow cast back onto the wall behind her.

He swallowed hard. "You what?" he asked hoarsely.

"I just want to spend every minute I can with you," she whispered.

Something in his chest swelled. He wasn't even sure he could speak. His fingers itched, his feelings consuming him. There was something about the way she stood, the play of light, what was passing between them, that made him want to capture the moment. He wanted to preserve her beauty, he wanted to share how he felt, what he saw. How when he looked at her, she was nothing but perfection, the rare person who was beautiful inside and out.

Frantic, he looked around the floor. He needed a pencil. A small brush. Something, anything. There was nothing but the wall paint supplies, and that wasn't going to work. He spotted Piper's purse and he went in it, the urgent need to sketch compelling him to do what he normally wouldn't, like ransack someone's private space.

"What . . ." she started to speak in confusion.

Brady found a pen at the bottom and a nubby pencil. With both, he'd make it work. "Don't move."

"Brady, what are you . . ."

He chose a spot on the wall, between the doorway and the window, just a few feet from her, and he drew his first line, starting with the shape of her face. The sense of relief he felt was catastrophic. He hadn't realized how much he had missed drawing, and he took a deep, shuddering breath. When he looked over at her, he saw that she understood. Her confusion had been replaced with sympathy, and maybe, some relief of her own.

"Don't move," he repeated.

"I'm not going anywhere," she said quietly.

It was exactly what he needed to hear. His hand moved quickly, capturing the shape of her head, the graceful arch of her neck. As the minutes passed and her image appeared before him, confident and flawless, Brady felt a mix of elation and arousal. Appreciation. And something that he was finally willing to label. He didn't understand it, didn't know how it was possible after such a short time, but given that he'd never felt it before, he knew exactly what it was.

There was no denying it.

"Piper."

"Yes?"

Glancing back between her and his sketch, he tried to emulate the soft flow of her wavy hair, wishing he had acrylics to really capture the subtlety of colors in it. "I'm not going back to Chicago."

He heard the sharp intake of her breath and he turned back to her, pausing his hand for just a second.

"What?" Her bottom lip quivered a little.

"I know it's crazy," he said quietly. "But what am I going back for? Everything I could want is right here, with you."

Her head shook back and forth. "I don't understand. You mean you're staying here . . . indefinitely?"

That was what he meant. It should scare the shit out of him, but it didn't. "Yes. I want to see where our relationship could go. Relationship, not affair. I want there to be a you and me."

Then he turned away from her, to the face he'd created on the wall, because he'd just made himself about as vulnerable as he'd ever been, but Brady felt an enormous sense of relief. He needed to be honest, with himself and with Piper. He didn't know where they could go with this, but he needed her to know that she was so extraordinary that he had fallen for her, that he had done a total free fall.

He knew he was asking her to defy her family's wishes, but Danny was a reasonable man. He would get over it, once he saw Piper was happy. Brady had every intention of making her happy, if she let him. Her silence was stretching out and starting to worry him.

"Piper?" He forced himself to face her, not her re-creation.

"I want there to be a you and me, too," she said.

Thank God. Otherwise he was going to be feeling pretty damn stupid and pretty damn heartbroken.

"I'm scared," she added, with an embarrassed laugh.

"Well, that makes two of us," he told her honestly. "I'm terrified. I've never felt this way and I know . . . I know that what I'm asking is a lot, that you could do better and your family has every right to be concerned because I've never been the settling-down kind, but—"

She broke her pose and reached out, her fingers softly covering his mouth. "Shh. There is no better man for me. You're what I've always wanted."

It almost undid him. The trust he saw in her eyes, the confidence, the gentle understanding of what he needed. His throat felt so tight he was going to need a crowbar to pry it apart to swallow.

But he managed to say, "There is no way to express how beautiful you are to me." He gestured to the rough sketch. "But I had to try. And it feels good. Everything feels . . . right."

Brady stared at the wall, at his representation of Piper. He would come back to it, would try to capture the glossy shine in her eyes, the wonder and conviction on her face. She deserved to be preserved in oil. He dropped the pen and pencil on the floor as he placed his hands on her waist and pulled her closer to him.

"It's lovely, and I'm honored." She glanced at his sketch. "I still have every sketch you ever did for me in my closet. I was in awe of your talent. Still am. And I wanted you to fall in love with me. Still do."

He brushed his lips along her jaw, loving the feel of her soft skin. "Oh, I think I'm well on the way to doing just that."

In fact, he might already have.

PIPER GLANCED BETWEEN THE IMAGE OF HERSELF Brady had created in such a short time and Brady himself, overwhelmed with joy and awe. This was the man she had been waiting for, the man she had been saving herself for, if not literally, then emotionally.

No one told her she was beautiful except for her family. Not only did Brady say it, he proved it by sketching her in a way that took Piper's breath away. She did look pretty in his rough sketch. Because she looked like a woman falling in love, and what could be more beautiful than that?

When Brady kissed her, his hands cupping her cheeks, she shivered, eyes fluttering closed.

In relief she realized that while her father might not initially approve, he would come around. She trusted that. She had trusted so few people in her life, really, but she trusted her parents.

And she trusted this moment, she trusted that right now Brady was sincere and that he wanted to stay with her here, in this house on Swallow Street.

"Let me see what you've done with the bedroom," she murmured to him, wanting to feel him inside her again, wanting to run her hands across his nakedness.

He gave a soft laugh. "I put your bed in it. And now I'm going to put you in your bed."

That sounded like a fantastic idea to her. Before she could respond with encouragement, Brady stepped back and peeled off his T-shirt.

"I can't be taken seriously wearing this," he said. "I don't want you laughing at me while I'm trying to get it on with you."

"Oh, trust me, I'm not laughing." Piper swallowed hard, realizing that this was the first time she'd really seen him in the light with his shirt off. Shelby's room had been moonlit, as had the orchard, and while she had felt his muscles, she hadn't really been able to see them in all their perfection. That first night, when he'd stripped off his wet shirt, she'd been aware that she couldn't really gawk at him. Now she had every right to, and she had an incredible view of all that definition, the lines of his abdomen that disappeared into his jeans.

Reaching out, she ran her hands over him, trailing her fingers across his chest, up and around to his biceps, marveling at how solid he was. He nuzzled her ear, his tongue slipping inside, while she continued her exploratory path down to his abs, then on to the snap of his jeans. She popped it open and he sucked in a breath.

"Bedroom, Piper," he said, hand coming to cover hers.

"Sure," she said, though she was feeling impatient, wanting to see all of him naked. Now. So she didn't wait for him. She just walked quickly to the bedroom, peeling off her tank top as she went, knowing he would follow right behind her.

Turning around at the foot of the bed, she kissed him again, deeper, embracing the plunge of his tongue into her mouth, her fingers taking down his zipper. Slipping inside his jeans, she stroked along the length of him, enjoying the low groan of approval he gave into her mouth.

"Take your jeans off," she urged him, stripping her own down to the floor.

Brady sat on the bed and did as she asked, taking his briefs off along with his jeans, before pulling her, still standing, between his thighs and kissing her. His head descended down onto her breasts one at a time, his tongue teasing across her nipple through her bra.

"Your breasts are amazing," he murmured, easily reaching around and undoing her bra.

"So is your . . ." Piper flushed, realizing she couldn't bring herself to say what she was thinking out loud.

Brady glanced up at her, amused. "My what?"

"This." Piper went down on her knees in front of him, nestled between his thighs, and enclosed his erection with her hand.

"Oh, yeah, that's perfect, baby," he told her, as she stroked up and down.

She was just getting started. Feeling emboldened, and wanting to do what she had been giving some considerable thought to, Piper bent over and slid her mouth down onto his smooth heat.

"*Fuck.*"

His agonized approval was exactly what she wanted to hear. There was something intensely satisfying about showing her appreciation for him this way, for resting her palms on his thighs and drawing him deep into her throat. It felt profoundly intimate, her surrounded by him, in her new bedroom that he had been sleeping in, like there was no denying the connection being drawn between them. Like the image of her in the living room, the strokes were getting darker and more obvious, bringing them as a couple into shape, into being.

When his groans grew more pronounced and he dragged his fingers through her hair, urging her to stand up, Piper didn't. She stayed down, on him, until his grip tugged her hair so tightly her eyes teared, and he exploded in her mouth with a hot pulse.

"Holy shit," Brady breathed. "I haven't done that in ten years. Fuck, fuck, fuck, you are hot." He just sat there for a second, stunned, staring down at Piper, her hair tumbling over his thighs, as she wiped her mouth, a sweet but satisfied smile on her face. The combination of sweet and sexy was going to kill him. Literally kill him.

He hadn't done anything to deserve this amazing woman, and yet, here she was, with him. It felt like a dream he didn't want to wake up from, and he wanted to hold on to it with both hands, both feet, and anything else he could use to grip her to him.

"I'm glad you liked it," she said, too damn cute for her own good.

Brady gave a soft laugh. Then he pulled her to her feet. Her bra was dangling on her breasts loosely, and he divested her of it completely. Then her panties. Goosebumps rose on her skin as he bent over, breathing deeply the scent of her, brushing his nose across the warm flesh of her stomach, teasing her. He slid his tongue up and down her inner thighs, moving his hands around to her smooth ass to grip it lightly. She had started to make quiet moans of anxious desire, wanting more, and he reveled in the sound, the feel of her. She got wet so easily for him. She came so easily for him. For him. No one else.

He slipped his tongue over her clitoris and felt himself start to harden again as she whimpered, and her tangy moist arousal greeted him as he moved further south, tasting her thoroughly. Her nails dug into his shoulders and her head fell back in abandon. When she came on him, he marveled that he could take so much pleasure in her pleasure.

And when he pulled her down onto the bed and rolled her beneath him, sliding his cock inside her welcoming body, he also marveled that so much could change in such a short amount of time.

And that it would be so easy to free fall with Piper like this, with no thought to whether or not he had a parachute.

PIPER SMILED AT BRADY AS THEY RINSED THE BRUSH and paint roller they had abandoned an hour earlier in the kitchen sink. She put the lid back on the paint can, her inner thighs pleasantly sore, her body satisfied.

"Well, we did about ten percent of the room," he said, with a grin. "It's a start, anyway."

"We could buy a new brush and roller and keep going tonight," she said, not wanting to leave him and go back to the farm.

"Nah. Screw that. It can wait. I'm starving. Want to go to the Bee and get some dinner?"

She would most likely go anywhere with him. "Sure. I'll text my mom and let her know I'm not coming back for awhile."

Brady, whose hair was sticking up from her fingers

racking through it, finished rinsing the brush and dumped it on a rag on the counter. "Are you ready to go out in public with me? Tongues will be wagging, you know."

"I can handle it." Tongues had been wagging about her since the day she'd shown up in Cuttersville. It was not going to bother her if they were talking about how had little Piper Tucker managed to get Brady Stritmeyer to stick around town for awhile. She almost welcomed it.

Brady leaned over and kissed her. "I bet you can handle anything."

She smiled. "Even you."

He laughed. "Oh, you handle me just fine. Better than fine. You have me firmly handled."

She wasn't sure about that, but she was sure she'd love to keep trying.

Brady hadn't underestimated the attention they would receive when they walked into the diner, his hand firmly in hers. Every eye in the place swiveled and settled on them, openly curious. For a split second, Piper worried about her father, and his opinion of what she was doing, but then she squashed it. She wasn't going to ruin the moment, and she was going to trust that her father trusted her, whether he was comfortable with Brady or not.

Fortunately, Brady shared none of her hesitation. He strode right in, giving everyone a charming smile. "Hey, Marge, how are you this evening?"

"Still above ground, so that's something." Then Marge noticed their hands. "So that's the way the wind is blowing, huh? I'll tell you what, Brady Stritmeyer, you hurt this girl here and you'll have a whole lot to answer to." She snapped her chewing gum in her mouth to emphasize her point.

Oh, Lord. Piper felt her cheeks burn. "Marge, I think Brady has been threatened enough already by my father, but thanks for the concern."

Marge barked out a laugh. "I bet."

Brady didn't look as annoyed as Piper felt. "How come no one is worried about me getting hurt?" he asked, the corner of his mouth turning up. "I bleed too, you know."

The waitress's answer was a snort of derision.

Tucking her hair behind her ear, Piper took the menu from Marge as she slid into the worn booth. She ordered a coffee and Brady ordered a glass of milk.

"Milk?" she asked him, amused.

"It does a body good." He smiled at her, the secret smile of someone who knew her intimately, and it warmed up her insides, the memory of what they had shared, what they were going to be. "I need to get my strength up these days."

"All this home improvement?" she asked, teasing.

"Uh-huh. Among other things." He winked at her, his knee bumping hers. "But in addition to all of that, I suppose I need to do some job hunting here in town."

Piper didn't imagine there was much need for full-time marketing employees in Cuttersville. Except maybe at the plastics plant. "You could talk to Boston."

He looked less than enthused at the prospect. "I'm not sure I want to dive right back into a corporate job, but I have to do something." Drumming his fingers on the table, he didn't look particularly upset or irritated. In fact, he looked very relaxed. Happy.

It made Piper felt squishy inside. "My mom has that cousin in New York who owns an art gallery. Maybe we could talk to him, send in some of your work."

She wanted him to be successful and she wanted him to stay. The minute the words were out of her mouth, she wondered if her suggestion was at cross-purposes with her desire to keep him in town, but it was too late to withdraw the suggestion.

"Sure," he said. "That would be cool."

Brady didn't think for one minute that anyone in New York would give two shits about his work, but it was sweet of Piper to offer. The only reason he was really agreeing was so they could close that subject and move on. It was easier to say yes than explain why it would be pointless. He didn't want to waste time debating his talent, or lack thereof. "Isn't there usually a fall festival? They still do that here?"

"Yes. It's this weekend."

"Will you be my date?" he asked, feeling ridiculously pleased with his life. No job, no money, but he was happy. Insane, that's what it was. "I want to kiss you on the hay ride."

She nodded her yes, but before she could answer, two women came up and spoke to her, asking about their students and how they were adjusting to Piper's class. Then a few minutes later, an elderly couple thanked her for raking their leaves. Followed by a girl around eight who looked thrilled to have run into her old kindergarten teacher.

Brady sat there and watched, proud to be with her. Impressed by the woman she had become.

Everyone loved Piper. Including him.

Chapter Thirteen

"I HOPE YOU KNOW WHAT THE HELL YOU'RE DOING," Shelby told him.

Brady eyed his cousin as they stood in the driveway, leaning on the U-Haul he had rented to drive back to Chicago and pack up his apartment. "I have no idea what I'm doing," he told her truthfully. "But I haven't been this happy in I don't know how long."

He and Piper had been basically living together in the little blue house for the last two weeks, painting walls, yanking weeds, cooking dinner together, sharing night after night in the little bedroom. She always got up and left and drove back to the farm, but after this weekend, she was moving in for keeps, and Brady felt that, for the first time in his life, he was where he was meant to be.

Shelby sighed. "Just please don't get her pregnant."

"What would be the big deal if I did?" he asked defensively. "She's the best thing that's ever happened to me. I want to be with her."

She just shook her head, lips pursed tightly.

"Is this how it's going to be for the rest of our lives? Everyone always telling Piper she could have done better? Everyone always making me feel bad?" He didn't want to have this argument repeatedly, and he didn't want attitude at every family gathering.

"Brady."

"Don't Brady me." He got in the truck. "I'll see you later." Annoyed, he slammed the door harder than was necessary. The file he had picked up from Bree with the hospital records on Rachel sat on the passenger seat.

As he drove on 77 North, he realized that the downside to being around people who loved you was that their opinions mattered.

It had been lonely in Chicago but he'd never had to deal with anyone's criticisms.

He didn't like it.

PIPER STOOD IN HER OLD BEDROOM AND RAN HER hand over a butterfly. It was a little faded, maybe slightly dingy, but it was still charming and whimsical, somewhere between cartoon and realism. Closing her eyes, she pictured the way she had looked that day, a grungy ball cap covering her bald head, brand-new sneakers too big on her feet, eyes wide with awe that something so pretty was hers. That this was her room, her very own private space, was almost incomprehensible to her.

Brady had been sporting blue hair and a lip ring at the time. He smelled like cigarette smoke and excessive cologne but that didn't bother her. Most of the adults in the trailer park had smoked and it was a familiar scent. What wasn't familiar was the casual kindness he had shown her, the way he had treated her like she was totally normal.

Now, fifteen years later, they were building a home together. The love shack, he called it. It was hard to believe.

Lifting her digital camera, she took several shots of the wall, both from a distance and some close up. These were going to be blown up and framed and hung in the guest room of the blue house, the room she secretly hoped would be a nursery in a couple of years. It was too soon to hope for anything like marriage or children, since Brady hadn't even told her that he loved her, but he spoke like their future together was a given.

The portrait of her in the living room had been shaded and painted in oils in the weeks since he had first scrounged that pencil out of her purse and started drawing. He had gone back to it again and again, adding to it until she was amazed at the detail he coaxed from his paints. He had also gone out and bought some canvases and paint supplies, and since then he had been painting in the upstairs bedroom. His skill and sudden drive amazed her, especially since he had shrugged and swallowed his pride and gone to Charlotte Murphy-Thornton for a part-time job at her coffee shop. He seemed to enjoy the casual interaction with people and not having to bring his work home with him. Just coffee beans.

Her dreams were coming true. And her nightmares had gone away. There were no sleepless nights, no ghosts. No stepfather shutting her in the closet.

Her phone buzzed, but when she glanced at the screen, it was an unknown number. She'd gotten several calls like that recently and she wondered what telemarketing list she'd wound up on.

Turning, Piper almost ran into her father, who was standing in the doorway, watching her, eyes filled with something she didn't understand.

"Hey, Daddy." She smiled, wishing away this sudden distance between them. Did it happen to all women when they fell in love? Did it make all fathers feel like they had been replaced? Her decision to see Brady despite her family's concerns was the first time she had ever willfully defied him. But this wasn't skipping school or running off with a criminal. Brady was the right choice for her, and she knew her father would come around when he saw that she was happy.

"Hey, baby girl. Grandma said you were in here. What are you doing?"

She held up her camera. "Decorating on a budget."

He nodded. "He's going to stay in the house with you, isn't he?"

There was no question of who "he" was or how her father felt about it. Piper nodded. "Yes."

Her father sighed. "If it doesn't work out, there's always a place for you at home. Just so you know."

"I know." She did. "I'm sorry that you don't feel good about this. I never wanted to disappoint you."

"Oh, baby, you could never disappoint me." He held open his arms. "Come here."

She did, because she was going to cry and she wanted to feel his big, strong hug surrounding her.

"I just want you to be happy. I don't want you hurt."

"He's not going to hurt me," she said into his chest, words muffled.

"You're special to me. You know that."

She nodded, but then she looked up and told him honestly, "I don't want to be special. I don't want to be the girl who got dumped in your driveway so you can never be hard on me. I want you to treat me like you do the boys, and I want to make my own mistakes and fall on my butt and have you tell me I'm being stupid."

His jaw worked. "Alright, you're being stupid."

Piper gave a watery laugh, stepping back away from him. "I didn't mean right now, not about this."

"As far as I can figure, this is the first dumb thing you've ever done besides letting Cameron talk you into going to the honky-tonk when you were eighteen. So maybe you're right. Maybe it's time for me to let go and let you fall in love with a man you just met." He studied her for a second, then threw his hands up. "Love is maybe the stupidest thing any of us ever do and it almost never makes sense. So who am I to say who you should be with? Would anyone have thought it would work out between me and Amanda? They were probably placing bets on how soon we'd wind up divorced, her hightailing back to Chicago, yet here we are."

"Here we are," Piper repeated softly, feeling the weight of his disapproval lifting off her shoulders. She cried a little harder, just knowing that she could love both the two most important men in her life. Because she did love Brady, whether the words had been spoken out loud or not. "And I'm the luckiest girl in the world to have a father who loves me like you do."

Now her father looked like he was working up a tear, only he pretended it wasn't there and said gruffly, "Come on, there's pie at home. Grandma and Grandpa are coming over for dinner."

If there was one thing Tuckers agreed on, it was that pie solved everything. Or maybe that pie went with everything, including the bittersweet.

"Sounds perfect."

BRADY STARED AT THE MOUNTAIN OF MOVING BOXES around him and rolled his shoulders. Every muscle from head to toe ached. Even his tongue ached. It was nothing but affirming that he was making the right decision to get out of town because none of his so-called friends had been willing to help him pack his stuff up and get it on the van. He had suddenly realized that what he had was a bunch of superficial relationships and nothing more. Not that he was blaming other people. Those were the friendships he had cultivated, keeping people at arm's length, never sharing much more than a drink or two after work.

For years, he had drawn it that way, but now it wasn't enough. It was black-and-white when he wanted color.

It made him all the more eager to get back to Cuttersville and Gran and his stepmom and Shelby and Piper. Most of all Piper.

Fortunately he didn't have that much stuff. He'd sold his couches and bed to a former coworker. So that was that.

He was going to sleep on the couch, then head out in the morning, so he was lounging on it with the file from Bree. This was the first opportunity he'd had to read it.

Rachel's death certificate was in the file. Intemperence was the official cause of death. Brady had had to look the word up on his phone and found out it meant "excessive consumption." So she had overdosed, in other words. Intemperence was a much nicer way to say she was a smack addict.

Flipping through the pages, he saw daily schedules for her, dosing charts, the bill her parents were sent for seven dollars and eighteen cents. When he came across a report written by a Dr. Cyrus Drummond, he thought he might have found something.

"I do not believe that Miss Strauss's insanity was caused by dissipation and menstrual derangement as was originally concluded. After extensive conversations with the patient, my conclusion is that she is wholly sane. Her current state of confusion can be attributed to grief and dependence on laudanum and chloroform. It is my opinion that Miss Strauss is just as much a victim as her dead fiancé."

Brady sat up, intrigued, chewing his fingernail as he read. "So what happened, Dr. Drummond? The dude didn't whack himself."

"The story that she tells is one of deception, manipulation, and violence, but none of it perpetuated by her. It was her understanding that her maid was of a duplicitous nature and was well acquainted with the male form. Miss Strauss had actually informed her earlier in the evening that she was being dismissed, as her conduct had been shy of appropriate. Then she went upstairs to fetch her bonnet at the last moment, and as she was returning down the stairs, she heard her fiancé spurning the advances of the maid. Though this distressed her, nothing could prepare her for the sight of coming around the corner and seeing her fiancé being bludgeoned with a candlestick. Miss Strauss was aghast, in shock, and as the maid repeatedly struck him, Miss Strauss rushed forward to assist and was herself hit upon the head. She sat stunned, whoozy, as the maid put the candlestick in her hand and began to scream, thus turning herself to victim. By the time help arrived a few moments later, Miss Strauss's mind had snapped and she was not able to coherently tell her story to a doubting witness and, later, the coroner. The maid, who was at once hateful and manipulative, successfully maneuvered herself into position as the district attorney's wife, and Miss Strauss's fate was sealed. I have repeatedly suggested to the board of directors here at the asylum that Miss Strauss be released to no avail."

That was interesting. The doctor in charge of her treatment thought Rachel was innocent.

The story sounded believable enough to him.

Did it matter? Brady wasn't sure.

Alone in this apartment, he suddenly found he wasn't entirely sure about a lot of things.

"YOU'RE LETTING HIM MOVE IN WITH YOU?" CAMERON said, sounding appalled. "Hello, can you say mooch?"

Piper flushed with anger. "He's not a mooch."

"You just said he lost his job and no one in his family would take him in. That's a little too convenient, in my opinion."

"I don't remember asking your opinion." Piper propped her phone with her shoulder and cut the daylights out of a piece of French bread, thoroughly annoyed. Everyone seemed determined to tell her that she was making a mistake. Given that she had never experienced that in her post–Mark the Butthead life, she wasn't really liking it. Her dad had finally come around a little, and now she had Cameron telling her she was being used.

"Yeah, well, here's another one—let's see how in love with you he is in six months when he's financially on his feet."

"That's the meanest thing you've ever said to me." Piper fought the tears that welled up in her eyes. "I'll talk to you later. Bye."

Slamming her phone down on the kitchen counter, she took a deep breath and tried not to cry. Her phone rang. It was Cam calling her back, most likely to apologize. But she didn't feel like hearing it. You could only have people telling you you've made a mistake so many times before you got sick of it. Plus, she hated to admit it, but without Brady there, showing her how much he cared, she was starting to feel some doubts creep in. Was she a phase or a fad for him? Would he get tired of her and leave? He had left Cuttersville with a fire under his butt the first time. It didn't seem likely that he would just be willing to settle back down in the town he couldn't wait to leave.

He'd been gone two days and she was already doubting that any of it was real. That frustrated the hell out of her.

With shaky fingers, she assembled her ham sandwich, jumping when her phone rang again. This time it was Brady.

"Hello?"

"Hey, babe, how are you?"

"Fine." Not really. She was starting to freak out that they were moving too fast and that he couldn't possibly care about her in any real way and that everyone in her life was turning on her. "Great. How did everything go?"

"I busted my balls and got it all done. I'm pulling into town now. Can you meet me at Shelby's?"

The relief she felt in hearing his voice, in knowing he was almost back, kind of scared her. She shouldn't be that dependent on his presence. "Why are you going to Shelby's?"

"I want to show you something."

It was hard to read his voice. He didn't sound flirtatious. More tired and agitated. "Okay. I can be there in twenty minutes." She wanted to eat her sandwich and brush her teeth.

"Good. See you soon, sex kitten."

"Okay—" Piper frowned when she realized he'd already hung up. "See you then. Bye," she told the dead phone. Then she made a sound of exasperation when her phone buzzed with a text message alert. It was from an unknown number.

It's on you bitch.

Piper dropped her phone. That couldn't be for her. She didn't get messages like that. She quickly deleted it and went for her purse, deciding to forgo the sandwich. She just wanted to see Brady. Get some reassurance.

Which made her wonder if she still was that needy little girl she'd been.

BRADY WAS IN SHELBY'S DRIVEWAY, CURSING THE FACT that he'd asked Piper to meet him here. Shelby and the kids weren't home, having stepped out for dinner at the Italian restaurant at the outlet mall thirty minutes away. Shel had told him where to find the spare key but suddenly he was wishing he'd just gone back to Swallow Street and taken a shower with Piper. This could wait until he wasn't exhausted.

But it was too late now. She'd be there any minute. He went into the house, and on cue, there was a knock at the door. Opening it, the smile fell off his face when he saw a thin brunette looking at him, not Piper. She was wearing a huge hooded sweatshirt and her hair was limp, her eyes frantic.

"Is Piper here?"

"No." Brady felt alarms going off. "Can I help you?" This did not look like the type of woman Piper would associate with.

"Yeah. Can you tell me where she is? I'm her brother's girlfriend and I really, really need to talk to her."

Piper had mentioned her half brother Marcus to him, had expressed how sad it made her that he had taken a bad path. Brady studied this girl, wondering whether he could trust her. "Where is Marcus?" he asked her.

"Jail. Possession of a controlled substance. That's why I need to talk to Piper."

By this time, she had entered the house. Brady cursed as she wandered into the parlor, her shaking fingers reaching out to stroke the end table. He sensed this girl was in desperate need of a fix. Great. He'd let a drug abuser come into his cousin's house. Thank God they wouldn't be home for another hour.

But Piper was going to be there any minute, and he did not want her to see this girl. "What's your name?" he asked her.

"Trina. Who are you?"

"Piper's boyfriend."

It took her two seconds to process this. "Got any money?"

"No. I lost my job."

"Oh." Standing in front of the fireplace, her eyes traveled over the array of brass decorative items.

No doubt she was gauging what she'd score in a pawnshop. Brady felt sorry for her but he was already thinking he'd call the cops if he had to. "Why did you think Piper was here?" He was suddenly afraid. Had she been to the farm? He was sure she hadn't because Danny would have called the cops, no doubt about it.

The girl was young, no more than eighteen, and now that he could see her in the light, it was obvious she was rail thin under that massive sweatshirt.

"The old lady in the diner told me."

Marge? Or more likely his grandmother. She was the only one who had known he'd asked Piper over to his cousin's. He had called her for her advice and she'd given him the thumbs-up.

"Listen, Trina."

She knew he was about to dismiss her. Her eyes shifted, and she came closer to him. Brady stepped backwards, but he was caught by the fireplace.

"I'll blow you. Just ten bucks, that's all I need. I'm pregnant. I need to get something to eat. Please. Everyone says I give good head."

It felt like it was happening in slow motion. Her hands going for his zipper. His hands reaching out to stop her. Her bending over. His hands on her shoulders, ready to push her away forcefully.

Piper in the doorway of the parlor, jaw dropping.

His thought that this could not be happening. His strangled, "Piper, it's not what you think."

Trina's hand continuing into his pants.

His jerking away, shocked, the blow coming to his head, and his going down like a ton of bricks.

PIPER HEARD THE VOICES AS SHE CAME ONTO THE porch, wondering why on earth the front door was open. One of the kids must have left it open, but she didn't see Shelby's minivan in the drive. She wondered again what it was Brady wanted to show her.

"Just ten bucks, that's all I need. I'm pregnant."

Who the hell was that?

Piper turned towards the parlor, and then what she saw made all thoughts vanish from her head. She couldn't move. She couldn't breathe. A thin girl with dark hair was unzipping Brady's pants. He was holding her like he was going to shake her.

And Piper was six years old again and watching her stepfather force her mother onto her knees to do things that seemed dirty and wrong to her, especially since Mark always said her mother owed it to him for paying for her pills. If he spotted Piper, he'd lock her in the closet, so she always tried to run away and hide first when it happened, to cover her ears so she didn't hear the sounds that were so strange and foreign.

Now there was this girl and she was clawing at Brady's pants, her thin, pale fingers reaching inside to touch what she should never touch.

Piper ran. She thought Brady said something but she

wasn't sure what it was. She just ran. She got in her truck and she drove home, to the farm, sobbing.

She fell out of the cab and tripped in the gravel before she made it to the door. When she got inside, she ran up the stairs as fast as she could and locked herself in her empty bedroom.

Chapter Fourteen

❧

BRADY GLARED AT THE POLICE OFFICER. HE VAGUELY remembered him from his childhood. "Can I go now?"

The officer nodded.

Thank God.

"You should go to the hospital," Gran told him.

"I'm fine. She just hit me with a vase. It's not that big of a deal." He didn't have time to go to the hospital. He needed to find Piper. He'd called her three times and texted her twice, and she hadn't answered. He had no doubt that she had gone to the farm, but he was worried about her driving so upset. Terrified that she might actually think he was on board with getting a blow job from a drugged-out teenager.

It must have looked bad from where she was standing, and he wanted to make sure she knew what was really going on.

"I can't believe it took the cops so long to get here." Gran glared at the two officers who were talking in the foyer. "I called them as soon as I realized what that girl was about."

"You shouldn't have told her where Shelby lives, Gran." Brady couldn't help but reprimand her even though he knew she felt terrible. Usually his grandmother was super savvy, but for some reason she had gotten her wires crossed and thought Marcus's girlfriend was one of Piper's friends. It made Brady concerned that she wasn't as sharp as she used to be.

"You don't need to tell me that, punk. I am well aware of that fact. Feel bad enough already."

Brady felt guilty instantly. His grandmother looked shaken to the core, her skin pale, her usual bravado missing. "I'm sorry, Gran, I know. I'm just worried about Piper." He was more than worried. He was freaking out on every level.

"I know, I know. Go get her. Fix this. The cops will have the girl picked up before the night is over, so don't worry about her."

Brady figured Trina was long gone and they wouldn't see her again anytime soon. After beaning him with a vase, she'd managed to snag five bucks from his pocket and a brass snuffbox off the mantel during the thirty seconds he'd been down. That smacked of serious desperation. He wasn't even sure he wanted to press assault charges unless he thought it might get her a spot in rehab. Otherwise, he didn't feel good about watching a young girl with some serious problems go to jail. But then he reminded himself that if she was willing to hit him on the head, she wasn't fit to be walking around with innocent people.

It wasn't his pressing concern right then, though. He kept thinking about that moment, turning and seeing Piper standing there . . . It made him sick. He loved her more than he could ever have imagined. He wanted to protect her, to take care of her, to love her day after day until he was a wrinkled old raisin of a man with erectile dysfunction. The thought that it could be slipping through his fingers, that he might have inadvertently hurt her, was killing him.

Kissing her grandmother on the cheek, he said, "Wish me luck."

He was going to need it.

PIPER HAD MANAGED TO STEM HER TEARS BUT SHE couldn't bring herself to explain to her parents what she had seen, despite their coaxing concern. Her mom had finally left her alone after stroking her hair back and washing her tears off with a washcloth. Piper wrapped her arm around Prada when the dog leaped into bed with her and cuddled the dog close against her chest, her head hurting, her sinuses swollen from sobbing, her stomach sick.

But nothing hurt as much as her heart. She felt like she had been kicked and stomped, like her soul had been wrung from her body and flung into a ditch. She wasn't sure what she had seen in Shelby's living room, but she kept hearing Brady tell her over the phone that he wanted to show her something. Why would he want to show her that?

Almost as disturbing to her was the realization that she had completely forgotten about seeing her stepfather using sexual favors as a control tool with her mother. Maybe she had blocked it out because she hadn't really understood what she was seeing. Or maybe she didn't want to remember that her mother had been subjected to such humiliation.

For all she knew, it was a game her mother and stepfather had played. Foreplay. That didn't change the fact that she hadn't remembered it. What did that say about her?

It said that the first eight years of her life weren't something she could easily shake off.

There was a knock on her open door. "Piper, Brady is here to see you," her mom said.

"I can't see him," she said. She felt too vulnerable, too hurt, too much of an idiot. How dumb was she to think that Brady Stritmeyer, who had access to a whole city of single women, would want her?

"Are you sure? He looks really upset, and you're clearly upset. You might want to talk about it."

"Not tonight." She would humiliate herself. She would show him the truth—that no matter how much she wanted to believe she could be like everyone else, she wasn't. She never would be.

"Okay."

While Piper lay there stroking Prada's soft flank, she heard murmured voices downstairs and the door firmly closing. A second later there was pounding. Then pounding again. And more pounding.

A tear rolled down her cheek.

BRADY KNEW HE WAS BEING IRRATIONAL. PIPER DIDN'T want to see him. Amanda had gently but firmly closed the door in his face. But he couldn't leave. He just couldn't. He hit the door with his fist again.

It flew open, and this time it wasn't Amanda, but Danny, looking furious. "My daughter does not want to see you right now, so I suggest you go on home."

Knowing he had only seconds before he was facing a solid wood door again, Brady put his hand on the doorjamb and started talking, desperate. "Danny, look, I really need to talk to her. It's just a misunderstanding. Please, just let me go up there and talk to her for two minutes."

"Don't make me throw you off my porch. I don't want to have to do that, but I will."

Given the look on Danny's face, Brady didn't doubt it for a second. Despite his hours logged in at the gym, there was no way he could match Danny in strength. But he had plenty of determination. Ignoring Danny, he pulled out his phone and dialed Piper again. For a second, he thought Danny was going to yank it out of his hand, so he turned, keeping his shoulder wedged in the door. He didn't have a plan, exactly, but he'd sleep on this goddamn porch all night if he had to in order to get Piper to talk to him. He'd risk Danny calling the cops on him because he was not going to just roll over and let the best relationship he'd ever had die.

"Piper," he said to her voice mail, knowing he was pleading. "Piper, please talk to me. I need you."

He didn't care whether Danny heard, what he thought of him. He just knew that he had finally come home with Piper and he didn't want to lose that.

"Brady, that's enough. You're disturbing my whole family. If Piper wants to talk to you, she will." With that, Danny gave him a firm shove on the chest, sending him back onto the porch, and the door closed.

Brady heard the lock tumble into place.

Shit.

He figured he had maybe ten minutes before the cops showed up. Sitting down on the steps, he sighed. The urge for a cigarette was strong again. The drive down from Chicago had been long, and he had a bit of a headache behind the eyes from the girl beaning him with a vase. Resting his arms on his knees, he tried to think, to plot a strategy, but nothing came to his weary and panicked mind.

It just felt like he'd been given a winning lottery ticket, then lost it. A sense of hopelessness settled over him, and he stared out into the driveway, to the cornfield beyond, and wondered what the fuck he was supposed to do now. It didn't seem right that the older he got, the less sure of his future he was.

His phone rang. Glancing down, he saw it was Piper.

Heart thumping painfully, he answered with a careful, "Hello?" His urgent need to explain had dissipated. If Piper wanted to talk, he wanted her to control the conversation, not feel like he was pressuring her or verbally vomiting on her. She had told him once that liars over-explain, so he wasn't going to do that, because he wasn't lying.

"Hi. Where are you?"

Her nose sounded stuffed, like she'd been crying. A lot. "On your front porch. I imagine your dad has called the cops by now."

There was a rustling, and her voice was muffled. "No, I don't think so. I'm coming out."

"Okay." He didn't say anything. He wanted her to look in his eyes when he told her the truth. He wanted to see that she believed him. He wanted to know that something wasn't so broken between them that she wouldn't accept the truth he told her.

The door opened with a slow creak and a dog came running out ahead of Piper. It blew past Brady and headed out into the yard. Piper came and sat next to him on the steps. Brady searched her face. What he saw made his heart break. Her face was swollen from crying, cheeks blotchy, eyes red.

"Piper, it wasn't—"

She cut him off, with a hand placed on his knee. "Shh. It's okay. I know. That was Marcus's girlfriend, wasn't it? I think she's been calling me because I've had missed calls from a blocked number, and today I got a weird text."

Relief surged through him. "Yeah, she was looking for money. It's pretty obvious she's doing drugs and she said Marcus is in jail for possession."

Piper sighed. "I'm sorry to hear that. But I don't imagine he's had a good life. I'm sorry for freaking out, but when I saw you like that, it just really shocked me. She was bending over, her hand . . ." Piper shuddered.

Brady took her hand in his and squeezed. "I understand. I'm sorry you had to see that. Bad timing. I was trying to get her out of the house without it escalating into something, but clearly I didn't succeed." Did this mean they were okay? He couldn't tell. Something about Piper didn't look quite right.

She nodded. "Seeing that, I remembered something I hadn't before. I remember my stepfather forcing my mom to give him oral sex, telling her she owed it to him for buying her pills. It just was an overwhelming moment for me, and I'm sorry I ran off."

Jesus. What did he say to that? "I'm sorry, that's terrible. And I'm sorry that you had to see what you did. No matter what the circumstances, it's awkward."

Something was still off, and he didn't know what it was, so he just waited.

"You know how I told you once that you're insecure? The thing is, it's really me who is insecure. I care too much what other people think of me. Why should I care that I was abandoned at eight, looking like a total ragamuffin? That's not on me. That was my mother and Mark's fault. Actually, mostly Mark's fault. Yet I still want to fit in, be like everyone else, not see ghosts. I shouldn't care."

"I think it's understandable that you do, but you're right, no one thinks any less of you for your parents' mistakes."

Piper looked at him, tears shining in her eyes. "I know what everyone has been saying, that you're not stable enough for me. But the truth is, I'm not stable enough for you. Woman-child, that's me. I'm a clinger, and I'm going to suffocate you."

That wasn't the sound of them being okay. That was the sound of nails being driven into a coffin. "I don't believe that. And it's my choice whether to risk it or not." The emotion of what she saw, her memories springing back to life, had her overreacting. She would be fine. They would be fine.

But she shook her head. "You didn't want any of this. It was me who talked you into an affair even after you said it wasn't a good idea. It's ironic, really. We both thought the biggest obstacle to our relationship was that I lived here and you lived in Chicago. That was never it at all. It's that we're both afraid and I still am. I . . . I did something I shouldn't have."

"No, you didn't." Brady wanted to shake her. This wasn't the Piper he knew. This was defeatist and resigned and he didn't like it.

"I did. I told you I was going to send that picture of the portrait of me to Amanda's cousin Stuart in New York at the art gallery, but I didn't. I put it off because I was worried that if you had some success, you'd want to move to New York." Her voice caught on a sob. "I was afraid you'd leave me, but that was such an awful thing to do, to hold down your dream."

Brady was stunned. It *was* an awful thing to do. He never would have thought her capable of such a thing.

"You deserve better than me." She paused, like she was waiting for him to argue with her, but Brady was so freaking stunned he couldn't think of a single word to say.

So she pulled her hand from his, walked into the house, and closed him out.

Brady stared out into the darkness for a minute, then stood up. There was nothing here for him.

Which made it horribly ironic that he was driving a truck full of all his worldly possessions. One of which was a ring he'd been planning to use to propose to her with.

PIPER WATCHED BRADY DRIVE AWAY, KICKING HIS truck tire first before he got in and started the engine. She had closed the door, gone into the dining room, and watched him, needing to see him leave. It hadn't been her intention to go out there and make him feel bad, but she was starting to realize that she hadn't been fair to Brady all along. She had asked things of him that were unrealistic, like moving back to Cuttersville, living her dream in the house on Swallow, not his dream. It seemed so obvious now, and she'd be right to feel insecure. How long would it be before he resented being stuck in a small town with her?

How long before she wasn't interesting enough for him?

Granted, it had been his idea to stay in Cuttersville, but that was because she'd made it clear she wasn't going anywhere. She had made it clear she wasn't going to see him or sleep with him anymore because her parents didn't approve. So this was her fault, and she felt regret grip her like the flu.

It didn't make sense to keep going down a path that would leave them both hurt. It was a path they should never have even stepped onto.

"Are you okay?" Amanda asked her from the stairs.

Piper shook her head, still watching the truck recede into the night. "No. I just shoved the man I love away from me because I'm afraid of being abandoned." She gave a shaky laugh. "I'm like a textbook case of kids who were dumped by their parents."

Amanda came down the steps. "Well, nine out of ten kids are going to carry insecurities because of that. Odds were you weren't going to be the lucky one, but I am really sorry to hear that."

"I thought I was over all that. I've had a loving life. You and Dad are the best parents I could ask for." Piper leaned on the window glass, feeling very small and sad and ungrateful.

"So on the other hand, maybe you're using that as an excuse. Most people have a moment of panic when they realize they're in love. Maybe you're being too hard on yourself and it's just your knee-jerk reaction to shove him away because it's scary to think that someone owns that much of your emotion. It could have nothing to do with your childhood."

"I don't know." When she had been little, her imaginary friend, Anita, had made all their decisions, had all the answers, never showed fear.

She wasn't a little girl anymore, and there was no Anita.

But that little girl was still part of her, and maybe for the first time, she really understood that she needed to respect her, not ignore her.

"I'm going to go back to my place," she told her mother. "There are some things I need to do."

Alone in her rental house an hour later, she had e-mailed a digital file of the portrait Brady had painted to Stuart in New York. She had e-mailed Bree for an appointment, not to have her tarot read but to ask her how to communicate better with the spirits who appeared to her. She searched her insurance for a therapist who dealt with childhood abuse, just to talk her situation through with a professional. She made a note to call the salon to get her hair trimmed. Two inches. She could manage two inches for starters.

Wandering around her house, she marveled that she and Brady had made it a home in such a short amount of time. His clothes were in the bedroom, his toothbrush on the counter, his laptop on the kitchen table. They'd painted, hung photos, put down area rugs. The wicker furniture her parents despised fit perfectly in this tiny cottage and her bed was snug inside their bedroom.

Her bedroom.

Piper stared at the painting of her in her living room. She wasn't sure how she could look at it every day. But she wasn't sure that she could ever get rid of it either. He had captured her love for him. It was in her soft smile, the tilt of her head.

How could she ever cover that with stark white primer?

She had made a mistake. It would be better to run their relationship into the ground, have whatever time they could have, before it ended. To steal those precious moments, to live happy, until they weren't anymore.

Piper called Brady with shaky fingers.

He didn't answer.

The background on her cell phone reflected up at her. Butterflies. The mural he had painted on her old bedroom wall.

Piper went into her photos and deleted it.

She had been carrying that fantasy entirely too long.

Chapter Fifteen

❧

BRADY SAT DOWN IN THE CORNER OF THE COFFEE shop on his lunch break with Shelby and the twins. Boston was at Zach's basketball game.

"How the heck are all you girls?" he asked, smiling. He was glad for the company while he ate his sandwich. Sometimes he enjoyed retreating into a moody corner and putting in his earbuds while he took his break. But most of the time he preferred company. It was one of the reasons he didn't mind the low-paying job he'd begged Charlotte to give him at her coffee shop. He got to interact with people, saw repeat customers over and over, and was reminded of the simple pleasure of doing something for someone else. Never in a million years would he have thought he would be content to do something like this, but he was. For now.

He had contemplated going back to Chicago after Piper closed the door on him, but he couldn't do it. Not when his family was here. Not when there might someday still be a chance for him and Piper.

"We started ballet today," Emily told him, managing to speak for once before her normally more aggressive twin. The ballet lessons were a little obvious, given they were both dressed in pink tights with black leotards under their thick coats, their feet crammed into rain boots.

"Cool. Sounds like a kick." He winked at them.

They laughed. Shelby rolled her eyes. "How are you?" she asked, and it was a fully locked and loaded question. Everyone wanted to know how he was. They all seemed to think he was going to dig himself a grave and dive into it.

He wasn't great. But he was okay. "I'm fine."

"I don't believe you."

"What, you want me to cry?" he asked her, holding his potato chip bag out to the girls to offer them one. "Yeah, I had my heart broken—is that what you want to hear? It sucks. What am I supposed to do about it? I can't make her talk to me, and believe me, I've tried." Brady couldn't even count the number of times he'd called Piper in the last two months. More than he could count. To be fair, she had called him back a few times, but they always missed each other. It was like it was meant to be that way.

"Look, Brady, I really owe you an apology. It was your right to date whoever you wanted and I had no business giving you a hard time. So I'm sorry. You're a good man, and you deserve to be happy."

Brady was touched. "Thanks, I appreciate that. That means a lot to me."

Emily and Lilly munched on his chips and thumb wrestled with each other. Brady watched them, very grateful that he was getting to know Shelby's kids on a more familiar basis. It was a gift that Piper had inadvertently given him. "Hey, I called my mom."

Shelby almost dropped her latte. "You did? I didn't even know you knew where she was."

"I found her on Facebook. It wasn't that hard." Hearing Piper express her fear that she was more messed up from her childhood than she had realized had made him wonder about himself. He liked to think he had no issues with his mother running off, yet he clearly had separated himself from the rest of his family. So he'd found her and called her and it had been just fine. A friendly, but not too friendly, conversation.

"So how did it go?"

"You know, it was fine. It wasn't like she pissed me off by telling me to take a hike. But I didn't get any warm fuzzy feelings of nostalgia either. I think we were both just mildly pleased with it. Content to talk, but not in need of doing it again anytime soon. Which probably sounds weird."

"Not really. Just because you want to know someone has thought of you doesn't mean you want to be in their life again. You just want to know that on some intrinsic level they care."

"Exactly. But I did ask her about my name." Brady shook his head, still not ready to accept he was named for such an incredibly stupid reason. "She says she had no idea there was a previous Brady Stritmeyer. She named me Brady because *The Brady Bunch* was her favorite show growing up."

Shelby's jaw dropped, then she closed her mouth tightly, like she was fighting the urge to laugh.

"I know. It's ridiculous."

"Oh, Lord."

"Exactly. She says that she always thought Greg Brady was hot."

"So why didn't she just name you Greg?"

"God only knows. So my name is a total coincidence.

There is no higher meaning." He bit his turkey sandwich and marveled at the sheer randomness of life.

Which became even more random when the door chime tinkled and he glanced up to see Piper coming in the door. The sandwich got stuck in his throat and he choked a little, trying to force it down. Shit. He had been waiting for a chance to see her, talk to her, and it had to be here, now? He had fantasies about being back in the apple orchard, proposing to her to show he was serious about being committed to her, giving her the gift he had picked out for her at a little artsy boutique in Chicago, the ring he thought suited her perfectly.

A mouthful of food and steamed milk on his shirt was not part of his vision.

Piper was wearing a red scarf wrapped around her neck, her hair pulled back in a ponytail. Funny how he'd never seen her wear her hair pulled back like that. But she looked the same. He wasn't sure why she would look different. It just seemed like something should visibly reflect that she was as devastated as he was.

Instead she was smiling and walking up to the counter.

Shelby followed his gaze and her eyes widened. "Oh, my word."

The twins looked, too, and they yelled, "Piper!" Chairs were shoved back and they went running to her.

Which was when Brady realized she was not alone.

She was with a guy.

PIPER HEARD HER NAME AND LOOKED UP TO SEE LILLY and Emily rushing towards her in pink tights. Looking behind them, it took her only a second to realize Shelby was sitting with Brady and he was staring at her.

"Cameron," she said, turning around in a panic. "He's here."

"Who?" Cameron frowned and looked around.

But by then it was too late. The girls were bouncing around her telling her about ballet class and she was giving appropriate responses and Shelby and Brady were standing up and she was trying not to panic.

This wasn't how she wanted to see Brady for the first time in two months. It was cold outside and she was wearing a scarf. Her nose was probably red. Her hair was pulled back because, with the scarf, the hair had to go away or she would suffocate under the double volume of hair and knit.

"We haven't seen you in forever," Emily said, and it sounded a little accusatory.

"Is this your boyfriend?" Lilly asked, eyeing Cameron with curiosity.

"No, this is my friend Cameron."

"Hello, small children," he said with a casual wave.

Then Shelby and Brady were upon them and Piper swallowed hard. Brady looked good. His hair was longer and he was wearing a coffee shop shirt. She'd heard he had started working here full-time but it was a little hard to believe. He looked content, though, a slight smile on his face, his biceps shown to advantage in his short-sleeved shirt. Biceps she had once had the right, however briefly, to touch.

She should have tried harder to speak to him. He'd called her. She'd called him. But they'd never spoken. That suddenly felt so unbelievably wrong she couldn't find any words to express all the thoughts and emotions that were kicking around her. Hell, kicking at her. She wanted to just grab him and kiss him and take him home to their house, the blue house they had fixed together. But she had screwed that up, probably forever.

"Hi, Piper," Brady said, and there was a tone she didn't recognize. "Who's your friend?"

Then she knew. Jealousy. That's what she heard. Maybe, despite her mistakes, there was a chance. She shouldn't hope. But she couldn't help it. "Oh, this is Cameron, my friend from middle school."

"Nice to meet you." Cameron stuck his hand out and shook Brady's.

"Brady Stritmeyer."

Cameron's eyebrows shot up as he caught on to what was happening. "So, I need a black coffee the size of my head before I have to help my mother figure out her new computer. Anyone else need anything?"

"No, no, we're good," Shelby said firmly, when the twins started to offer their needs.

"I need to speak to Piper for a second," Brady said suddenly. "Alone."

Piper tried to tamp down the hope that bloomed in her. It could be anything. He might have heard from Stuart. He might want his toothbrush back, the only thing still left at her place after she had sent the rest of his things home with Shelby a few days after their breakup. Just because he wanted to talk here, now, didn't mean he wanted to talk about them. It was probably about the toothbrush.

"Sure." She moved over to the stone fireplace in the center of the room and turned back to him. "How are you?"

He shrugged. "I'm okay. How are you?"

Her answer was the same. "Okay." That was what she was. Fine. Okay. Hanging in there. Making progress. Coming to terms.

But she wasn't great, amazing. Happy. None of those.

Brady crossed his arms over his chest, like he was uncomfortable. "I wanted to tell you that I don't want you feeling guilty about not sending a picture of my painting to Stuart. That was your idea in the first place, not mine, and I didn't really care one way or the other, so truthfully, I think it was your dream for me, not mine. I don't need to hit it big in the art world to be content with what I'm producing. And I am, for the first time in a long time, and I owe that to you."

That surprised her. She had been carrying a great deal of guilt around over that. But he was right—it had been her idea. Nodding, she said, "Thank you. I'm glad you're still painting."

He nodded.

They were both a couple of nodding fools.

"I'm only on break, and I should probably get back to it, but are you coming to Shelby's party?"

"Yes." Boston was having a forty-first birthday party for Shelby because he'd taken her literally the year before when she'd said she didn't want a fortieth party. This was an attempt at rectifying that mistake. "Of course."

Brady gave a look she couldn't decipher. "Save a dance for me?"

As if there was any way she could say no to him. "I'd love to."

TAKING A PULL ON HIS BEER, BRADY LOOKED AROUND the yard at Shelby's and was satisfied with what he saw. He and Boston had spent the day pitching a tent and stringing it with lights. They had rolled out a couple of kegs and put down plywood boards duct taped together for dancing while Gran and Amanda and Willie Tucker and Piper and Shelby's mom had lined up tables by the house and piled them with food. Now the party was in full swing, and Brady was amazed to realize how happy it made him to see that he knew every one of these people.

No matter what happened with him and Piper, he wasn't going anywhere.

But if he had anything to say about it, a whole lot would be happening between him and Piper. Watching her all day, seeing how she smiled at all her relatives, how she entertained and counseled the kids, the way she followed directions and never got stressed, it just confirmed for him that she was an amazing woman.

He knew what he'd known all along, and while he'd stepped back for a while, given her the space she'd asked for, he wasn't doing it anymore. Tonight he was throwing it all out there and she could either take it or leave it. But he had to try.

The air was crisp, and the bonfire he and Boston and Danny had built was blazing away. Kids, jacked up on soda and birthday cake, were tossing marshmallows into the fire and watching them explode. Piper was supervising, keeping the overexcited single-digit set from falling face-first into the flames.

They had of course spoken, greeted each other, made various random comments to each other as the day had gone by, just like anyone else there. But that was it, and Brady had been waiting for just the right moment to approach her.

When the music blaring through the speakers changed from fast-paced country-line dancing to an old-school eighties love ballad, Brady knew this was his chance.

Since he'd never gotten anything by hanging back and waiting for it to fall in his lap, Brady went over to the fire and moved in close to Piper, too close for two people who weren't dating. Her reaction was what he expected. She turned, flustered, and grabbed her throat. She was bundled up in a winter coat with a fake fur collar, and he wanted to grab those lapels and kiss her until the sun came up.

God, he had missed her. He couldn't live without her. He

couldn't. She was a doorway to the purest happiness he'd ever known, to a contentment he'd never even known existed.

"Oh! Brady."

Intertwining his fingers in hers, he said, "Dance with me?"

With a flustered look at the children, then over to the dance floor, she took a deep breath and said, "Yes."

For the first time Brady realized Cameron was on the other side of the fire. "Watch the kids, Cam," she said. "And hold my drink, please."

"Yeah, because that's exactly what I want to do," Cameron said, looking anything but pleased as he took the cup from her.

Brady led her to the dance floor. Piper's cheeks were pink from the heat of the fire, and she looked so alive, so juicy, he was having a hard time holding an erection at bay. When she wrapped her arms around his neck and they started to sway, Brady was overcome with a sense of certainty. This was the woman he was meant to be with.

"I miss you," he told her simply as he stared down at her.

Piper swallowed hard. Her voice was hoarse, tight. "I miss you, too."

"See, the thing is, Piper, nobody is perfect. I think there probably isn't a person alive who is totally and completely done growing and changing as a human being. So I don't see any reason why you and me can't do that growing and changing together."

He figured he had about three and a half minutes left of this dance, and he wanted to just get down to it. He was in love with Piper and he was going to tell her before the night ended.

Staring up at Brady, her hands on his waist as they made a halfhearted attempt at dancing, Piper wanted to cry. After she'd broken things off with him so unceremoniously, in a five-minute conversation on the front porch, he still wanted to be with her. After two months apart, and countless flirty girls in the coffee shop, he was here, with her. Her counselor had told her that it was normal for her to doubt the sincerity of people's affection for her, that she needed time to establish trust given her early years, and she supposed that was true. All she really knew was that she loved Brady, she missed him, and she'd have to be the stupidest woman on the face of the earth to say no to what he was offering.

"I don't suppose there is any good reason why we can't." She felt a surge of love for him. God, he was so amazing. A man, not a boy. He had never once played a game with her or been anything other than totally honest.

"For real?" He looked astonished.

That made her laugh. "Yes."

"Well, shit, that was easier than I thought. I still have a good two minutes left to this cheesy song. I was planning to use the whole thing to talk you into being with me."

"I don't need to be talked into it. I'm sorry I got scared."

"It's okay, babe. But the thing is, if you get scared of the dark, you don't need to hide under the bed. Just tell me and we'll turn on the light together, okay?"

Oh, now she was going to cry. She nodded furiously because she couldn't speak.

"I don't have to move into the house. We can take it slow. Gran is tolerating me well enough for now. When push came to shove and I was homeless, she gave me a room."

"We can play it by ear, do whatever feels right." Piper shook her head, in awe that it was that easy. That here they were. "This feels right. I was so miserable without you but I thought it was the best thing for you."

"I know what's the best thing for me, and that is you." Brady bent over and brushed a soft kiss over her lips. "I've missed your lips. Let's go behind the garage and make out."

Piper laughed. "Are you serious?"

"Dead serious. No one can see us back there."

She surprised herself by saying, "Okay."

She'd shocked Brady twice in two minutes. His eyes widened. "Hell, yeah. Perfect timing—the song is over."

Pulling her by the hand off the dance floor, Brady led her past a half dozen people, who all noted their hands clasped together. Piper didn't care. She didn't blush or demur or feel like a teenager sneaking off. She felt like an adult, like a woman who made her own choices. Her mother was sitting on her father's lap, looking a little drunk given all that hair flipping, but despite having his hands full, her dad definitely noticed who she was with, and he just nodded to them.

"I'm sure Danny is going to be thrilled about this," Brady said.

"Actually, he probably will be just fine. We came to an understanding that I'm an adult." He would be there for her no matter what. She knew that, trusted it. He just wanted her happy.

"Excellent."

They cut around behind a jumbo pine tree and darted behind the garage. Only to almost run into a teen couple doing just what they wanted to be doing.

"Oh, shit, looks like someone beat us to the punch," Brady said, clearly amused.

The teens sprang apart and Piper almost croaked. It was Shelby's son, Zach, and Georgia, Charlotte and Will's daughter.

"We were just . . ." Zach tried to feebly explain, before giving up. "Don't say anything to my parents, okay?"

"We won't say anything," Brady reassured him. "Just remember that her daddy is sheriff, though. He carries a big gun."

Even in the moonlight, they could see Zach's face blanch. Georgia was staring at the ground, her hair disheveled.

"Got it," Zach muttered, and the two shuffled off.

Piper shook her head. "Good Lord. I still think of Zach as being a kid, and Georgia even more so. I watched them both when they were babies."

"Face it, Tucker, you're old," Brady told her.

Laughing, she smacked him in the chest. "Hush. And if I'm old, guess what that makes you?"

"Damn, you're right. Old enough to know better."

"Better than what?" Piper let Brady pull her into his arms.

"To know that I shouldn't lure a girl off behind the garage."

He kissed her, and Piper sighed. She had missed him more than she had even realized. The feel of him against her, despite her coat and his sweatshirt, was perfect. The kiss was deep, true, passionate, filled with all their pent-up emotions.

"You taste like whiskey," he whispered, hugging her tightly. "Has my grandmother been fixing your drinks?"

As a matter of fact. "Yes. I had two sips and I swear I started slurring my words."

"She should be banned from bartending." Then he shook his head. "But what the hell am I doing talking about Gran? I brought you here to make out, yes, but also because I need to tell you something."

"What?"

"I love you."

Piper sucked in a quick breath. Her heart swelled. Her lip started to quiver. His expression was so sincere, so earnest, so matter-of-fact. She had never heard anything more beautiful. Just three simple words that meant everything.

"I love you, too. I've always loved you," she whispered.

"I know it sounds crazy, but I've always known I was meant to be with you."

Brady's throat felt so tight he was going to need a crowbar to pry it apart to swallow. But he managed to say, "Damn, I wish someone had told me. Could have saved myself some trouble." He was only half kidding. The path he'd taken to get here was more than a little potholed.

Piper smiled. "Where would the fun be in that?"

"Did you cut your hair?" he asked suddenly, realizing that whereas before her hair had skimmed the bottom of her rib cage, as he held her now it seemed just a little shorter.

She nodded. "Two inches. Nearly killed me. But I did it."

"It always looks beautiful. You look beautiful. Why would you love me?" he asked her in all seriousness, having a moment of doubt. She was so . . . special. Why was he entitled to her?

Cupping his cheeks with her hands, she gazed into his eyes. "'When he shall die, Take him and cut him out in little stars, And he will make the face of heaven so fine, That all the world will be in love with night, And pay no worship to the garish sun.'"

Piper kissed him softly. "You have a beautiful heart that is as bright as those stars above us in my truck. I have always seen that."

Brady knew that he was going to spend the rest of his life trying to live up to the trust in those words. He had never understood how falling in love would be so much bigger than himself, that he would care more about someone else than about himself. It should have been obvious, but he had never gotten it until that very moment, and he kissed Piper back, his hands on her waist pulling her as close as four layers of clothes would allow.

Her lips were soft and pliant, and he closed his eyes and gave in to everything that he was feeling.

"I'm sorry," he told her, kissing her over and over between his words. She smelled like bonfire and whiskey and sweet country air, and he knew that as soon as this party started winding down, they were going back to her place.

"For what?" Piper opened her eyes and stared up at him, guileless and open.

"Sorry that I'm broke and basically homeless." It wasn't exactly a pretty package at the moment.

"I don't care about your bank account. And stop insulting the man I love."

Brady laughed. Then he picked her up and squeezed her so hard she squealed.

Gasping and laughing, she said, "You're crushing me."

"I did strike a deal with some of the local antique shops to carry my work. We'll see if anyone actually buys it." If he made enough to pay for the paint, he was happy.

"Really? That's fantastic. I'm so proud of you."

She was. He could see it. Brady dug into his pocket. "So I got something for you a while back. I saw it and I thought of you."

"What is it?" she asked, eyes wide with anticipation.

"I've been carrying it around this whole time. Guess that makes me a little pathetic. I prefer to think of it as being romantic."

"What is it?" she asked again.

Brady drew the moment out just a few seconds longer. "Well, it's not a poke in the eye."

She was about to smack him again, but he caught her off guard by holding up the ring in front of her.

"Oh, my God," Piper breathed, taking it and turning it around and around to study it, stunned by his gift.

She started crying, tears blurring her vision. "Brady," she breathed, started to choke on her tears. He had gotten her a pewter ring that was shaped like a butterfly, the gems in its wings a perfect match to the purple of her childhood bedroom.

"My plan was to tell you that I love you, then ask you to marry me. I thought this ring suited you more than a fancy diamond. It's delicate and feminine and it's not traditional, but I thought you'd like it. You don't have to wear it, and— shit, I'm just going to shut up now."

She was sobbing. She couldn't help it. "I love it," she managed to blubber, hugging him tightly, letting the feel of him, the smell of him, wash over her so that she would always remember this moment.

"But that was before that night, so even if it doesn't make sense for me to propose right now, I still want you to have it." He wiped her tears off her cheeks. "It's been like carrying a piece of you with me, but now I have the real deal."

He just made it worse, in the best way possible. She just cried harder, then she shoved the ring back at him. "Do it."

"Do what?" he asked, bewildered, enclosing his fist around the ring.

"Propose to me."

"What? Are you serious?"

Oh, hell, yeah, she was serious. "Yes, I'm serious. And in case you're wondering, I'm going to say yes." Maybe it was crazy, and maybe she was jumping way ahead, but she knew how she felt and that wasn't going to change. They didn't need to get married tomorrow, but she wanted to hear him ask.

Brady grinned. "Well, alright, then." He held the ring up, and what she saw on his face quieted her tears. It was such a look of total certainty, Piper saw him by her side fifty years down the road. "Piper, will you marry me?"

She nodded. "Yes."

Then he put a ring on it.

Chapter Sixteen

❧

"ARE YOU SURE YOU WANT TO DO THIS?" BRADY ASKED Piper. She looked pale. Hell, he wasn't sure he wanted to do it.

But she nodded. "It's the right thing to do."

"Okay, then." He turned to Bree. "Should I go somewhere else?"

"No." Bree handed her baby to Shelby, who was watching with a baleful expression. "You're integral to the unrest these spirits feel."

Brady rocked on his feet in front of the fireplace at Shelby and Boston's and tried to think whether there was anything particularly intelligent about allowing his fiancé to harness a spirit. Nope. Not smart at all. But Piper wanted to do it.

"So you think just by the accident of my name I became connected to the spirits here?"

Bree was burning some smelly herb all around the parlor.

Brady wondered whether the baby needed to be taken into the kitchen. He'd be happy to volunteer. That stuff didn't seem great for a baby's lungs, and he didn't really want to be here.

"Your name, and the fact that Piper is a medium. The universe chose you two for each other, and to release the original Brady and Rachel from their bonds here on earth, in this house."

Brady was an open-minded guy, but sometimes Bree made his bullshit meter go off. But given that he had seen what he had with Piper, he figured he couldn't really dispute any of it. He and Piper had been together again for three months and he accepted her for who she was, and the truth of it was, she saw dead people. He was just glad she'd finally come to terms with it and had stopped trying to hide it. It wasn't something she advertised, because most parents of kindergartners wouldn't want to hear their kid's teacher talked to ghosts. But Bree had taught Piper how to gently but firmly tell them when they needed to give her privacy.

For the most part, it hadn't been an issue. The house on Swallow seemed empty of anything other than their own vibe, which was a happy and sexy one, he was grateful to say.

"If it wasn't for Rachel, you and Piper probably wouldn't have gotten together," Shelby said. "I could say the same for me and Boston."

Brady thought he and Piper were together more because she had dropped her robe and they'd had sex on Shelby's bed, but he wasn't about to share that.

"I think I always knew Rachel was innocent," Piper said.

"So you believe the doctor's report Brady found?" Bree asked.

Piper nodded. "Absolutely."

"I think so, too." Given all that bogus reporting, Brady was way more inclined to trust the doctor than the Keystone cops who had investigated Brady's murder. "So what exactly are we trying to do here?"

"Bring them both into the room at the same time, so they can see each other. It might bring them peace. At the very least, we can tell Rachel we know she didn't do it."

Figuring he might be needed to protect Piper from flying objects, Brady stayed, but he really wanted to make off with the baby like Shelby was doing.

"I'll be in the kitchen with Iona if you need me."

Piper saw Brady studying Shelby's retreat with a fair amount of longing, and she was grateful that he was willing to stick it out. Not every man would tolerate a woman who was a ghost magnet.

Bree had prepped her on the spells they would be speaking. She didn't consider herself Wiccan or a witch, but she trusted Bree, who had become a mentor of sorts to her, reassuring her that she was in fact completely normal, just more aware than others.

The candles were lit and Piper closed her eyes and murmured, visualizing both Rachel and Brady in the same place, standing next to each other. The Blond Man and Red-Eyed Rachel, facing each other for the first time in one hundred and twenty years. Expressing their love for each other. How would she feel if Brady were taken away from her?

It would be a physical pain. It would be agony, like losing an arm or a leg. She would survive, but she would be damaged. Just the thought made her melancholy. Since Shelby's party, she and Brady had been happier than she could have dared to hope for. He'd won her parents over by proving himself a hard worker and very loyal to her and to his family. If that was suddenly taken away from her? When she'd just started to be able to enjoy it?

That was Rachel's pain, and Piper felt immeasurable sympathy for her.

She sensed it was time to open her eyes.

There they were. Both of them. Standing in front of the fireplace, their spirits more opaque than usual, as if they were afraid to fully appear, afraid it wasn't real. Brady's hand stretched out for Rachel.

A shiver rolled up Piper's back. "He says he loves her," she whispered, not hearing the words, but reading them off his lips as he spoke.

Her heart broke even more for them as she felt like she was watching an incredibly private exchange.

Rachel's sigh was so pronounced, Piper felt her own skirt swirl around her boots from the sudden breeze. Then Rachel mouthed the words back to her fiancé, her hand lifting to touch his, palm to palm.

Then they were gone. There was no sign that they had ever been there, and Piper turned to Bree. "They're gone. Is that permanent?" Part of her was relieved for them, and yet part of her suddenly felt like she was going to miss them.

"I don't know, honestly," Bree said. "I don't feel them anymore. What's this?" She bent over the fireplace. "This just fell down from the chimney." She brushed some ash off the object and unfolded it and frowned. "Do you know what this is?"

She held it out and Piper took the paper. It was yellowed, a page torn from a decade-old sketchbook. "Oh, my God," she breathed, her hand starting to shake. "Brady, look at this."

"What?" He leaned over her shoulder to see. "Holy crap."

It was Rachel and the Blond Man, standing right in front of this very fireplace, smiling, standing close to each other, Brady's arm crooked to allow Rachel to rest her hand there. Piper knew without a doubt that it was a sketch the current Brady had done. But she turned it over just to confirm what she already knew.

"By B. Stritmeyer," Brady read, tracing his fingers over

his own signature. "As described to him by Piper Danielle Schwartz Tucker."

"I remember this now," Piper said, a lump in her throat. "It was the first time I used the last name Tucker. I was kind of trying it on for size, wanting it to be mine."

"Now you're really going to have a hell of a name when we get married," Brady said, teasing her. "Double hyphen and everything." But he also took her hand in his, like he understood how hard that had been for her. "I don't remember sketching this specifically. I remember doing a half dozen ghost images for you."

"I have the others," she admitted. "I kept them. But I haven't seen this one in years. I'd forgotten about it."

"That's a crazy coincidence," Brady said, feeling under the fireplace mantel. "Why was it in here? Who put it there?"

"There are no coincidences. Only a design whose pattern we don't recognize. I don't think we can dismiss that you were assaulted right here by a duplicitous woman, just like the first Brady. Fortunately, your story has a better ending." Bree blew out her candles. "I'm going to check on Iona and Shelby."

"Sometimes she scares me just a little," Brady said, watching Bree retreat.

Piper laughed. "I think she has a point."

"What, that ours has a happy ending? I'll absolutely agree with that." Brady folded the sketch back up and put it in his pocket. He took her left hand and ran his fingers over her engagement ring. "Want to go home and add another page to your diary?"

The diary was still fictional, but the desire never was.

Piper nodded. "I thought you'd never ask."

TURN THE PAGE FOR A PREVIEW OF
ERIN McCARTHY'S NEXT EBOOK

True

COMING IN MAY 2013 FROM INTERMIX!

NATHAN'S APARTMENT WAS ON MCMICKEN STREET, off-street parking only. Tyler's car was a rusted-out sedan, at least twenty years old, with a maroon door that stood out in stark contrast to the white car.

"It's unlocked," he told me as he stepped into the street.

So I pried open the passenger side and climbed in, shivering, crossing my arms over my chest. I checked for a seat belt, but there didn't seem to be one, and so I just sat there, stiff, my rain boots shuffling through a pile of discarded fast food bags and Coke cans. I didn't know what to say to Tyler. I wanted to thank him for rescuing me. Because that's what he had done. I wasn't sure I could have gotten away from Grant on my own.

I forced myself to glance at him, but he was just looking back over his shoulder as he pulled out of the spot. He had a strong jaw and a little bump in the center of his nose that

I had never noticed before. With his sweatshirt swallowing him, and in profile, somehow he looked younger, less intimidating than when his tattoos were on full display and his dark eyes were staring at me, inscrutable. It gave me the courage to say, "Thanks."

My voice came out like a hoarse whisper and I cleared my throat, embarrassed.

"No problem," he said. "You can't walk through this neighborhood by yourself at night. This fucking hill alone would kill you if the ghetto rats didn't."

Whether or not Straight Street got its name from the fact that it was virtually a 90 degree incline or not, I didn't know. It was definitely unwalkable, even during the day. But I wasn't talking about him giving me a ride, though I was grateful for that. "Yeah. But thanks for . . . Grant." I didn't want to get more specific than that.

He turned now, and I was sorry that he did when he gave me a look that I couldn't read. "Sure. If you find yourself in that situation again, punch him in the nuts. But you can do better than Grant, trust me."

"Yeah." I wasn't sure if it were true or not, but I did know that I would much rather be alone than have those wet, narrow lips anywhere on me, and that demanding grip on my arm, the back of my head.

"I mean, you've waited this long to have sex, you shouldn't waste your virginity on an Oxy junkie."

So he had heard me talking to Jessica and Kylie. I gripped my purse tighter in my lap, that churning sensation in my stomach starting again. The car was heaving and bucking as it struggled to make it up the steep hill, and the engine whined as Tyler gave it more gas. The street was empty, most of the houses darkened since it was after two, and I suddenly felt as trapped in the car as I had in the apartment. I didn't want to talk about this with Tyler. Or anyone.

"Oxy?" I asked, to buy time. Dodge and weave when the subject was uncomfortable. But I'd never been particularly good at dodging anything. I was the girl in grade school gym who didn't move fast enough and took a rubber ball in the nose.

"OxyContin. Grant likes to snort it. When he can't get his hands on any for awhile, he gets a little edgy. I told Nathan he shouldn't let him come around anymore, but Nathan is loyal."

So Grant did drugs. I guess I wasn't surprised, not really. He had the requisite dysfunctional family, the nervous twitch. It made sense. I was disappointed, though, because it meant that I had inaccurately assessed Grant. I had seen him as a male version of myself, quiet from a lack of social skills, nervous. But it wasn't that at all, and I had projected what I wanted onto him.

The thought made me want to cry again.

"So you're not?" I said, then immediately regretted it. It sounded almost accusatory, when the truth was, the silence was stretching out, a long rubber band that snapped with my unintentionally harsh words.

"Not when you're doing drugs and kicking girls."

That made sense to me.

I didn't really know Tyler at all, other than that he was Jessica and Kylie's party buddy, and on occasion he and Jessica hooked up. He almost never came to our dorm room and I had only been around him a few times at parties and at the apartment. We didn't share any classes and he'd never made much of an effort to talk to me.

But suddenly I liked him a whole lot better.

Unsure what to say, as usual, I tucked my hair behind my ear, but I was spared from having to talk by his phone ringing. He glanced at the screen and swore.

"Yeah?" he said, after tapping the screen, turning the steering wheel with his left elbow, heading towards campus.

I wondered if it was Jessica. But I realized that it couldn't be Jessica because she wouldn't have called him. She was a texter and she always used an absurd shorthand with acronyms that no one but she understood, like *LULB*, which she insisted stood for *Love You Little Bitch*. Or my personal favorite, *W?* Jessica sometimes meant it as a general question, as in she didn't understand what was happening, which most people would assume, or sometimes as "what time," but no one but her ever knew which one she intended.

"No. In the kitchen. No," he said into his phone, more emphatically. "I didn't take it. The cat probably ate it."

The woman talking to him was so loud that I could hear her, though the words were garbled.

"Well, stop leaving your shit laying around," he said, and pulled his phone from his ear and dropped it into a dirty change compartment next to the gear shift with a sound of disgust. "Moms are a complete pain in the ass."

If I hadn't been drunk I probably wouldn't have said anything at all. I would have just agreed or, most likely, just nodded. But my mouth seemed to move faster than my brain. "I don't remember my mom being a pain in the ass at all. She was always smiling."

Tyler glanced at me. "Remember? She run out on you or what?"

I wondered what the statistical odds were that someone would assume abandonment over death. "No. She died. Of cancer. When I was eight." The beer was working overtime. I never told anyone that unless they really pressed me because the *C* word immediately brought both sympathy and fear to people's faces. They felt instantly bad for me yet at the same time they were momentarily afraid that it would touch their life like it had mine, and they had to whisper the word. *Cancer.* Like if they spoke it too loudly it would be conjured up in their bodies like a destructive demon direct from hell. People had told me that straight out, that cancer was from the devil, a horrible affliction of otherworldly implications, unstoppable.

Others had told me that the government probably had a vaccination for cancer but was keeping a lid on it, to drive the medical economy. This seemed unlikely to me for more than a dozen reasons, not the least of which that it didn't make sense on a cellular level. It wasn't a virus but a mutation, yet I understood people wanted an answer for the randomness of why it struck, why it killed.

I had stopped asking why a long time ago.

Tyler seemed to get that. His response wasn't an uncomfortable apology. He said, "Well, that's about as fucking unfair as it gets, isn't it? My mom is a selfish bitch and she'll probably live to be ninety, and yet yours died."

It was kind of nice not to get the same pat response of sympathy, the one where everyone was sorry but at the same time so damn glad it wasn't them. I appreciated his matter-of-fact attitude. "You don't get along with your mom?"

"Nope." Tyler pulled into the driveway that led to my dorm. "She's not all bad, though. She did give birth to me." He turned and shot me a grin.

It was so unexpected that for a second, I blinked, then I let out a startled laugh. The sound was foreign and awkward to my ears but Tyler didn't seem to notice. His face changed when he smiled, and his eyes warmed. In the dark they still looked like deep black holes, but with his lips upturned and the corners of his eyes crinkling, he wasn't so intense, so remote.

I realized that was why I'd always been slightly nervous around Tyler. He was what people always accused me of being—there but not present. Easygoing, but distant. Smiling, but intense. Maybe it was the alcohol, my ears still buzzing, my insides hot but my skin cold and clammy, but for the first time I didn't feel uncomfortable around him.

"So are you really a virgin?" he asked, sounding genuinely curious. "Or were you just saying that?"

No longer comfortable. It went away faster than you could say Awkward Moment.

Why he thought I would want to talk about that made no sense to me at all. I was drunk, but I wasn't *insane*. If I hadn't even told my roommates until that night, why the hell would I sit in Tyler's car and spill my guts? I wasn't the confessional type. I never had been.

So I just looked at him.

"I'm going to take that as a *yes*."

I wanted to tell him to mind his own goddamn business. To stop pressing a girl he didn't know for intimate details about her sexual experience. That it was rude. But I remembered that he had in fact saved the very virginity he was questioning, so I didn't want to be a bitch. I just shrugged. Really, what difference did it make? I was already a collegiate abnormality. Likes to study! Hates to talk! Won't go tanning! See this freak-show exhibit in her natural dorm habitat . . .

But I actually surprised myself by opening my mouth and saying, "Yes, I am."

My admission silenced him for a second, but then he drummed his thumbs on the steering wheel as he put the car in park in front of my dorm, which was a seventies-built tower of glass and steel, the light from the lamppost flooding into his car, showing even more clearly how dirty and ancient it was, the slot for a cassette player crammed full of what looked like parking tickets.

"Do you have a purity ring or whatever?"

Now that I was in, and the beer had loosened my lips, I

said the first thing that came into my head. "I prefer to call it my hymen."

Tyler let out a laugh. "No, I mean one of those rings you wear on your finger . . ." He looked at me, comprehension dawning. "Oh, wait, you're being sarcastic, aren't you?"

I nodded.

Which made him laugh harder. "Rory, you are an interesting chick."

Interesting wasn't exactly a riveting compliment, but he hadn't called me a freak, which was how I felt sometimes. Like I had been assembled in a different way altogether from everyone around me, and while I liked the end result, everyone else was confused as to how to interpret my very existence. They watched me, suspicious, as if I were a Transformer and they were waiting for metal arms to spring out from my chest cavity.

I didn't think that I'd ever seen him laugh before, or maybe I had just never noticed, my attention focused on Grant, who I had thought was more likely to fall in with my plan of exploring human mating and relationships. But then again, Jessica and Kylie tended to dominate all conversation in a group setting, so maybe their own perfectly affected laughter had drowned out Tyler's.

But for some stupid reason, I liked to think that he was laughing just for me.

Which was when I knew I was even more drunk than I had realized and I needed to get away from him before I sat there blinking at him like a baby owl indefinitely. Before I put some sort of hero worship onto him that he might deserve, but which didn't mean a damn thing. Before I substituted one pointless crush for another.

I shoved open the door, half falling out, clinging to the handle and the remnants of my dignity, like he could hear my stupid thoughts. "Thanks," I said over my shoulder, barely glancing back as I exited the car, clutching my bag.

There was no response, and when I struggled to slam the heavy door, which seemed to weigh a million pounds and required more coordination than my icy fingers had, I realized that he was just staring at me. There was a cigarette in his mouth, and he was lifting the car lighter up to it, his hand guiding it to its destination without thought. As he sucked on it to catch the paper and tobacco on fire, his eyes never left mine.

The smile was gone. There was nothing but a cool scrutiny.

I shivered.

Then I walked as fast as I could to my dorm, digging in my bag for my swipe card.

Once inside, I paused at the front desk to check in and I glanced out the front doors.

His car was still there, and I could see the shadow of his outline, the tiny red glow of his cigarette.

TURN THE PAGE FOR A PREVIEW OF
ERIN McCARTHY'S NEXT NOVEL

Full Throttle

COMING IN DECEMBER 2013
FROM BERKLEY SENSATION!

"I DOUBLE DOG DARE YOU."

Shawn Hamby stared at Eve Monroe-Ford and remembered exactly why they had gotten in so much trouble together back in the day as the only two girls on the tween racing circuit. Eve had grown up with brothers and was a master at taunting manipulation. Shawn had grown up an only child and was eager for camaraderie, with an inability to keep a straight face. The combination had resulted in broken bones and many a grounding from their honked-off parents.

"I'm not falling for that," Shawn told her now, with a laugh. "I'm not going to talk to a random guy in a fetish club because you dared me to." She wasn't twelve anymore, and she didn't need to prove anything to anyone.

Which didn't explain why she was here in the first place.

Damn. Maybe she hadn't changed all that much.

"Oh, come on," Charity Mclain said, lifting her cocktail towards her mouth as she leaned against the bar. "We're here because of you, so you might as well have the full experience."

They *were* here because of Shawn, in a roundabout sort of way, and as she looked around at the dimly lit club, she fought the urge to giggle, which was her usual reaction to situations that made her uncomfortable. How a book club meeting had resulted in her and three friends at a place called The Wet Spot—and no, they weren't talking about spilled beverages—she couldn't imagine.

"All I said was that people don't really do what the chick in that book was doing. I didn't say let's go to a fetish club and see if it's true or not." It had just been a little hard for Shawn to believe that their fiction selection for the month had any basis in reality whatsoever, regardless of how enjoyable a read it had been. Average suburban women didn't just up and go to a sex club after years of lame sex and let a total stranger blindfold them. She was sure of it. Not in Charlotte, North Carolina. Not in a day and age when true-crime shows about serial killers and date-rape drugs were on TV every day, all day.

Not only did it seem dangerous, but it seemed kind of silly. She wasn't so sure what would be hot about having a man boss her around. Hell, she had that every day at the track and it just frustrated her. There was nothing sexy about it in the least. Not to her anyway. Hence the curiosity.

Harley, Charity's twin, tucked her blond hair behind her ear, glancing around nervously. "Let's just leave then."

"No!" Charity rebuked her. "Shawn needs to admit that this is real, that people go to clubs like this."

"I admit it," Shawn said easily. She wasn't exactly sure what people were doing here, or what drew them to the club, whether it was curiosity like it was for the four of them, or a genuine interest in BDSM or other fetishes, but she'd seen enough.

There were only so many adult men and women being pulled on dog leashes she could see before she lost it and started laughing. It wasn't like she found other people's choices amusing. It was that it just looked . . . fake. Like a movie being filmed. Like a giant skit being played out for her benefit. None of it seemed real, from the girl on the red velvet sofa allowing two different men to swat at her backside with a paddle to the extremely thin man who was shirtless and wearing nipple clamps, SLAVE tattooed across his chest, a lollipop in his mouth.

"This isn't really what I pictured," Eve said, scrutinizing the room. "I guess I thought it was going to be more tawdry. Nobody is having sex or anything."

"Do you want to see people having sex?" Shawn asked, because she didn't. She didn't even really get the appeal of mirrors in a bedroom. Sex was not a spectator sport. Not that she remembered what sex was like, given how long it had been since she'd had it. Eve, on the other hand, was married to a sexy jackman, so she had no business being curious in Shawn's opinion.

"No, I do not. I don't even want to be here. My husband's going to start to think our book club is a front for checking off items on my Bad Girl Bucket List. Last month we got drunk on margaritas and took a pole-dancing class, which was a huge leap from reading Margaret Thatcher's biography. The month before you goaded me into waxing my cooter, though Nolan wanted to write you a thank-you note for that one."

Eve had a point. Shawn wasn't sure how this kept happening. She thought it had something to do with the prevalence of wine at their book club gatherings and the fact that she and Eve felt every one of the five years they had on the twins. Or maybe they were just repeating their childhood of stumbling into Bad Ideas together, though she had to primarily blame Charity for this particular outing. She was the one who had asked Siri on her iPhone where to find a fetish club in Charlotte and suddenly here they were.

"We can go at any time," Shawn said. "And I get to pick next month's book selection. Plus it's my birthday month so you'd better have cake for me." She was turning thirty-three, which while not noteworthy, was fairly appalling. "Red velvet."

"Fine. I'm going to the restroom first," Eve said, setting down her beer and heading off.

Shawn wasn't sure going alone was totally wise, but Eve could take care of herself. She was known around stock car racing as having a razor-sharp tongue and no hesitation whatsoever in using it to slice offenders to ribbons. It was a talent Shawn did not possess. She was the goofy girl, the one who cracked a joke at the wrong time, who no one took seriously.

"I'm kind of disappointed," Charity admitted. She and Harley were identical twins, but only in appearance. While she was outspoken and wore significant makeup and teased and highlighted her hair, Harley was quiet and completely natural-looking. When they stood next to each other, it was like seeing a before-and-after pageant shot of the little girls on *Toddlers & Tiaras*. "I was hoping for something more glamorous."

"I think if you join one of those members-only clubs, you get glam. Otherwise you just get skimmers," Harley said. "People dabbling in the scene. Not that I know anything about it, really. I'm just speculating."

"None of these guys are even cute," Charity complained.

Shawn would have to agree, except right at that moment, a guy came around the corner from the other room, and he wasn't just cute. He was beyond cute. He was smoking hot. He was wet-panty-producing sexy.

"Hubba hubba," she said, before she could stop herself. "Now there's a fine male specimen."

He was ripped, but not bulky, filling his button-up shirt and jeans to perfection. Just a perfectly hard, muscular, lean man with a confident step—and an intense stare that swept the room and landed on her.

"Oh, damn, he *is* hot," Charity said.

"And he's looking at us," Harley breathed, sounding panicked.

He was.

And then he strode right over to them, his eyes locked on Shawn. On her. Yikes. She swallowed and tried not to fidget. She didn't really want to do this. She wasn't really prepared to talk to a guy here. It was a dumb idea to even set foot in this place, and she certainly didn't want to encourage any attention from a guy who would clearly be interested in areas outside her expertise and comfort level.

She would have to politely dissuade him.

Before he even spoke, his hand slid out and took hers, his thumb stroking across her palm, causing a shiver of arousal to take her totally by surprise.

"You should dance with me," he said, already pulling her towards him.

"Okay."

So much for turning him down flat. Why the hell had she just agreed to dance? Because he was hot. And there was something commanding about him that appealed to her. Which was annoying.

"I'm Rhett," he told her.

Of course he was. Shawn squeezed her mouth shut so he wouldn't see her desperately trying not to laugh. She imagined using a fake name was what you did in a place like this, but seriously? Rhett?

"Well, then I guess that makes me Scarlett," she told him.

RHETT FORD SAW THE BRUNETTE THE MINUTE HE CAME around the corner. She was smiling at her friends, and she looked relaxed, casual, dressed simply in jeans and a purple sweater that had fallen off one shoulder. Her friends were dressed similarly, and given that he'd never seen her at The Wet Spot before, he suspected she was someone just like him—curious and turned on by kink, but not sure where to start.

Aside from the fact that he was immediately attracted to her, she also didn't appear to be the type that he'd always gone for, and which had always resulted in total disaster. He had a firm habit of choosing the shy, unassuming girls—like the blond twin currently standing next to the brunette—and invariably he scared the shit out of every single one of them. They all ran, terrified. Like his latest disastrous relationship with Lexi.

So this was a conscious choice, to be approaching a woman who looked confident and amused by her surroundings. He didn't even mind that she thought he was giving her a fake name. Though God knew, if he had a choice of names, he never would have picked Rhett. It had been the bane of his existence almost since birth. If he went for an assumed identity he would probably pick Bill or Dave. No one could poke fun at a Dave.

Leading the woman by the hand to the back bar where there was a dance floor, Rhett glanced back at her. She was checking out his ass. Now that was promising. He had never actually hooked up with anyone he had met here, since for the most part, he had just been observing and working out his own personal sexual interests, but he was definitely intrigued by this so-called Scarlett. When they got to the small, dark room where only half a dozen people were moving to the baby-making music, he pulled her into his arms and studied her face.

She met his gaze steadily, her hands snaking up to wrap around his neck. He was tall, but so was she, and while he had to bend down to make eye contact, it wasn't significant. Her eyes were an amber color, and they were shining with amusement and, if he wasn't mistaken, attraction. As they swayed, his hands resting lightly on her trim waist, he gave her a slow smile.

"So what brings you here?" he asked her.

Her response wasn't flirtatious, nor was it cryptic. It was just matter-of-fact. "Information."

"Are you a reporter? A blogger?"

"No. We're four women who like to be right. This is my friends' attempt to prove me wrong."

Interesting. Bored housewives? He couldn't check her ring finger to see if she was married, but then again, if she was looking for a good time, she would take her ring off anyway. If she was, he would be disappointed. Married women weren't his thing. He was loyal and committed to a single woman at a time, and he had no desire to serve as an itch-scratcher for a restless spouse.

"How so?"

"I didn't think people came to places like this. Apparently they do." She gave him a wry smile. "So why are you here?"

He had no problem being honest. Another lesson hard-learned. He needed to be upfront about his desires. "I'm looking for the right woman for me. One who likes to be led in bed."

She gave a little laugh. "Oh, really?"

"Really."

"Uh-huh."

Rhett wasn't sure if he should be offended or not. He did know he was turned on. There was something very compelling about the way she never broke eye contact. What could be hotter than a woman submitting to his desires but doing so out of titillation, boldly? Nothing, as far as he was concerned. But he was getting ahead of himself. Which was evidenced by her dropping her arms to halt his creeping progress lower and lower on her back. He was at the curve of her ass when she reprimanded him, gripping his hand to stop it.

"Hey now, sport, watch the sticky fingers."

Rhett grinned. "Don't you mean wandering hands? I'm not trying to steal your wallet."

"Whatever," she said dismissively. "You know what I mean."

"I do." He kept his hands far above the erogenous zone, wanting to respect her limits. "So give me your number." The song was almost over and who knew what would be played next. She might use a booty-grinding song as an opportunity to leave the floor and return to her girlfriends. He didn't want to waste time.

Her eyebrows shot up. "That's a little presumptuous, don't you think?"

"You never get what you want if you don't ask."

"How old are you?" she asked suddenly, putting more space between them as they swayed to the bass-pumping R&B.

So that was it. She was older than him. "Old enough to know what I want."

"You're younger than me." It wasn't a question. She seemed certain of it.

"Frankly, Scarlett, I don't give a damn." Might as well make his stupid name work for him.

She gave a short laugh, smiling at him. "Nice. Corny, but effective. What's your real name, by the way? I only give my number to Clark Kent, not Superman."

He liked the sound of that. She was going to cough up her phone number, and he was suddenly glad she'd shifted away slightly because he was getting hard. There was something about her that he found seriously arousing, and she didn't seem intimidated by what he'd told her, which further turned him on. "It really is Rhett."

A flicker of annoyance crossed her face.

But before he could pull out his driver's license and prove it, her friend approached them. "Shawn!" she said, urgently.

So her name was Shawn. It suited her. Unusual, unique. The tomboy who grew up to be a sexy woman. Or so he would guess given the muscle tone of her waist and arms, and the perky lift of her backside. This girl liked sports, or at least the gym.

"Sorry to interrupt," her friend said, "but we need to leave. Emergency. Let's go, now."

Shawn stopped moving to the music entirely and dropped her hands to her sides. "What's wrong?"

"Nothing. We just have to go. Come on." The blonde wouldn't face him at all, and when there was a hesitation on Shawn's part, she actually took her friend's hand and pulled her away.

"Wait," Rhett said. "I still want your number."

But to his disappointment, Shawn just gave him an apologetic smile and a wave. "Nice to meet you," she said, as she was dragged away.

Rhett was left standing on the dance floor feeling a whole hell of a lot of sympathy for Prince Charming when he'd been ditched. But unlike Cinderella, Shawn didn't leave any clues behind.

* * *

"WHAT IS GOING ON?" SHAWN ASKED CHARITY, FIGHT-ing the urge to glance back at the hot hunk of man flesh she'd left on the dance floor. Despite ticking her off a little with his refusal to give a real name, she had to admit, her interest was piqued. Along with her nipples.

"We have to go because of that guy you were talking to."

"What? Why? And where are Eve and Harley? And stop yanking on me. You're going to pull my arm out of the socket." Shawn followed Charity out the front door, the cold February air hitting her with a smack.

Eve was pacing to the left of the door, looking anxious. She darted her eyes behind Shawn. "He didn't follow you, did he?"

"No. Why would he follow me? And what is the big deal about that guy?" Had Eve seen him on *America's Most Wanted*? Was he a *Gone With the Wind*–inspired serial killer? First he dressed you in drapes, then threw you down the stairs?

As they started walking towards the car, Eve said, "*That* was my brother-in-law. When I came back from the restroom I saw you with him. There was no way I could let him see me there. And there was no way I wanted him to know I saw *him* there."

"Your brother-in-law? You mean, like Nolan's brother?" She could see how that would be more than a little awkward for Eve. It wasn't just the corner pub they'd been in.

"Yes." Eve beeped open her SUV and they all climbed in. She turned towards Shawn in the backseat and gave a snort of laughter. "Nolan's little brother, Rhett."

"His name is really Rhett?" she asked in amazement. Now she felt like a jerk for doubting it. "I thought he was making that up!"

"No, it's really his name. He's twenty-five years old and he's in a sex club. Oh, my God, how am I going to look him in the face?"

"Twenty-five?" Shawn squawked, horrified. "Good Lord, he's a fetus!" Who she had been contemplating pursuing so she could get a serious look at him naked. Her cheeks burned.

"What the hell was he doing there?" Eve asked, pulling out of the parking lot.

Oh, Shawn had a funny feeling she knew exactly what he was looking for. She might not be particularly knowledgeable about the lifestyle, but she could pick up on a clue or two. "I think he was a Dom looking for a submissive," she said, not at all sure how she felt about any of this.

"*What?*" Eve said, moaning. "Oh, shit, I'm going to die. I do not want to picture that. God!"

"I should have let you give him your number," Charity said ruefully from the front passenger seat. "But I panicked."

Still stunned, she murmured, "I told him my name was Scarlett. I thought he gave me a code name."

As Eve cruised to a stop at a red light, they all looked at each and burst out laughing.

"So what are we reading next month?" Harley asked.

Shawn figured it could only be a letdown after this selection. She settled back into her seat, shivering, and tried not to think about a certain guy who was too young for her with the most intense blue eyes she'd ever seen in her life.

It worked for about three whole seconds.

FROM *USA TODAY* BESTSELLING AUTHOR

ERIN McCARTHY

SLOW RIDE

A Fast Track Novel

Legendary sports journalist Tuesday Jones can't deny
the attraction she feels to ex–racing star Diesel Lange,
but the recent death of her father has left her fragile.
Now, he'll need to do the one thing he'd never been
able to do on the track—take it slow—if he wants to
shift their romance into high gear.

PRAISE FOR THE FAST TRACK NOVELS

"Steamy . . . Fast-paced and red-hot."
—*Publishers Weekly*

"The sexiest series I've ever read."
—*Carly Phillips*

erinmccarthy.net
penguin.com

M1032T0312